I0586129

Inside The Maelstrom

Part One

Grace McGinty

For the ones who are lost inside the maelstrom.

Also by Grace McGinty

Hell's Redemption Series

The Redeemable/The Unrepentant/The Fallen

The Azar Nazemi Trilogy

Smoke and Smolder/Burn and Blaze/Rage and Ruin

Dark River Days Series

Newly Undead In Dark River/Happily Undead In Dark River/Pleasantly Undead in Dark River

Black Mountain Mates

Hunting Isla

Eden Academy Series

The Lost and the Hunted (Prequel)/Heart of the Hounded (Prequel)

Rebels and Runaways (Book 1)/Sweethearts and Savages (Book 2)

Shadow Bred Series

Manix (Book 1)/Frenzy (Book 2)/ Feral (Book 3)

Stand Alone Novels and Novellas

Bright Lights From A Hurricane/The Last Note/Castle of Carnal Desires/ Inside The Maelstrom(PT 1)

Inside The Maelstrom

Trigger Warning

The very core of this book centres around mental illness. References include suicide, eating disorders and bipolar.

However, at its roots, this is a book about hope, and while no one is ever "cured", they do find contentment, however that looks for them.

"If at every instant we may perish, so at
every instant we may be saved."

— Jules Verne, A Journey to the
Centre of the Earth

"The world breaks everyone, and
afterward, many are strong at the
broken places."

— Ernest Hemingway, A
Farewell to Arms

Prologue
Aviva

I turned up the music, ignoring the harsh way my breaths were falling from my lips. I ignored the clank of empty bottles from the passenger footwell. Ignored the check engine light on my dash that had been on for the last twelve months. Ignored the flashing of my phone, with my mother's face glaring at me from the screen.

Instead, I drove down the quiet back streets of my middle class neighborhood. I chewed my lip incessantly, but enjoyed the way it stung and the slight metallic taste of blood. I'd told my parents that I was going to my friend Alison's house, but we hadn't been friends in two years. They didn't know that—how could they?

I was an adult. I went to college. The need to police my friends had ended after my brief goth stage during middle school. So they didn't know Alison had gotten a boyfriend in freshman year. She had a life now, and we'd drifted apart. Or maybe I'd just stopped talking to her. I couldn't really remember. Everything blurred together now.

I watched the people stroll down the sidewalk, their dogs on long leads, frowning as they glared at their phones. Were they happy? Was that what happy looked like? Did they wake up in the morning and want to shower, want to go to school or work, want to talk to other people and eat breakfast and make plans?

I dragged my eyes back to the road. The Petersons lived right at the end of this block. I knew it was their house because I'd dated their son in senior year. Lost my virginity to him in a truly uninspiring way. Later on, he got accepted into Harvard. He was a good guy. Beige. Safe.

The Petersons as a whole were unremarkable. The only exceptional thing about them was the magnolia tree in their front yard. It was huge, bigger than it should have been in this climate. It must have been thirty feet high. It was in full bloom right now, and it was something bright and magnificent in a world where it didn't have any fucking right to be so extraordinary.

It was in the front of a freaking box house, architecturally designed to be devoid of personality. I could relate to the house, but that fucking tree taunted me. It sometimes caused accidents, because it was just so beautiful, and that was wrong.

Suddenly, my chest felt tight, and my blood turned hot. Scalding, even. It chased away the deep chill that had permeated my bones for years. No, a chill would insinuate that I felt something underneath this cloak of numbness.

I had felt nothing for so long. But now, I felt rage—and it was glorious.

I pressed my foot further to the floor, my shitty, mid-priced car revving with a high, tinny sound. I unclipped my belt, letting it whip back up to where it belonged, safe and secure.

I pointed my car at that magnolia tree, and I grinned. It felt wrong on my face, but it didn't matter as I reached down to turn the music up as loud as it would go, then slammed my foot onto the gas pedal until it hit the floorboards.

I mounted the curb, my car flying high as it hit the outer branches of the magnolia tree before slamming into the trunk.

My head collided with the steering wheel, bouncing off to hit the side window, as the front of my car crumpled in slow motion.

The last thing I saw before everything went black was a downpour of perfectly waxy magnolia blooms.

Good. Now we were both ugly and dead.

The neck brace ruined the lines of my responsible white blouse, and my head wound ached. The judge's eyes saw too much. My mother sobbed softly into her linen handkerchief behind me.

"Aviva. It's the opinion of the doctors who admitted you that you require treatment in an inpatient setting. That you pose a significant danger, not only to yourself, but to the wider community." He looked down at the paperwork in front of him. "Looking at the police reports, I have to agree. Your blood alcohol level was twice what it should have been. If anyone else had been involved, if you'd hit a pedestrian, you'd be going to jail right now. But it is your apathy regarding the seriousness of this situation that concerns me."

I'd never wanted to hurt anyone else.

The judge gave me a look that was part jaded, part desperately sad. I knew the look. "The Petersons are generously not seeking any remuneration or pressing any charges for the property damage you caused. But I don't believe you'll be so lucky next time. And Aviva, there will be a next time. Until you get the help you need, there will *always* be a next time. I am committing you to a mental health facility for ninety days. At your parents' request, I am happy for you to undertake this involuntary treatment at a private facility."

The judge took a deep breath, her eyes filled to the brim with compassion. I couldn't comprehend how she still felt compassion after sitting in this courtroom day after day, seeing the worst of humanity up close. I zoned back in and realized she was still speaking.

"I know this feels all-encompassing. That you feel like you're drowning every time you take a breath. But believe me, you just have to wake up every morning and put one foot in front of the other. Then one day, you'll look back at this moment right now and realize it was exactly what you needed. I'm throwing you a life preserver, Aviva, and I need you to grab it with both hands."

The rest was a blur as the case wrapped up, and my parents stood beside me, my father's hand on my shoulder and my mother gripping my fingers tightly, like she could feel me slipping away already. It wasn't their fault, but I knew they wouldn't believe me if I told them that; they'd still blame themselves. That's just what parents did.

But something was broken inside me, and it wasn't anything they could have fixed with more family dinners and quality time.

People buzzed around me like flies in the wide halls of the Court building, and a nice-looking police officer with a soft face was murmuring promises to my parents about how I would be fine. That was audacious of him, if not an outright lie. But I was glad he could give them something that I couldn't right now—assurances that I was going to be okay.

I was put in the back of a police car, and I let my eyes drift to my parents as they cried on the sidewalk. I watched them get smaller and smaller, and saw the moment my mom collapsed into my father's arms when she thought I was out of sight.

Guilt washed over me. I was a failure, really. I couldn't even die right. It was all cry for help bullshit—at least, that's what they told me. They were wrong, but I'd fucked it up.

The policeman thankfully didn't try to talk to me, didn't give me any of the reassuring words he'd laid on my parents. He just drove quietly out of the city as I stared blankly out the window. The houses became more sparse, the trees thicker, hours passing until we rolled through a set of heavy wrought iron gates.

The sign on the gate said 'Heath Buckley Center.' It had manicured gardens, with artificially planted palms along the edges that carefully obscured the fences. The illusion of freedom. The policeman drove down the long, graveled driveway, and I was kind of glad that this was an unmarked police car. And the cop was in plain clothes. Made it feel less like the first time I was being delivered to a mental health ward.

The cop climbed out, opening the rear door for me. He gave me another one of those smiles that didn't quite reach his eyes, and tilted his head for me to get out. I was probably the most docile person he'd had in the back of the police car, doing exactly as I was told, pulling my backpack out after me. Everything here was supplied apparently, but my parents had packed me a few things they thought I'd need.

I didn't really *need* anything, especially not the stuffed toy cat I'd had on my bed since I was five, or three battered paperbacks. But it made them feel better, and I was enough of an emotional black hole that I could let them have this comfort.

The cop held open the front door for me, and I stepped into the foyer. A plain woman bustled over, smiling politely at me and beaming at the cop. I looked over my shoulder at him, and I guess he was handsome in a plain, moon face kind of way. So was she. They'd have plain, round-face, average-looking kids.

The cop grinned back at her. "Hey, Peaches. Got another Invol for you. This is Aviva. She's a good kid."

I tilted my head at the smiling woman. She had orange-blonde hair that kind of resembled the fruit. "Peaches? Is that a nickname?"

The woman shook her head, gently taking my bag

from me. "Nope, just my parents being crazy stoners from Georgia." She pointed to a sunshine yellow door. "Come on, we'll get the initial paperwork done, and then I'll take you to your room. Dave, there's cupcakes in the break room if you want to have a coffee before you leave?"

There was a desperate hopefulness in her voice, and I let it wash over me. But I felt nothing for their budding romance. Not giddy excitement or embarrassment for Peaches or jealousy. Nothing.

I signed my name on a bunch of paperwork. I was officially an adult and just because I was here involuntarily, it didn't make me medically incompetant. Go figure. While I signed and initialed six hundred pieces of paper, Peaches went through my backpack, searching for contraband or anything I could finish myself off with, I assumed.

Giving it a tick of approval, she led me from the office with a calm efficiency. Peaches was a little bit like a balm. Her nonchalance was refreshing. She didn't look at me like I was a waste of potential, or like I was broken, or like I was some tragic statistic. She just shooed me along like she'd seen a million girls just like me. There was something reassuring in that.

She used her ID card to go through a locked set of doors. It opened into a short hallway, and then another set of doors opened into a bright, sunny room filled with recliners and bookcases, a huge TV, and dozens of round tables.

"This is the common room. You're welcome to come here and relax at any time."

I looked around at the other inhabitants of the room. They ranged in ages, from a gray-haired old man to a few middle-aged women, to a guy who had to be my age, or maybe a year or two older. He watched me closely, the look in his eyes predatory.

A shiver ran down my spine. I dragged my eyes away, but watched him in my peripheral vision. He was cruelly beautiful, his lips full and twisted into a sensual expression that still somehow managed to be harsh. It was like he was appraising my weaknesses in that fifteen second stroll across the common room, and he'd pinpointed every single one.

When I looked back over my shoulder, his derisive pout had formed into a grin, and if it was possible, that scared me more. When the double doors slid shut behind us, I almost sagged with relief.

My heart was thudding, and I realized it was out of fear. I frowned, unsure if I should be happy I felt something at all, or if I should run away screaming.

Chapter 1
Aviva

Two Months Later

"How could anyone not look at me and be disgusted?"

The slightly nasally voice grated inside my skull, and I looked over at Yvonne, who was fucking beautiful. You could tell her mother was a former Eastern European beauty queen—her cheekbones were so sharp, they all but glinted like blades in the stark fluorescent lighting.

Yvonne would be a knockout too, if she weren't so thin she looked like the walking, talking skeleton of a runway model. Eating disorders had no rhyme or reason though; they just warped your vision like a hall of mirrors.

There were mutters of protest, but I tuned them out. Group therapy was the worst part of the day, and considering this treatment center was basically a glorified prison, that was saying something. I tucked my legs up until I could rest my chin on my knees. Turning my face to the side, I looked outside at the beautiful sunny day I probably wouldn't get to appreciate if everyone was feeling as chatty as Yvonne. Once upon a time, the pool that shimmered on the grounds of the facility would have called to me like a siren song, but not today.

It was stupid, really. Why put a pool in a rehab filled with people who wanted to off themselves? It was almost a self-fulfilling prophecy. Except the pool was locked up tighter than Alcatraz, and Corey—who was the nurse/lifeguard who patrolled it when it was open —was built like a fucking wall of muscle, and would drag your ass up from the bottom, then give you mouth-to-mouth.

Corey was a nice guy. He'd give you mouth to other things, if you knew the right words to ask.

I should know. A girl had to get her kicks somehow in here, and my roommate was a bit of a downer, so it wasn't like I could flick the bean while she was in the room.

My eyes snagged on a golden back and broad

shoulders flexing in the sun, making the water drops shimmer like diamonds on his skin in the Florida sun.

I curled my lip in disgust. Hendrick fucking Kenley. Of course he'd be outside enjoying the fucking day, instead of being stuck in hours of group therapy. I didn't know who he'd paid off to be exempt, but he only ever had to go to his one-on-one sessions. Even then, I was fairly sure he just napped on the couch and Dr. Arubat signed off on it.

I'd found out he was the youngest in a dynasty of tycoons. The Kenleys literally had their hand in every big business maneuver in the US. We'd done a case study on his grandfather in my Econ class. Rumor had it that his daddy wanted to upgrade from senator to President, and that's why Hendrick was here getting clean.

Well, I assumed he was here for drug abuse. His file was closed, and not even Corey could tell me why. I'd asked him if he could find out, while he'd been fucking some feelings into me. Never worked, but at least I got some form of release from the whole experience.

No, I was just guessing about the real reason Hendrick was here, and I wasn't the only one. There were a lot of rumors flying around; I'd heard everything from a cocaine habit to a sex addiction.

Considering I'd seen him fucking Flora the nurse

in the supply closet last week, it could be sex. He didn't even shut the door. He just stood there fucking her where anyone could see and report her. He obviously didn't care if she lost her job, because what did the lives of everyone else matter to a boy who was richer than the Queen of England?

A part of me—the part I liked to think was still clinging hopelessly to mental stability—piped up and said I was doing the exact same thing with Corey. But Corey was a whore and was fucking half the female inmates, and if those pesky whispers were correct, some of the male patients too. Corey was like a dumb Golden Retriever; he thought he was doing a public service. Like treating hysteria patients in the olden days—nothing that a good dicking couldn't fix, right?

So if Corey got caught, it would be his fault. But Flora was a sweetheart, who'd obviously just got caught up in the magnetic bullshit of Hendrick Kenley.

"Aviva, do you have anything to add to today's discussion?" Dr. Arubat's voice pulled me away from my mental crucifixion of Hendrick.

I stared him dead in the eye and shook my head. "No." I looked over at Yvonne. "You're beautiful. It's the eating disorder that's ugly. Shake that fucker out of your head, and you'll be all good."

Dr. Arubat's lips pursed. He didn't like profanity in his sessions, but really, fuck was a perfectly fine word. It was the tone that made it a problem. "Thank you, Aviva. Let's not try to diminish anyone else's experience though, okay?"

I mentally gave him the finger and tuned back out. Ten minutes later, we were set free, and I couldn't get out of there fast enough. Swinging past my room, I grabbed a book.

Maybe I'd head outside anyway. Find a tree to read under, and pretend I was somewhere alone, rather than at a wellness center that was bankrupting my parents one day at a time.

I knew the reason I was so angry today was because it was visitation day tomorrow, and no one would visit me. Again. It wasn't that my parents didn't *want* to visit—they called me every single night. I'd never tell them, but their voices were the only thing keeping me afloat some days. No, they were great people, but were working day and night to keep me in here, and out of jail.

Fuck, I loved them, and that made me feel so goddamn guilty.

I couldn't even die right.

I found a palm tree with grass that managed to creep right up to the trunk, and decided that was my spot for the day. I'd quickly run through everything decent in the small library of books the center had. We weren't allowed electronics, so no eReader. Like, what the fuck was with that?

I'd hit the under-read classics now, and I was reading Jules Verne like this was an English Lit class. *Twenty Thousand Leagues Under the Sea.*

Scribbled on the title page in marker were the words:

Man gets hijacked by a submarine? If this isn't a euphemism for Verne's repressed sexuality, nothing is.

I let out a laugh. Well, they probably weren't wrong. Jules Vernes, arguably the godfather of steampunk literature, was not a riveting read. He was scientific and technical, and honestly, if I wanted to listen to an old white guy yabber on endlessly, I'd go back to group therapy.

But the notes in the margin? They were amazing. Sometimes serious, sometimes poking fun at the story. I found myself becoming immersed in the story just so I could understand the mystery commenter's notes scribbled across the page.

A shadow fell over me, and I looked up. Hendrick fucking Kenley stood over me, his face silhouetted by the sun.

"What are you doing?"

I screwed up my nose. "Masturbating." I rolled my eyes. "Obviously, I'm reading."

He tilted his head at me. "I think you're masturbating wrong. Want me to show you how it's done?"

I flushed all over, but gritted my teeth at him. "Not if you were the last discombobulated head on Earth."

I climbed to my feet, pushing down the skirt of my dress. Hendrick didn't move a muscle, and I huffed as I stepped around him. Tucking the book under my arm, I strode away, not giving him the satisfaction of looking back at him, even though I could feel his eyes burning into my spine.

As I walked past the pool, Corey was just locking up. He grinned when he saw me, and I gave him a smirk back. "Finishing up early?" I asked, and he lifted an eyebrow.

"Yep. Though I still have a little time until I clock out. I might have to do some paperwork." His eyes dipped down my body, letting me know that I was the paperwork he wanted to do.

Honestly, I expected so little from Corey that I actually laughed at his bad metaphor. "Need a hand with that? I'm good with numbers."

His eyes hooded, and he sucked his bottom lip between his teeth. He had perfect, straight white teeth that flashed in the warm afternoon sun. "I might just take you up on that, Aviva," he purred, and it went straight to my core.

Corey headed to the pumphouse beside the pool, while I moved casually over to the pool fence, watching the turquoise water ripple softly in the breeze as I counted to sixty.

Turning back the way I came, I sucked in a breath as I noticed Hendrick still watching me. Fuck him though. I met his eyes and held them as I turned on my heel and followed Corey toward the pool shed. Let him think that the smile on my face was because I was excited about fucking Corey, and not because I was happy to get one up on Hendrick Kenley, the entitled, arrogant, asshole.

Chapter 2

Hendrick

I watched the girl head toward the pumphouse with that fucking dumbass Corey. He was a goddamn idiot, but she wasn't. She was... annoying. Honestly, I'd kind of thought she was a lesbian, but apparently she just hated me. I don't know why though. I hadn't spoken to her in the two months she'd been here. I didn't pay any attention to her until last week, when she'd stood in the hallway and watched me fuck the nurse in the supply closet. Not gonna lie, I might have put a little extra enthusiasm into it, knowing there was an audience.

And when I'd looked over my shoulder, all I'd seen was a swirl of skirts and those bouncing golden curls as she stomped away.

Mmm, she was an enigma, and I was bored as fuck.

Still, it burned to watch her strut away with that shit-head after rejecting me so solidly.

The phone in my pocket buzzed and I pulled it out. Otto's name flashed on the home screen, so I tapped the group chat icon.

Otto: Ready to bust out yet?

I huffed a laugh and sat down in the spot that the girl, Aviva, had just vacated.

Me: Nah. At least Dad isn't riding my fucking ass in here.

I didn't use standard texting abbreviations because that shit pissed Otto off. He was a stickler for the written word, and I owed him enough that I wouldn't give him shit about it and I'd use my words properly.

Sam: Wrd on the st is that he's busy riding his secretary's ass, nasty af.

Yeah, Sampson didn't give a fuck what anyone wanted, not Otto and not me. I gritted my teeth at the news my father was screwing his secretary, but I wasn't surprised. She would have signed an NDA before he got into her panties, and therefore, she'd be too scared to go public with that shit, so it would always just be rumors.

My mother wouldn't care either because she was fucking the driver, the pool boy, and her yoga instructor. She was a cliché, but what could you expect? My father was an asshole, and she was a drunk.

Otto didn't rise to Sam's baiting, and a pain stabbed me in the chest. I missed these guys down here in my parental-ordered isolation. I didn't say that though.

Me: Fuck you guys. It's nice here. Like Aruba without the gold diggers. Might hit up the beach.

Sam: We'll be there in six hours. I'll take the jet.

I laughed low, stuffing my phone back into my pocket. Sampson didn't screw around. I leaned back against the tree, watching the pumphouse out of the corner of my eye.

Fuck it.

I climbed to my feet, brushing the grass from the back of my shorts and strolling back toward the main building of the treatment center. Honestly, it must have been a former mansion—it looked like something that should be in Hollywood Hills rather than Florida, and was filled to the brim with drug addicts and social media influencers with eating disorders.

My feet slowed as I passed the path toward the pool pumphouse, hidden away as it was by lush gardens. Turning, I walked around the side so I was standing at the back of the building. It was dark in there, no windows, so maybe they weren't even in there. Maybe she'd just walked through the gardens toward the center's side entrance.

But as I leaned closer, I could hear it. The soft moans of a woman. My dick instantly hardened in my shorts, and I gripped it through the material. Looking around, I made sure no one could see me back here. Luckily, it was pretty covered by the overgrown bamboo screening.

The mechanical whir of the pump covered most of the noises coming from within, but when I rested my ear against the sheet metal, I could hear it so clearly that she must have just been on the other side.

"Yes," came another breathy moan, and then the distinctive sound of skin slapping against skin. More moans, and my dick throbbed. Looking around again, I reached into my shorts and dragged out my dick. I listened as she moaned, imagined it was me fucking her, her skirt flipped up around her waist as I pounded into her.

"Harder," came the breathy command, and the snapping sounds got louder. Yeah, he definitely had her bent over the workbench in there. I'd fucked a nurse there the other day. It made it easy for me to imagine wrapping my fingers in those golden curls and gripping them in my fist as I pounded away.

I stroked my dick as her moans got a little more frantic. "Don't stop," she panted, and then I heard an annoyed sound. "No, no, go back to how you were— Umph."

Yep, that was definitely an annoyed groan. When I heard a masculine grunt afterwards, I knew that Corey had blown his load before she'd even gotten off.

I grinned as I stuffed my dick back in my pants, tucking it under the waistband of my pants and fluffing my shirt over it to hide the raging erection. I shuffled back to the main path, sitting on the seat by the back door like I'd been there the whole time watching my phone.

A couple of moments later, when Aviva—fucking hippy ass name if you asked me—appeared, I smirked at her flushed cheeks and irritated expression. Her steps faltered when she saw me there, and I gave her a knowing grin. "Sure you don't need any help?"

She huffed and marched past me, slamming the door so hard it was a wonder the plate glass didn't break.

Oh. Maybe little Aviva would be fun. Standing, I sauntered into the main rec area behind her, but turned off toward the rooms. I didn't have to share and even had my own ensuite—perks of paying off the admin staff. It was almost dinner time, and I needed a shower to take care of a problem that was still achingly hard in my pants.

I had a feeling that when I closed my eyes under the warm water of the shower, it was a certain pissed off face that I would see when I came.

. . .

I didn't need to check my phone to know that my friends were on the other side of the perimeter fence that ran around the center. It was the only prison-like feature of this place. I knew without a doubt they were there, because Sampson was allergic to being late. Or being early. He was exactly where he needed to be, whenever he needed to be there. Not a moment before or a moment after.

Me: Jump the fence. We'll hang by the pool.

I slipped from my room and out into the main hall, nodding at the night nurse and giving her my signature cocky grin. Otto always said it was an expression that made girls swoon, and it didn't matter if the girl was seventeen or seventy.

Combined with the shitload of money I was putting into her retirement fund, it was enough for her to ignore the security monitors for the night. Plus, I'd solemnly sworn that I wouldn't do anything crazy like escape, or try and off myself. I snorted internally. Because crazy people and addicts didn't lie. Yeah, right.

Lucky for Nurse Becky, I didn't intend on doing any of those things. My father put me in here to get me out of the way, and honestly, it was better than being at home, with the constant fighting and arguing. Then there was the political trail and the false smiling that was so goddamn tiring. I'd rather stay here and talk bullshit to Dr. Arabut, which he'd feed back to my dad, despite all his Hippocratic oaths and statutory non-disclosure provisions.

At least the food was good and the view was nice.

I slowed near the room that I knew was Aviva's. She was... interesting. Unpredictable. And she seemed to hate me, which I kind of found refreshing. She didn't want to fuck me, or try and marry me. At least, I didn't think so. Hell, if she was playing the long game, getting thrown in here for whatever terrible thing she'd done, all in the hopes of intriguing me enough to put a ring on it... Well, I liked her dedication.

Opening her door quietly, I was glad the lights were dimmed at bedtime. She had the bed by the back window, which meant I had to creep past her room-mate, whose name I didn't remember. Standing over Aviva's bed, I reached down and slapped a hand over her mouth, dragging her from beneath the covers and into the hall before she was even fully awake.

Then the bitch bit me.

"Fuck! That hurt." Dropping her to her feet, I looked at the crescent-shaped dents in my hand. Which was why I didn't see the punch coming until it cracked into my nose.

"What the fuck is *wrong* with you, you goddamn psychopath?" she screeched, and I hushed her.

"Be quiet. Fuck. I just thought you'd like to hang out, not maul me like goddamn Jeffrey Dahmer. Christ, that's going to get infected." It was definitely beginning to bleed. I looked up just in time to catch the next hit in my hand. "Woah, calm your tits."

Her chest was heaving as she panted through her teeth. "You pulled me out of bed in the middle of the night, covering my mouth and dragging—" She paused, like she was trying to collect herself. "Dragging me into the hallway. Because you want to *hang out*?"

"Well, when you put it like that, it sounds dumb."

She stepped closer until her finger was in my face and I could feel the hot gusts of her breath on my chin. She was kind of short, and it ruined the intimidation factor. "I don't want anything to do with you, let alone to spend time *at night* with you. Fuck, I thought you were dragging me out here to rape me, you fucking entitled Neanderthal."

I took a huge step back, flinching from her words in a way I'd never flinch from her fist. "You think I'd rape you? Or any woman?" Okay, maybe it was my turn to get a little angry now. "Listen, and listen good. I have never, and will never, force myself on a woman. I get enough pussy thrown at me."

She snorted, narrowing her eyes. "You don't have

to be Dr. Arubut to know that rape isn't about sexual satisfaction, dickhead. It's about power. And for a guy like you, who's had everything handed to him his whole life? Trust me when I say it isn't a mental stretch to imagine you wanting something that isn't freely given."

I blinked at her in shock. I wasn't an idiot. I'd gone to private school with the exact assholes who Aviva just described, right down to their trust fund legal teams. But I wasn't like that—surely anyone could tell that, right? But just in case...

"I'm not like that."

She rolled her eyes so hard that she probably saw Jesus. "Sure. I believe you. Now I'm going back to bed, and if you sneak into my room again, I'm going to cut off your balls and really give them the Dahmer treatment."

She spun on her heel, and my hand flung out to grab her wrist. I don't even know why. Because I felt something? Even if it was just pain from a bite and some words that were sharp enough to cut.

"I'm sorry. Just come and hang out with me and my friends. We'll hang in the pool, swim under the moonlight, and pretend we're just normal people for a minute, okay?"

"Your friends? Oh sure, allow me to go into the unsupervised darkness with an undisclosed number of probably men, who are strangers. What could possibly go wrong? God, you can't be that oblivious, can you?"

I gritted my teeth. "I promise they're good guys too."

"You're a fool."

"My business degree would say otherwise."

"I didn't say you were an idiot. I said you were a fool."

"Just five minutes. They say it only takes twenty-seven seconds for you to form an opinion of someone, so if you don't like them in five minutes, you can walk right back inside. What do you say, Aviva?"

Chapter 3
Aviva

This was fucking insanity. Absolute insanity. But when was the last time I'd felt anything at all, let alone the very real fear that had crawled through my veins when this dickhead dragged me out of bed?

Not in years.

The fact my heart was still racing was exhilarating. I felt alive. But I couldn't let this pompous asshole know that I didn't hate this at all. I crossed my arms over my chest, just so he couldn't see my heart trying to beat out of my chest.

"Fine. Five minutes. Why is this so important to you? I'm pretty sure Nurse Flora would follow you out into the dark and happily have an orgy."

He raised both eyebrows and grinned. "Who said anything about an orgy, Viva?"

I flipped him the bird. "Are we doing this or not? Because I'm tired and I want to go back to bed. Not all of us are insomniacs."

He frowned. "What makes you think I'm an insomniac?"

I shrugged, embarrassed. "Lucky guess?" I'd actually watched him through a crack in the door as he paced up and down the hallways at night a few times.

Hendrick didn't say anything, just herded me through the back door, the nurse behind the night desk purposefully not looking up as the door whooshed shut behind us.

The night was bright, and it made the darkness more magical than it had any right to be. Hendrick stepped up to the gate and held out his arms. "I'll lift you over."

I knew this was crazy. Knew that climbing into a fenced pen on the word of someone I didn't know—and who I didn't particularly like—was lunacy. But I was in a center for the mentally unstable. And I was here for not giving a fuck about my personal safety, so that fit too. I shrugged, stepping toward him, and he grinned again.

"Otto!" he called, and someone appeared on the other side of the fence. I didn't get much of a chance to see anything as Hendrick picked me up and physically tossed me over the fence like I weighed nothing.

Holy shit.

I let out a squeal as I flipped over the bars, but two arms grabbed me from the air like I was a football. I was deposited back onto my feet, and I fell into the chest of a huge guy. A huge guy with a bright smile and soft eyes.

Fuck, now a different part of me felt alive.

Hendrick took a run up and vaulted the fence easily. When he landed on the other side, he gave his friend a considering look.

"Oh, so me you hate, but this guy you stare up at like he's the best thing since the clit? That would be right; middle class attracts middle class."

"Fuck off, Drix," the guy grumbled. He looked back down at me, a dimple flashing in one check. "Hi, I'm Otto. Do you need me to punch this asshole in the face?"

Well, swoon.

"No, it's fine. I've already been there and done that tonight." I stepped away from Otto before I did something embarrassing, such as climb him like a tree, and make myself look like an idiot. Especially considering I'd just spent ten minutes acting like a repressed virgin at the mention of an orgy.

On a chaise lounge on the other side of the pool was another guy, his face illuminated by his cellphone.

He was swigging a beer as he scrolled, and I looked over my shoulder at Hendrick.

"Really? Beer in a rehab? That's a little insensitive, don't you think?"

The guy looked up from his phone, and I swear his eyes were entirely black in the darkness. He looked like a demon from hell.

"Are you in here because you're an alcoholic?"

I couldn't look away from the guy's eyes, like I was trapped. "No."

The guy stood, tossing his phone down on the lounger. He sauntered toward me with that cocky rich boy swagger he seemed to have in common with Hendrick. "What are you in here for then?" He stopped a foot in front of me, close enough to tower over me. I lifted my chin and glared back, my eyes briefly dipping to the small scar that crept across his bottom lip.

Swallowing hard, I met his eyes again. This close, I could see they weren't black pits, but they were still dark. I wished it was the middle of the day so I could see exactly what color they were. "That's none of your fucking business."

He didn't move. "Not drugs. You don't have that strung out look about you, like you're coming down. Unless Mommy and Daddy were worried about you taking E at your sorority parties."

"I'm not a drug addict. Or an alcoholic."

He looked me up and down. "You still have tits and ass, so it isn't an eating disorder. You try and kill yourself?"

I tried to stop myself from reacting to his gruff words, but I still flinched. It wasn't because I was remembering the pain. No, it was because that shit was embarrassing. I took failure to a whole new level.

"No."

The guy lifted an eyebrow. "Yes."

Hendrick slapped the guy on the shoulder. "Leave it, man. We're all here for something."

Otto touched my lower back, and I dragged my eyes away from the demon to look over my shoulder at him. "Sorry, he's an asshole too. This is Sampson. He was clearly dropped on his head as a baby, and it made him lose what little tact he was born with."

Otto guided me to one of the chairs, like we were in a formal living room rather than around the dark depths of a pool. Hendrick grabbed a beer from the six-pack beside the pouting Sampson, holding my eyes as he cracked it, like he was daring me to say something about him being in this wellness center for substance abuse. I honestly didn't care though. He was an adult, capable of making adult decisions.

Otto made a noise under his breath, but smiled in my direction when he caught me looking. "Now that

Sampson has rudely discovered you aren't in here for a substance addiction, would you like a beer?"

I shook my head. Otto was dangerously disarming. In close proximity to the other two—who were obviously predators—Otto was like a Venus flytrap, luring you in with a place to rest until he snapped his jaws shut, leaving you trapped.

Even knowing this, I didn't leave.

"Why'd you bring the girl?" Sampson asked Hendrick, who shrugged. That was it. I don't think he even knew why he wanted me here.

"He kidnapped me from my bed."

Sampson raised an eyebrow. "You fucking her?"

I snorted. "In his fucking dreams. I have no interest in rich assholes who believe the world owes them a good old-fashioned dick sucking."

Otto laughed, and Sampson turned his dark gaze on me again. "I see."

That was it. Like I hadn't just disparaged his friend's character. They moved on to talking about people and things that didn't involve me, but I still knew the names. That was the thing about being rich and famous. Everyone knew your business. So when Sampson said a producer had been fired by his firm and blacklisted from Hollywood for having his hands down his proverbial—and literal—pants, I knew who they meant. Same with the socialite who'd been caught snorting coke by the paparazzi. But they interspersed it with talk about UFC fighters, and apparently Otto had a love of bull riding, because he waxed lyrical for ten minutes about a female bull rider coming up in the ranks. I mentally gave her a high five for fucking with all those bigots.

"What about you, Viva?" Hendrick sneered, though I was beginning to understand that sneering was his default setting. He wore his pompous attitude like a shield; he even sounded like that with his friends.

"What about me?"

He rolled his eyes. "Who were you before you were here? Any deep, dark secrets you want to share?"

Hell no. I wouldn't bare my soul to these piranhas. "I was no one."

Sampson leaned forward, steepling his fingers. "Everyone is someone."

"How profound." I flicked my fingers dismissively in his direction, and enjoyed the slight tensing of his jaw at the gesture. "Not me. Beige. Good girl, good grades. Lost my virginity to someone who was on track to be an accountant."

A hand shot out and grabbed my chin, and then Sampson was dragging my face to his, slamming his lips into mine and sucking down my gasp. It was over before I'd even managed to get my synapses firing.

"You don't taste beige, Good Girl."

I shot to my feet, my heart pounding, my mouth hanging open. I could feel the heat surging through my cheeks and I felt all wrong. Or all right. I clutched at my outrage.

"How fucking dare you?" I hissed, striding away but I didn't get very far, because the fucking gate was locked.

Then Otto was there. I tensed as he stepped in close, but he didn't touch me. "Sorry, Aviva. Here, I'll lift you over," he said softly, and it sounded like true regret in his voice.

I gave him stony silence because I didn't know what would come out of my mouth if I spoke. When he lifted me gently over the fence, I clung to the top and carefully lowered myself down.

I stopped and stared at him, while he gave me a soft smile. "Be seeing you, Aviva."

I blinked at him slowly, then fled back inside the safety of the main building.

Chapter 4
Sampson

I watched the girl flee. Probably a safe move.

Otto strode back over with a frown on his face, which meant I was about to get a lecture. Sometimes I thought we kept Otto around because he acted like the conscience that had been burned out of me and Drix from a young age.

"Is that who you are now, Sam?"

"What?"

He sat down, schooling his face into something carefully blank. "I just want to know if that's your new thing. Sexual assault."

Hendrick sucked in air through his teeth, but didn't say anything.

"Fuck off, Otto. I didn't sexually assault anyone."

Otto just gave me that look that said *I think you're a fucking idiot,* but didn't say anything else. I took a long sip on my beer and forgot about the girl. Aviva. Pretty name for an average chick.

I looked around this prison masquerading as a McMansion. It was pretty nice, and honestly, Hendrick had been booted from most of the ones on the West Coast, where we all went to school. About as far as we could get from NYC and our families. Except Otto, of course. His parents loved him, and by extension, probably us.

"How long until you're out of this fucking place?"

Hendrick shrugged. "Whenever I buy my way out, I guess. At least it keeps me out of Dad's way, and I don't have to do any of those goddamn campaign rallies."

Hendrick's dad was a cunt. There was no other word for him. Mine was an asshole too, but he was an asshole in a negligent way. He didn't care if I lived or died, as long as I didn't upset his lifestyle. He would never put me in one of these facilities, even if he found me smacked out on horse tranqs in our foyer. No, he didn't care enough to even pretend.

Honestly, he'd probably be happy.

But Hendrick's dad was a sociopath in a nice suit, ruthlessly trying to obtain the usual things: pussy or power. Always one or the other, and it was Hendrick who suffered. Otto and I were his real family, anyway.

I'd walk through fire for them both—or even worse, sit through one of Otto's lectures on morality.

Otto lifted an eyebrow. "Nothing to do with the pretty Aviva you just dragged out here?"

Hendrick shook his head, taking another sip of his beer. "Nope. Only met her today. She's just something shiny to pass the time. I have been fucking a pretty nurse though. She's very interested in my treatment pathways."

Otto shook his head, letting Hendrick's bullshit slide. "They alter your meds?" A sharp nod from Drix. "You're taking them?"

This time, Hendrick grinned wide. "Some of them."

Poor Otto. Burdened with the need to do the right thing. Quite frankly, I didn't care if Hendrick went unmedicated. I would wreak havoc right there beside him, for no other reason than he was my brother and needed someone to watch his back.

That was Otto's M.O. too, but he did it in a bit more of a conventional—and probably caring—way. He gave a shit if we lived or died, and honestly, he was the only one. Other than the tabloids, that was. Pretty sure they'd be excited if we died.

I emptied my beer and tossed it into the pool. It sank into the dark water with ease. "Then let's get the fuck out of here. We can head to Cabo or something, live it up in the sun. Your dad can pretend you're still here. Or rot in fucking Hell, where he belongs."

I didn't care either way.

Hendrick sighed, leaning back on his elbows. "I'll give it another week. At least the food is better than the last place." Hendrick had been in and out of these facilities since he was twelve. Everyone thought he was a drug addict, and he didn't correct them. Honestly, in the darker hours of the night, I wondered if his father was just setting a precedent so he could off him and point to his history of rehab.

Hendrick didn't need rehab. The guy barely drank, and Otto was way too much of a nagging wife to let either of us take drugs, outside of a little weed. No, Hendrick's parents had no fucking idea that he just hated them. Or maybe they did and this was a convenient excuse to ship him somewhere while they went skiing in Switzerland. Or sailing around Ibiza. I don't even know where his mother was at the moment, but it wasn't anxiously worrying about the health of her son.

I hated people.

"We should go back to college," Otto added, though I knew he was doing his courses online, since being friends with us didn't lend itself to a healthy class schedule. He never complained though. Otto was a saint.

Hendrick was a demon.

And me? I was the fucking devil.

I took what I wanted, because who would stop me? My father was rich, but he wasn't influential. And my grandfather had left me all his money, because he knew that his own child would have blown it all in a decade, leaving us all destitute. I'd invested it, my accountant doing what he needed to do. A second accountant made sure the first one didn't rip me off, and now I was one of the wealthiest men under twenty-five, without working for a cent of it. I kind of knew why people like Aviva were pissed at us. They worked hard, to the point of a mental breakdown apparently, and would never have enough.

I was born with enough and I'd die with enough.

We shot the shit for a little longer, giving Hendrick the normalcy he so desperately needed. He was a fucking asshole, of that there was no doubt, but he needed us. He'd never really admit it, any more than I would, but it was true.

The sun began to peek over the horizon, which was our cue to leave. I stood and hugged Hendrick. I hated he was in here without anyone to watch out for him, and I knew Otto felt the same. But Hendrick wasn't some weakling; he'd been running this place within twenty-four hours, because money talked. But still, there was a difference between getting your dick sucked by a nurse, and being with your boys.

"I'll give you a week and then we're breaking you out of this shithole."

He laughed like I was kidding. I wasn't.

I watched as Otto gave him a hug too. We hugged like we meant it—doing weird, one-armed hugs in case one of you thought the other was gay was ridiculous. Science said we needed ten minutes of human contact a day for mental health, and I wasn't going to hug any other fuckers, especially not my parents. If I hugged a girl for too long, she started thinking we were more than we were.

So that left these guys, and they both hugged like they were touch-starved.

We went our separate ways, jumping the pool fence and then the back security fence. It wasn't really meant to keep people in. If the inmates of this facility wanted out, they could walk out the front doors, or hop the back fence without much problem. But when it came down to it, you couldn't help people who didn't want to help themselves in places like this, and if their symptoms were any worse, they'd be in a psych facility and not in a resort masquerading as a medical center.

"He looks good," Otto said, and I grunted my agreement. We'd seen every side of Hendrick. Sometimes I'd been too scared to leave his side; sometimes I'd rescued him from situations that only had the potential to be bad. Sometimes he'd done the same for me.

But he did look good tonight, his face alive and animated. And with the way he'd looked at that girl, I knew he was on the hunt, which made me feel a little bad for Aviva. Didn't matter, I would sacrifice a hundred good girls to Hendrick's beast to keep it at bay for another day.

I was surprised my rental Maserati was still parked under the streetlight where we'd left it. This really was a nice neighborhood. "Wanna go get breakfast?"

Otto smiled at me, and I once again thought he had an almost feminine prettiness about him. Don't get me wrong, he was tall and broad, but he had soft, full lips, long eyelashes and kind eyes. It was catnip for women; I didn't get it, but Otto had it in spades.

"Hell yeah, I'm dying for something deep-fried or smothered in syrup. Mom is on another juice cleanse, so the whole time I was home, it was kale three meals a day."

He shuddered, and I huffed out a laugh. It wasn't quite right when it was just the two of us—we were always meant to be a trio—but still comfortable. One more week and things would be back to normal.

As I started the car and roared away, I couldn't wait.

Chapter 5
Aviva

I'd purposefully avoided Hendrick like he was the plague. If I so much as saw a glint of golden hair, I turned on my heel and went the other direction. If he was in the dining room, I ate in my bedroom. At least he didn't go to group therapy.

I'd managed to avoid him for four whole days. Those days were spent hiding in the chapel, reading Verne and the margin notes of the guy I'd started to think of as Captain Nemo. Which was dumb, but he and Nemo seemed to have the same views on humanity and life. They both loathed it, yet were drawn to protect it. In my head, he was Nemo. His words, written in scratchy black ink, slightly smeared like he was left-handed, they spoke directly to my soul. Like he was talking to me.

· · ·

Can you imagine loving someone so much that you couldn't stand the idea of humanity without them? I want that kind of love, and nothing else will do.

I couldn't imagine it, no. I didn't even love myself like that. But one thing I did know was that I wanted to meet Nemo. I wanted to understand him. Wanted to hear him speak the words he wrote down in that slightly tragic voice.

When the door to the chapel opened and closed softly, I shut the book and looked over my shoulder. I groaned at the sight of Hendrick. It wouldn't matter that he was an asshole, if he wasn't so damn pretty on top of it. My body thought he was sexy as hell, even as my brain rebelled against finding anything redeemable about him.

My hate for him was visceral, and probably unwarranted. But like having a crush on Nemo—who I'd romanticized so much that he may as well be a fictional character in a Verne novel—my loathing was irrational.

I sighed heavily as he came and sat beside me. "I'm praying here, Hendrick," I said testily, and he grinned.

"Didn't take you as the religious type, Viva," he purred. I really wished he wouldn't say my name like that. Like it was foreplay.

I gave him a dead-eyed stare. "You don't know a thing about me."

He quirked an eyebrow. "I know you're here because you almost mowed down your neighbor. I know it was either here or jail for you. I know your parents work average jobs, a medical receptionist and the manager of a hardware store. I know you tried to kill yourself when you ran into that tree, or at least it was a cry for help. Nice girls don't slit their wrists in bathtubs for their mamas to find."

My whole body went ramrod straight. "How fucking dare you?" I said, my body trembling with rage.

He shrugged like he had every right to my history. "I know that you've got a failing GPA, and you're lost, Aviva Robinson. So hopelessly lost, there's no way out."

He turned back to the front of the pulpit, staring at the cross that hung on the wall like a grim reminder of our sins. I tried to ignore the ache in his words. But no matter how much he tried to hide the pain, and I tried to ignore it, it sat between us like a deflated balloon.

Finally, he turned those bright blue eyes that saw too much back to me. "So it looks like Sampson was right. Not so beige after all."

My body was still so stiff that my muscles were beginning to ache. The mention of his asshole friend, and that kiss, was like pulsing electricity through my body. "What do you want, Hendrick?"

"I'm bored."

"Then go fuck the nursing staff. Or hell, Esther van Wold is in here, and she's been eyeing you like you're a popsicle she'd like to deepthroat."

A laugh burst past his lips. "You have a dirty mouth, Viva. I like it." He watched me for a few more seconds, and then faced back toward the non-denominational pulpit. "You leave in a few days, liberated early for good behaviour. What are you going to do?"

I shrugged. I knew what I wanted to do, but I wasn't going to tell Hendrick. "Go back to school, probably."

"Mmm, predictable." He stood, petting me on the head like I was a wayward poodle and not a human being. "Good luck, Viva." He snorted. "The irony though, right? Viva means 'long live,' and you tried to kill yourself. Life is a funny thing."

I narrowed my eyes at him. "Hilarious."

He just chuckled and left, leaving me in the silence of my thoughts. Fucking Hendrick, he was in my head now. Standing with a sigh, I left the chapel and went to the phone room. We got five minutes a day, and it was about time my parents were waiting for me to call.

I waited for the guy in front of me to finish with the phone. He wasn't doing anything but grunting occasionally, but I pretended to fuss with my book to give him the illusion of privacy, even though he stared at me the whole time.

Finally, he ran out of time, slamming down the phone without apparently saying anything to the other person on the line. He continued to glare at me until he left the room, and I went over to the phone. You had to lean in real close, because the cord couldn't be long enough to... you know.

I dialled my parents' home number, the only number I knew off by heart. They answered on the second ring, which told me they'd been waiting around for my call.

"Hello?"

My mom's voice was always like a soothing balm to my soul. "Hey, Mom."

"Aviva! How are you doing, baby?"

It didn't even matter that we had essentially the same conversation every day. "I'm doing good. Excited to leave in a few days."

I heard my dad's low hum in the background. "Not as excited as we'll be to have you home. Just in time for the new semester too. Get back to normalcy."

I hesitated. "I don't think I'll go back this year, Dad. Just give myself some time to figure out what I want to do." I paused, the idea I'd been formulating all week on the tip of my tongue. "I thought I might travel a little bit, find out... I don't know. Find something."

There was a long, silent pause on the other end of the phone, making me wonder if it had disconnected. No, the silence was way too loud. I could almost see my parents looking at each other, having a silent conversation about me. I'd seen it a million times.

"I'm not sure that's a good idea, Aviva," Mom said gently, like giving me the slightest bit of bad news was going to send me back into a manic episode.

Past Aviva would have let it go at that, not wanting to burden her parents anymore. Hell, even now I had to resist the urge to tell them that it was okay, it was just an idea.

But no, I really wanted this. "I was thinking about doing a tour around the world, uh, like a literary tour or something. You know I like books."

A choked noise came from the other end of the line. "Where do you suppose we'd get the money for that? We already took out a second mortgage so you could get the help you needed to find yourself in there."

"Thomas," my mom chastised, but guilt was already washing over me like a wave. They'd given up so much, working twice as hard now to cover the bills.

"No, Mom. Dad is right. You guys have done enough. It was just an idea." I cleared my throat. "Tell me about Dr. Stefan. How's his wife? Has she had the baby yet?"

Mom, bless her heart, grabbed the conversational olive branch and ran with it. I listened to their lives for another four minutes until I ran out of time.

"I love you guys. You know that, right?"

They wasted no time echoing it back to me. As I hung up, sadness washed over me. They were right though—it would be better if I got back to my life. Leave this whole thing behind, with the joy of a good antidepressant and a smile.

I handed over the phone to the next person waiting in the room, a girl who was in one of the other group therapy sessions so I didn't know her name. I stepped out of the room, looking up and down the hallway.

I thought I saw a flash of Hendrick's gold hair in the rec room, so I turned and went the other direction. I didn't need any more headfuckery from that asshole. Moving down the labyrinth of halls toward my room, I didn't meet anyone's eyes. My room was empty when I got there, and I breathed a second sigh of relief. It wasn't that I didn't like Tova, my roommate. Well, actually it was exactly that. Her parents thought she was an addict, but really, she was just an asshole. She hadn't come down at all, so obviously she was either still getting high in here, or she was just a selfish jerk with no morals.

She probably said the same thing about me. I was so ready to leave this place. I didn't feel any more 'healed' than I did when I first entered, but the antidepressants were good. Made me feel more balanced. That was something.

Something to keep me comfortably numb.

Chapter 6
Hendrick

I'd eavesdropped outside the phone room yesterday. I didn't feel guilty; it was a room with no door. Anyone could listen. But Aviva's soft conversation sparked something in me, or maybe it was the look of desolation on her face. Maybe it was the idea that someone who hoped for nothingness could still be disappointed. Which then gave me an idea.

I just had to convince the guys. And by the guys, I meant Otto. Sampson wouldn't give two shits. After I convinced them, then I had to convince Aviva.

Me: Hey, leaving Friday at four a.m. Pack for a trip to Europe.

Otto: The fuck?

Sam: Want me to organize the private jet or are we going commercial?

I chewed my lip.

Me: Let's go commercial. Don't want dear old Dad ordering the plane to turn around.

Sam: Fuck your dad, we'll take mine.

Otto: This is the most ridiculous conversation. We're still in Florida. Want us to come and see you?

Me: Just get us flights to JFK, I have to stop and grab some stuff first. Four flights.

Otto: Four?

I stuffed the phone back in my pocket. I'd answer all their questions later, but there was no point if I couldn't get Aviva to agree. I didn't examine why I wanted to sink a fuckload of money into traveling around the world with a girl who hated my guts, but at least it was interesting.

Pulling the door of my suite closed, I was glad that I didn't have to share my space with some fucking Neanderthal. Starting my search for Aviva, I worked from the outside in. She was hard to track down, and I was starting to get the idea that perhaps she was avoiding me. A smile curled my lips. This was why I liked her.

Esther appeared in front of me, like the ghost of girlfriends past. Aviva hadn't been wrong about Esther wanting to fuck me; we'd hooked up at a party once, and now she thought I owed her something—mostly my dick. Her desperation clung to her like an oil slick, and it made my stomach turn.

"Hendrick," she whined.

"Esther," I whined back as I continued to move toward the back door. But Esther gripped my shirt and dragged me back.

"Wanna go to my room? My father made a sizable donation so that I could get my own suite."

"No."

She huffed and strode away, in sneakers instead of her normal stilettos. No wonder she seemed so short. Otto would be happy she was in here—she'd been snorting so much coke lately, it was a wonder she still had a septum.

I checked outside, under all the trees, knowing that was where Aviva liked to read. I even checked the pumphouse in case she was in there with that dumb-shit. But I was pretty confident she wasn't outside. I started inside, checking the dining and rec rooms, and then the chapel. Still nothing. Maybe she'd left early?

I didn't want to analyze the thump in my chest at that thought. It was probably just disappointment that I couldn't use her as an excuse to fly around the world on a whim.

I also ignored the relieved whoosh of breath that flowed from me when I finally spotted her wild blonde curls. Ducking into the infamous supply closet —because I knew she'd probably turn tail and run if she spotted me—I watched through the crack in the door. I waited until she was just passing by, then threw it open, grabbed her arm, and dragged her in with me.

She let out a scream, and I slammed my hand over her mouth. "It's me."

I'd learned my lesson from last time because I pulled my hand away before she could bite me.

"Honestly, you are so fucked in the head, Hendrick Kenley. You need way more therapy than you're getting. What did I say about dragging girls into dark-ened corners?" she hissed, and I would be damned if her chastisement didn't just amuse me more.

I shrugged. "You were hiding from me."

"Most people would know that meant I didn't want anything to do with you, dickhead."

"Not even if I fly you around the world on your literary search for salvation?"

Her whole body froze. "What?"

"I will pay for your entire trip. First class. To what-ever destination you need to see to 'find' yourself."

She stared at me again, her mouth falling open. "No."

Now it was my turn to gape. "No?"

She shook her head, taking a giant step away from

me. Well, as far as she could go in a tiny closet. "No. Do you need me to say it in Spanish? No."

I smothered a smile. That was pretty fucking cute. "Why not?"

"Are you serious right now?" She took a deep breath. "Why do you think? I am not prostituting myself for an around the world trip. Ask Esther. She'd happily do it, and you'd probably only have to take her to Vermont."

I snorted. "Viva, that was unnecessarily catty." She snorted back, giving me a glare that burned even in the darkness. "There's no strings attached to this. Except that you have to let us tag along."

"Us?" she squeaked.

"Me, Otto..." I paused. "And Sampson."

She went to step around me but slammed straight into my chest, and I wrapped an arm around her back to hold her steady. It made her body press against mine, and I resisted the urge to push her against the door and grind against her until she was mewling.

Instead, because I wanted something, I gently set her right. She was shaking her head, though I could tell she was turning over my offer in her brain. "You don't even know where I want to go."

I shrugged. "Doesn't matter. Anywhere."

"That's insane."

I sighed; this part was dull. "Look. I wasn't kidding

about being bored. Plus, I saw your face when I assumed your parents refused to pay fifty grand for you to galavant"—I looked down at the book in her hand—"around the world. Maybe in eighty days?" I paused, and tried to be as earnest as possible. "I want to just *do* something. Preferably somewhere outside the country."

She hesitated then, like taking this thing for herself was too much, but if she was doing it for me, it might be okay. She looked like the type, really. Bleeding hearts, or maybe people who never believe they're worthy of getting what they want unless it also benefits someone else. A poor person's problem—not an affliction I suffered from.

She chewed her lip. "My parents won't go for it."

I lifted my hand and let my fingertips trace the curve of her cheek. She stiffened but didn't move away. "Better to ask forgiveness than permission."

"There'll be rules."

I snorted a laugh. "I wouldn't expect anything else. Hit me with them."

"No sex."

I screwed up my nose. "No sex unless you give express and enthusiastic consent." I grinned. "Gotta keep your options open. I saw you eyefucking Otto."

"Fine," she huffed. "But I'm going to pay you back."

I rolled my eyes. "Sure, I'll even do low interest so you can finish paying me back when you're sixty-seven."

She crossed her arms, which made her breasts sit up higher, and I tried not to look. Emphasis on *tried*. "And you don't ask questions. We go where I want, when I want."

I nodded, my grin growing wide. "Done. We leave Friday at four a.m." I stepped closer to her, boxing her between my body and the door. "But to keep up the ruse and maintain my reputation, I'm going to have to kiss you a little, make it look like you were just in here giving in to my charm, rather than planning a great escape."

"Fine." She pouted like it was a hardship, obviously not realizing I could feel the racing of her heart against my chest.

I grabbed her chin and tilted her face up, only just seeing the outline of her features in the light through the cracked door. "Remember what I said about express and enthusiastic consent?"

She gnawed her bottom lip. "This isn't sex."

I grinned again. "It's going to feel like it." I leaned forward until my lips just brushed hers. "Say it, Viva."

She didn't sound like she was even breathing as she whispered, "Fine. You can kiss me. Enthusiastically."

I smirked at her snark. The girl obviously didn't

know that the chase was the best part of this. And she was a juicy gazelle.

I pressed my lips to hers, running my hand up the back of her neck to bury my fingers in her riotous hair. Then I kissed her hard. A bruising kiss, that's what they'd call it in romance novels. The type that makes you pant and your lips get all pink and swollen, and you look thoroughly fucked. We hadn't got to that last part yet, but soon.

She let out a small moan as she kissed me back, angling her mouth so she could suck my lip between her teeth and bite down. I hissed and pulled away a little, chuckling deep in my chest.

When she stumbled out of the closet two minutes later, she looked thoroughly debauched. I was patting myself on the back for a job well done, ignoring my own thundering heart that threatened to beat out of my chest.

Chapter 7
Otto

Electric cars made subversive getaways much easier. They idled silently, or the battery turned off, or something. I wasn't a car guy. But the Tesla we hired did its job perfectly as we waited outside Hendrick's rehab at the asscrack of dawn. I was glad we'd decided to hang around. Despite seeming really good, there'd been something about him the other day that had compelled us to stay. In fucking Tampa.

I was pretty sure Sampson had drunk every fancy ass country club out of top shelf whiskey, and fucked every single waitress while he was at it. And it had only been three days. He was asleep in the passenger seat. Sam didn't do early mornings, but had still insisted we be exactly on time.

The Pixies played softly from the speakers and I

tapped my fingers on the steering wheel to the beat. I watched the front doors, the lights still on the lowest setting in there, no one ready to get out of bed quite just yet.

I was watching those doors so hard, that when someone knocked on the passenger door, I jumped so hard my seat belt locked around my neck and I made a choking sound. Sampson, however, just opened a single eye like a sleeping dragon.

Outside the window was Hendrick's grinning face. Fucker.

I unlocked the doors, and he opened the rear passenger one. I really hadn't expected Aviva to climb in though. I don't know why; it fit with Hendrick's usual method of act first, think later. But she didn't seem like that kind of girl—the type who'd be taken in by Hendrick's innate charm.

I popped the trunk and climbed out to help Hendrick load the bags. "The fuck, man? Is this why we're leaving so goddamn early? Are we abducting her?"

He raised an eyebrow. "Does she look unwilling? Besides, she's twenty-one. I checked. It isn't kidnapping."

I took several fortifying breaths. "I thought you said she was here for a court-mandated period of time."

"Runs out today for good behavior."

Deep breaths, Otto. Deep fucking breaths. "Then why are we sneaking out of here at dawn like you just fucked the preacher's daughter?"

He snorted and slammed the boot closed. "I'm cutting off your romance novels, you sappy bastard." He walked around the driver's side with me, still muttering. "Look, her parents were coming to pick her up at lunchtime anyway. She just has other plans. I'm giving her a ride."

I narrowed my eyes. "A ride to where, exactly?"

He grinned, opening the rear door. "To Europe."

With that, he ducked into the backseat, leaving me gaping after him. What the actual fuck was going on right now? Opening my door, I climbed in, and looked over my shoulder at Aviva. She was as pretty as I remembered, although maybe her hair was just a little more chaotic this morning, her grin a little more manic.

"Are you being held hostage? Blink twice if you are."

She laughed, a soft sound that seemed almost too throaty. "No, I'm here voluntarily."

Sampson grunted something under his breath and then gave me a pointed look. "You can interrogate her later. We have a plane to catch and civilization to return to."

We rode to the airport in silence, returning the car

to the valet, and checking our bags ourselves to skip the unnecessary human interaction. When we made it to the first class lounge, Sampson dived on the breakfast buffet like it was an actual lifeline. I directed Aviva toward a comfortable set of couches, and Hendrick flopped onto an armchair sideways.

"Fuck, it's early. Why did we get flights this early?"

"Because you said you wanted to leave at the first sign of dawn, remember?" I looked at the girl beside us. "If I'd known you were stealing a girl, I would have been a gentleman and booked a flight at a more respectable time."

Aviva let out a strangled noise that could have been a cough or a laugh. "Not stolen, remember? Adult."

"Well, obviously not in your right mind, if you're going along with whatever half-assed plan this asshole talked you into."

Hendrick just shrugged, not even defending himself. "I told you to get four tickets. Who did you think the other one was for? My invisible friend?"

"You stopped seeing Jeffery when you were six." Hendrick glared at me, and I gave him my own smug smirk back. "No, I foolishly believed you were bringing Nurse Ratched, or whatever her name was that you've been fucking for weeks. Convinced her to give you a little in-home care, one-on-one."

Aviva flushed, and I chased away my guilt. She should know what she was signing herself up for if she went along with this. Hendrick just waved a hand like that was yesterday's news, which obviously it was.

Sampson broke the tension of the conversation by returning with a huge tray of pastries and a single coffee. He sat it in front of himself, obviously not willing to share.

I stood with a sigh. "You guys have the manners of barbarians."

Sampson glared up at me from sleep-hooded eyes. "What? I'm not your fucking bitch, Otto."

Still shaking my head, I looked at Aviva. "Come on, we'll get you some breakfast." Aviva went to grab her purse, which was cute, but I waved it away. "Nah, it's all included in the ticket." I led her through the line, collecting the things she pointed out and putting it on a tray. Fruit salad and yogurt. Healthy.

"So, what's actually going on? Last time we met, I got the impression you hated Hendrick and everything he represented."

She eyed a roast vegetable quiche. "Can I have three things?"

Her eyes were too big for her face. That's what gave her that fragile doe-eyed look, even if her gaze was shrewd. "You can have one of everything if you want."

She gave me a quick grin and put the quiche on the tray too, grabbing a tiny bottle of hot sauce. "I still hate everything he represents. But he made me an offer I couldn't refuse."

I knew all about Hendrick's deals. My jaw tensed at the idea of Aviva being one of the girls who threw themselves at Hendrick for his old ass family name and bulging trust fund.

She looked over, and I mustn't have kept my thoughts off my face well enough, because she frowned too. "Not that kind of offer. I didn't prostitute myself for a first class trip to New York, Otto. Jesus, you guys are all the same."

She stepped around me and over to the beverage section, pulling out a herbal tea bag from the carefully curated collection of artisanal teas. She ignored me as she filled a cup with hot water and strode back to the couches.

Halfway there, she stopped and doubled back, not stopping until she was in front of me, as close as she could get with the tray between us. "Let's get this straight. This isn't some bad reboot of Pretty Woman. This wasn't my fucking idea, but when life hands you an all-expenses-paid trip around Europe, you damn well take it. But there were three rules, and I'm gonna make them really clear to you and Sampson as well."

She spun on her heel, marching back toward the guys until she was standing in between all the couches, her knees bumping the coffee table.

"Listen up. Rule number one: I'm not fucking *any* of you, so you can stop looking at me with those damn bedroom eyes," she hissed, pointing at Sampson.

He grinned, and it was a shark smile. "Didn't want to screw you anyway, Good Girl. You aren't my type."

I saw her shoulders stiffen, but she didn't snark back. "Two: I'm not freeloading this. So, no paying for my food, or anything else. I'm paying Hendrick back the flights and hotels... eventually."

It would take her a decade to pay off this flight from Tampa to NYC, let alone Europe, but I didn't tell her that.

"Third thing?" I prompted. She looked at me over her shoulder.

"No questions. We do what I want to do, and go where I want to go, without the psychoanalysis."

Yeah, that one might have been aimed directly at me.

"Viva, as long as you don't wanna go to my place for dinner with my folks, I don't care where the hell we go," Hendrick joked, drinking some of Sampson's coffee, and nearly losing a hand by way of a butter knife.

66

I waved Aviva into a seat and handed her the things she'd chosen for breakfast. "Sorry, Aviva. I wasn't implying you were, uh, swapping one service for another. I just know Hendrick, and he could talk a nun into a tango between black silk sheets, you know?" I said in a low voice, because we were beginning to draw attention from the surrounding travelers. "I know you said no questions. But where are we going first?"

"New York City."

Hendrick lifted his head up. "I need some stuff from there too."

I hummed low. I was anxious to get out my journal and write notes, but I resisted. "And what about your passport?"

She froze, and her face turned down, like sadness was dragging it low. She looked like a kicked puppy. "I don't have it. It's back home in Columbia." She gave me a sad smile, waving a hand like it meant nothing. "It was a bit of a crazy idea anyway."

Sampson grunted, though he looked like he was back to dozing. "Don't stress it, Good Girl. I'll take care of it."

She blinked at him, where he was strewn across the couch in uncaring insouciance, and then looked over at me, like I was the calm voice of reason. "Can he do that?" she whispered.

"Don't know if you fully comprehend this yet, Aviva, but once you spend some time with these two, you soon will. There is no obstacle that money can't overcome, and Sampson is richer than God." I nudged her shoulder with mine. "Welcome to how the other half live."

Chapter 8
Aviva

First class was an experience. Actually, being with the guys in general was an experience. They were moved to the front of lines, given extra attention, given the best of everything because they oozed two things. Money and good looks. I tried to ignore the incredulous eye widening that all the customer service people got when they saw me tagging along at the back, and after one gate assistant tried to stop me going on with them—because I was an obvious interloper—Hendrick had taken to throwing an arm around my shoulders and holding me close, like we were lovers. The incredulous looks got worse, and some were downright catty, but at least no one barred my entry anywhere.

But first class itself? It was a little slice of luxury,

even though it was only a two and a bit hour flight. We were seated immediately, in seats that were as wide as a recliner and with enough leg room for an NBA player. It was better than being crammed in economy, but the guys still looked reasonably disdainful. Hendrick raised an eyebrow at Sampson.

"What? You said I couldn't bring the jet. I'm not your travel agent, asshole." He slumped down in his seat, with Otto sitting next to him, and Hendrick and I across the aisle.

Once we were seated, a pretty hostess came down, greeting us with champagne and 'fuck me' eyes cast in the direction of Sampson and Otto. At least she kept them to herself in regards to Hendrick, who I assume she thought was my boyfriend.

"Please, enjoy the complimentary champagne as the flight is boarding. If you need anything further, don't be afraid to press the assistance button."

She bustled off to greet other passengers, and I belted myself into my seat. I turned off my phone, knowing I only had a few more hours until my parents arrived at the center and realized I wasn't there.

Otto leaned across the aisle. "Now, I know you said no questions..."

I grinned at him. He was really easy to like, dammit. "You're going to struggle with that one, aren't you?"

Sampson snorted a laugh, and Otto elbowed him in the ribs. "I have to email our travel agent about a destination, even if it's just for the first leg."

I chewed my lip, pulling out the copy of Jules Verne that I'd stolen from the center. Hendrick raised an eyebrow. "Didn't see anything about being a klepto in your medical files, Viva."

"Of course you read her medical files," Otto groaned.

I ignored them both, and flicked the book open to the last page. I'd read the note over and over before deciding to do this, talking myself in and out of it several times before committing. It read:

Come and find me, and if our destinies are meant to intertwine, I'll be waiting with the Francs at the corner of 5th Ave and E79th.

Hendrick read over my shoulder, then gave me a look that I knew too well. I'd given it to myself in the mirror numerous times since I read the words.

"We're traveling around Europe because you're chasing someone who could've written in that book five years ago? You know how that sounds, right?"

It sounded crazy, I knew that. But I tensed my jaw

and glared at the three of them. "Rule number three." Otto was looking at me, not with incredulity, but with actual concern. Like I was actually mentally unwell still. Heat flooded to my cheeks and I doubled down on my stubbornness. "Maybe he'll be in New York and this will be a very short trip, okay? Or maybe he won't be there at all and we've had a great trip around the world. Just... let it go."

Hendrick shrugged, and grabbed the book, flicking through the pages. The Captain came over the speaker and gave the usual speech, while the flight attendants ran through the safety briefing that no one in the first class section actually watched.

Finally, we were taxiing down the runway, and I gripped the seat as we lifted into the air. It always terrified me, this moment where you were hurtling down the asphalt in a giant tin can only held to land by some tiny wheels that they literally pulled off the ground.

We jerked up and down a bit, bumping across the runway, and my heart stopped. This was the part where we hurtled off the end of the runway and into a steep embankment, where the plane snapped in half, and the front—with all the first class passengers—burst into flames.

A warm hand covered mine, and I realized I'd been gripping Hendrick's forearm like a vice. "It's okay, we're in the air now. Safer than driving a car."

I unclenched my fingers from his sleeve and gave him a tight smile. "Sorry," I mumbled, and when the hostess came back around with a bottle of champagne, I gladly held my glass out for more.

Two episodes of some cop show, one gourmet snack of cheese that smelled like ass, three complimentary chocolates and too much champagne later, we were touching down at JFK. We alighted first, and I swerved a little bit as I stood. The champagne had definitely gone to my head. Otto put his hand out to steady me as Hendrick carried my duffle bag.

I dreaded turning my phone back on, but as we stood at the baggage claim, I switched it off airplane mode.

Still nothing. I breathed out a sigh of relief, then guilt washed over me. They were going to drive all the way to Tampa and I wasn't going to be there.

Me: Checked out early. Going to take some time to sort some things out. I'm fine, I promise. I'll text every day. Love you xxoo

Then, because I was a chicken, I turned my phone back off. Our bags came onto the conveyor belt first, and the guys plucked them off. A driver waited with a sign, 'Kenley' printed across it, and Hendrick went over and spoke to the man in a low voice. There was a tenseness in his shoulders that hadn't been there before, and when he returned to us, his face was grim.

"I have to go home first. I've been summoned." He looked over at Otto. "Take her to the St. Regis. And to wherever she wants to go. I'll meet you guys later." He paused and looked at me. "If we could leave for Europe sooner rather than later, I'd appreciate it."

I tried not to feel extremely awkward as we slid into a town car, with rear-facing seats and everything. I sat beside Sampson, who was on the phone again, this time booking a room at a hotel.

For me.

"Don't you all live in New York?"

Otto nodded. "Yep."

"I don't need a fancy hotel. I'm pretty sure I could stay at a Motel 6 or something around here." I looked out the window as we passed a number of budget hotels that surrounded the airport.

Otto gave me a bright smile. "Don't worry about it, Viva," he said, adopting Hendrick's shortening of my name. "Sampson lives at the Regis permanently, so it isn't a big deal. We'll just get you a room near his."

We fell silent again and I watched the city through the window. I'd never been to New York City. Tampa was the furthest I'd ever been from home. I even went to college near home. Went home every summer.

New York was insanely busy, but as we crossed into Manhattan, I began to see things I'd only seen on TV, and excitement ran through my veins.

When we pulled up in front of the St. Regis, I gasped. It was beautiful. And I was in leggings and an oversized hoodie. As a woman in a gorgeous dress—the kind that I'd only ever wear to a job interview, or maybe a wedding—walked past and up the stairs, I realized that I did not belong here.

Otto slid out, heading over to talk to the doorman, while Sampson held open the door. He put his hand on my lower back and propelled me up the stairs to the front desk. I stood there, gaping at the beautiful fresco that flowed from the ceiling and down the walls. It was opulent in the extreme.

"This is Aviva Robinson. She's checking in."

The woman gave Sampson a tight smile. "Apologies, Mr. Rubio, but we haven't had her room made up yet. It will only be—"

"She'll be in my room. Call up when it's ready and have her things sent straight to her room."

"Yes, sir."

God, that must grate. A grown woman having to call Sampson sir, when he was what, twenty-three or twenty-four? Hell, that would drive me nuts.

Sampson ushered me into the elevator, Otto joining us a second later. "Her room isn't ready. We can chill in mine until it is."

A part of me—probably the remaining sane part—said going to a hotel room with two men I'd known for a sum total of two hours plus a plane flight wasn't a great idea. But that same part had also warned me that galavanting off to Europe with three strangers—who clearly had enough money to buy off the authorities in whatever country we ended up in—was probably not the safest move.

I'd ignored her then and I'd ignore her now. I was going to give these guys the benefit of the doubt, and if they chopped me up and put me in a barrel to drop into the Hudson river, then so be it.

I could hear Dr. Arubut's dry voice droning on about risky behavior. At least I didn't actively want to die anymore—that should count for something.

The doors to the lift opened and we stepped out into a hall, walking toward the door right at the end. Sampson opened it and strode in, not waiting for me to go first. Fair enough, he didn't seem the chivalrous type.

When I stepped into the room, I gasped. It was beautiful, and also completely impersonal.

"Welcome to my humble abode, Good Girl. Make

yourself comfortable. I need to shower." And then he disappeared into a gleaming marble bathroom.

Holy shit.

Chapter 9
Hendrick

The driver pulled up to my family's brownstone, and I slowly climbed out. Fuck, I hated this house. "Thanks, Reynolds." I'd left my bag with Otto, just in case shit went bad. And when it came to my family, it always went bad.

I knocked, and the butler opened the door. He was a new one; they never stayed around for long. They came and went. Either my father fired them in a fit of rage because they laid out the wrong tie, or my mother got caught banging them in the pantry.

I strode straight upstairs to get the shit I needed, so when I inevitably stormed out, I'd have it with me. Taking the stairs two at a time, I was relieved to make it to my room without running into either of my parents.

My room was immaculate, untouched. More like a hotel room than my bedroom, considering I never stayed here if I could help it. I didn't stop to look at the small pile of letters on my dresser, or bother to pack any clothes. Money could buy me that shit. Instead, I walked right to the end of my walk-in closet, pushing open the false front on the very end cabinet. If you opened the drawers, you'd see my collection of Rolexes and cufflinks. But if you pushed it into just the right position, the false front opened, revealing a safe behind it. Wasn't much there: important documents, a couple of photos from when I was a kid. Ten thousand in cash. My passport.

Grabbing a couple of bundles of cash and my passport, I grabbed a jacket and stuffed it all into the pockets. That was it. All I needed from this place.

I briefly wondered if I could sneak back out again before my father found me, but his voice bellowing up the stairs killed that dream dead. Dad was good at crushing dreams.

"Hendrick!" he yelled again, and I unconsciously walked faster. Old habits died hard. He was sitting in the den, in his chair, sipping what was probably forty-year-old scotch for no other reason than he could.

"You hollered?"

He narrowed his eyes at me, and I resisted the urge to needle him more. I needed to get in and out of here, back to Sampson and Otto. And Aviva. The addition of her company was like throwing fireworks into a whorehouse. Just Sampson's response to her was worth the chewing out that I was about to get any second now.

"The rehab called me."

Yeah, he refused to call it anything but rehab, like I was a junkie instead of...

"Oh yeah, what did they say?"

"That you bought your way out of therapy and abducted another patient when you left."

I snorted. "That's not true. It was her release day and she came willingly. And a lot." I gave him a smarmy grin, because Dad only knew two things in life. Power and pussy. He never saw the woman who existed above the tits. He wouldn't understand the thrill I got from the fact that she couldn't stand me.

He chuckled low, and took a swill of his scotch. "I need you on the campaign trail with me."

"I can't. I have college."

"If you can buy your way out of rehab, you can buy your grades, son."

I shook my head. "I promised Sampson I'd go to Europe with him, and you know, his company pays a lot in political donations."

My father ground his back teeth, because he knew I was right and he didn't want to piss off Sampson. "I'm sure Mr. Rubio can go to Europe without you holding his dick." I didn't say anything, just gazed around the room looking bored. "I need you back here before the primary elections, Hendrick."

I huffed out a sigh. "Can't you just tell everyone I'm dead and get the sympathy vote?"

The coldness in my father's eyes should have chilled me to my bones, but he'd been looking at me like that for as long as I could remember. "I could, if you stopped getting drunk and fucking debutantes in the back of Bentleys and letting the paparazzi photograph it for prosperity." He sucked in a breath. "You will be back here in three weeks for the primaries, or I'll cut you off."

A laugh burst from my chest, and I knew it was a bad idea as soon as I did it. But fuck it, I was all in now. "Cut me off from what? The money is mine, remember? We just aren't telling your constituents that."

In a love story as old as time, my father came from a good, all-American, blue-blooded family—who were poor as fuck, their money squandered away thanks to bad stock portfolio management and too much pride. It was my mother who had all the money. She came from new money, and my grandfather had been a wily old fuck. I missed him.

Still, he'd left me the money and not my parents, a small fact that pissed Dad off every day. I funded his shit, he left me alone, and together my parents burned through my mother's very ample trust fund.

"How about I get your psychiatrist to declare you mentally unwell and put you under a conservatorship?"

Ice ran through my veins, but I'd been preparing for that too. Since the first time he'd put me in rehab when I'd been fourteen, I'd been gathering my own case, ensuring that I had my own expert witnesses to confirm I was of sound mind and body. There were medical files, police reports that never went anywhere, recordings of shady shit and double crosses, all stashed in a lockbox beneath Otto's childhood bed. Even back then, I'd known Otto was the one person I could trust above all else.

Father didn't know any of that though. If he did, I'd already be dead. Still, the thought that he could take over my life by convincing one of his judge buddies that I was nuts terrified me.

My father stood, walking over to me, a smile on his face. "We both know that I could." He lifted his glass and smashed it against my temple.

I staggered to the left, reaching out to grab the armchair as stars danced in my vision. Adrenaline burst through my veins as he stepped closer, leaning over me. "Listen to me, you little fuck. You'll do what you're told or I will make your life so fucking miserable, you'll have a reason to hang yourself from a shower curtain rail."

I could feel the slow trickle of blood down my temple as I cowered. I hated myself. Hated myself for shrinking away, when I knew I could punish him right back. I could smash his head in with the crystal ashtray on the occasional table beside me, just keep beating until his head was mush.

In my head, I did just that.

But my body stayed frozen, my head throbbing from the cut that he'd opened in my scalp, until he strode out of the room like it was nothing. Like he didn't beat the shit out of me whenever he felt like it, didn't make my life so damn miserable that I hadn't considered ending it numerous times. I'd never give the fucker the satisfaction of dying though. None of that changed the fact that I was crushed beneath his five thousand dollar oxfords.

I uncurled myself and stood, resetting my fucking backbone. I needed to get out of here, out of this house, out of this city.

Grabbing my coat from where I'd laid it over the hall table, I slipped on my shoes. I paused at the front door. I didn't want to ever come back here—not in three weeks and not in three decades. I raced back up the stairs, not even trying to be quiet this time. Tearing open my bedroom door, I walked to the back of the closet again, grabbing a duffle and flipping open the safe. I unloaded everything; I'd store it at Otto's house.

I couldn't trust it here with them and I never wanted to come back.

In went a photo of me and Otto as kids, and of my grandparents in the kitchen of their home in Martha's Vineyard. The rest of my money went in there, as well as my grandfather's 1971 Rolex Daytona and my grandmother's Cartier engagement and wedding ring set. My mother had been pissed when I'd inherited those rings.

I hitched the bag over my shoulder and took off out of my room like the hounds of Hell were biting at my ass. I strode past my mother coming out of her bedroom —before lunch, shockingly.

"Hendrick? When did you get home?" I didn't stop, didn't even slow my step. Just took the stairs two at a time and burst through the front door.

Hailing a cab, I climbed in the back, directing him to the St. Regis. I pulled out my cell and called Otto. He answered on the third ring, probably because I never called. Calling was for doctors' offices, serial killers and emergencies.

As if to prove my point, Otto's first words were, "Are you okay?"

Despite the thumping pain in my head, I smiled. "I'm good, man. Can I stash some stuff at your house?"

"Sure. Put whatever you want in my room. Are you sure you're okay?"

"Never better. I'll see you soon." I hung up and leaned toward the cab driver's seat. "Actually, take me to Bayridge."

I spent the thirty minute cab ride scrolling through social media, deleting the DMs from ugly Instagram girls and social media influencers who wanted to use my clout for their own gain. Not going to lie though, I answered a couple of the prettier Instagram models.

When the cab pulled up in front of what had to be the all-American dream house, I smiled. Everything from the manicured topiaries, to the bright lace curtains, to Otto's cat Steve McQueen sitting in the driveway, made me happy.

Otto's family had always been comfortably well off. This house had been in their family for generations. Love and laughter seeped into the walls, and everything was bright and well loved. In summary, it was the antithesis of my own family home.

I paid the cabbie and climbed out, walking up the manicured path to the front door that I knew better than my own. Pulling out my keys, I hesitated, before stuffing them back into my pocket and knocking.

Letitia, Otto's mom, opened the door. "Hendrick! How... What the hell happened to your head?"

Ah shit. The blood from my temple. I swiped at it with my jacket sleeve, and she slapped at my hand.

"Don't do that! You'll stain your jacket and get

cloth fibers in the wound. Come in, I'll clean that up."
She grabbed my arm and pulled me into the house.
"Hendrick..."

I knew what she was going to say. She'd been
gently saying it to me for years. Since the first time I'd
turned up on her doorstep with a fat lip, she'd given me
the same advice. Call the police. Talk to someone at
school. Move in with them. So many solutions to a
problem that had no solution.

"It's fine, Letitia. Never again."

She gave me a sad smile. "Come on. Put that in
Otto's room, and I'll get my llama bandaids to patch up
your head."

Chapter 10
Aviva

Sampson stepped out of the bathroom in nothing but a towel, already on the phone. He had ink across his chest, up over his shoulders and down his arms to his elbows. It was like a dark swirling cape across his body.

I tried not to stare, but between the tattoos and the abs... I was only human, okay?

"I don't care how long it normally takes, I need it tomorrow," he snapped, walking to his giant closet. I breathed a relieved sigh when he covered up. He was too pretty, like a rough-hewn ancient warrior beneath a rich boy facade.

"We should go check out your bookstore," Otto said right behind me, making me jump. I whirled around to see him standing there, grinning. "Better to get it done, don't you think?"

My face flushed hot, and I nodded quickly. "Yes, of course." I picked up my purse, and bounced toward the door, hoping that Sampson hadn't caught me perving on him too. I cast a quick look over my shoulder, and crashed straight into his dark, intense gaze. My eyes fell to his full lips, twisted in a self-confident smirk.

Yeah. He knew. Fuck.

I hustled out the door after Otto, pretending it never happened. Being purposefully oblivious was a skill I'd mastered over the years. Otto didn't speak as we stepped into the elevator, but the silence wasn't awkward. It was oddly comfortable, considering I didn't know this guy from Adam. We walked through the beautiful lobby of the St. Regis once again, and I gasped a little more. I couldn't help it. It was gorgeous.

Out on the street, Otto turned to me, his smile bright. "It's about a twenty minute walk, or we can catch a cab?" He indicated a cab that was coming down Fifth Avenue.

I shook my head. "Let's walk. I've never been to New York before."

Giving me a nod, he started off up the street. "Nice. It's a pretty walk along Central Park." He held out his arm, and I stared at it. He let out a snort of laughter that I could hear even over the traffic. "You're meant to hold my elbow. It'll help me keep track of you in the crowd and ensure that I don't out-pace you. You're kinda short."

I frowned at him, but it was hard not to get caught up in his sparkling baby blues. "Jerk." I slid my hand in the crook of his elbow anyway as we strolled along the sidewalk. We didn't talk, because we spent most of our time maneuvering between groups of tourists and people in business suits power-walking angrily to wherever the hell they had to be.

Finally, we reached the leafy trees that marked the boundary of Central Park. I could comfortably drop his arm now, but I hesitated. It was nice. He must be a foot taller than me, his body broad and lean, like a swimmer. He didn't pull his arm away either, so I decided to go on pretending that I forgot I could walk on my own.

"So, how long have you guys all been friends?" I asked, finally breaking the silence. He looked down at me and smiled.

"Too long," he said with a laugh. "I was a scholarship kid at Hendrick's fancy private school. I mean, I was hardly a rags to riches story—my dad is an architect and my mother is a general practitioner. But I'm not Hendrick and Sampson rich. I'm not a trust fund baby."

We paused as we crossed the street, Otto's fingers closing over mine as he made sure I crossed the road safely, and something in my chest thumped painfully. Any little hint of care, and I was like a lovesick cat.

He dropped his hand as we reached the other side, but kept his arm tucked tightly to his body, keeping my fingers trapped in the crook of his elbow.

He cleared his throat. "Anyway, when I arrived, I knew no one, and Hendrick took a shine to me straight away. He said it was because I looked at him and had no idea who the fuck he was. Everyone had been clamoring all over him since orientation day to get in good with Hendrick Kenley, probably because their parents had told them to." He shook his head. "My parents aren't like that."

Well, obviously not. They'd raised Otto, and I might've only known him for a short amount of time, but I could tell he was a genuinely nice guy. Or he was a really good liar—you could never tell until it was too late.

"So a long time then. Must be nice."

He nodded. "It is. Sampson came along later, after his grandparents died. Before that, he'd been over on the West Coast, but once they passed, he had to move here to live with his dad. He hated everyone and everything, which is basically catnip to Hendrick. It was a bit rough at the beginning, but now I'd jump in front of a bullet for either of them, and I know they'd do the same for me." He smiled softly, the way you do when you're imagining people you love. "What about you? Siblings? Friends you wanna drag across Europe? I'm pretty sure I could convince Hendrick to let them tag along. If you just bat those pretty eyelashes, he'd even pay for it too."

I tried to wrack my brain for someone who would drop everything and travel around the world with me the way Otto and Sampson had when Hendrick suggested it. Sure, they had the luxury of money—well, at least two of the three did, though it didn't seem like Otto was hurting either, judging by some of the labels on his clothes.

But there was no one. And if I was honest with myself, that was my own fault. I'd been steadily extracting myself from people's lives for a year or more, not answering messages, cancelling plans at the last minute. Everyone had moved off to college, but I just shuffled my way through college on my own. I worked at a cafe, did my classes, and went home to not really sleep. I didn't want to admit that out loud to Otto though, and seem any more pathetic than I must already be.

So I just shook my head. He shook my hand off his arm, and I frowned. Shit, maybe he thought my loser-ness was infectious... Then I felt his arm wrap around my shoulders and he dragged me into his body for a quick side hug.

"Doesn't matter, Viva. We'll go on this adventure with you. Can't say it'll always be pleasant with those two; they can be assholes. But you won't be alone."

As my gut clenched and my chest felt too full, I just nodded. Fucking Otto—I knew he was the dangerous one.

He dropped his arm and stopped in front of a hotdog cart. "I'm starving. Want one?"

A hotdog from a cart outside Central Park was basically bucket list stuff. "Yes, please. I'll have whatever you have on it." Gotta trust the New Yorker on this one.

Otto ordered for us, while I looked through the entrance of the Park. It was a gorgeous paradise in the middle of a concrete jungle, and you definitely appreciated it as an escape from the gray wash of steel and stone. Maybe I could ask the guys to come for a walk through there, or maybe Nemo would be waiting for me at the bookstore to walk me through there himself.

My heart raced at the idea of meeting Nemo. Logically, I knew he wouldn't be everything I'd built him up to be in my head—hell, he mightn't even be a *he*— but what if he was? How would I even know what I was looking for? Should I just go up to random people and say, "Hey, were you in a mental health facility in Florida, by any chance?"

Panic began to wash over me, but I pushed it down.

No. I had this under control. I wouldn't let this blow out into a full anxiety attack.

When Otto turned around to hand me my hotdog, I had my smile firmly back in place. His eyes searched my face, though I might have been imagining that. "Prepare yourself for the best hotdog of your life."

I took a huge bite and moaned. Holy shit. "Why is this so *good?*" I said around a mouthful of food. The guy at the hotdog cart chuckled, but he'd already moved on to serving someone else.

Otto shrugged as he walked, eating his own dog. "I think it's the New York water. It makes bagels and hotdogs better. They never taste quite the same anywhere else. Sampson says it's because they use the same water for like a week and what you're tasting is the beginning of salmonella poisoning."

I laughed, sucking back a stray piece of bun, and Otto thumped me on the back as I coughed. We walked in silence again, eating our food and watching the people go by. I looked over at him, at his sharp jaw and soft eyes. "Don't you have school or something? Do you have time to be chasing after Hendrick and me as we go on this wild goose chase? Won't your parents be mad?"

Otto grinned. "That's a lot of questions. I do most of my classes online. I can do that from anywhere in the world. My parents think of Hendrick and Sampson like sons, and they understand Hendrick is... Hendrick. He's a complicated guy."

I snorted. "That's a nice way of saying he's an asshole."

Otto shrugged. "Can't change the man, and besides, he's different if you know him." He left it at that, putting a hand on my lower back and turning me to face a beautiful stone building, coated in curling ivy. "We're here."

Oh shit. My heart started racing again, and I felt clammy. Otto reached down and grabbed my hand, helping me across the road and inadvertently anchoring me to sanity. Bet he'd once been a boy scout.

He frowned at the building. "I'm going in with you. I won't encroach, but if this guy is some kind of fucking weirdo, I want to be close by."

I shrugged, because I didn't have that much of a death wish. A little extra support would be good.

This was it. Nemo might be in here. I didn't know if I was happy or sad about the idea, but that was nothing new either. We stepped into the store, and a girl stocking books smiled at us in that pleasant, customer service expression.

"Excuse me. Do you have a section with Jules Verne?"

"Second floor, on the left."

"Thanks." I looked over at Otto. "I won't be long."

It was insane to think he'd just be here. But maybe he'd left a hint? Like times he visited or where he was going after here. Something. Nemo was clever; he'd leave clues behind, just like he did in *Twenty Thousand Leagues Under the Sea*. I raced up the stairs, gasping at the beautiful painted ceiling. There was a woman here, browsing the shelves, as well as another couple. But no single men, no one who looked like they were waiting for someone. I let out a breath, and walked toward bookshelves that held the letter V. This place was breathtaking; I was half tempted to climb into one of the armchairs and never leave.

Suddenly, my heart stopped as I felt someone pause behind me. "No luck?"

I let out a choked sound as I looked over my shoulder at Otto. "No. I didn't think he'd just be here waiting, you know? I hoped... but that's pretty stupid." I skimmed along the book spines until I found what I wanted. "Help me check these?"

Otto nodded, squatting down and grabbing out a small handful of Verne novels. "What am I looking for?"

I shrugged. How the hell would I know? "Notes, maybe? Something between the pages?"

He didn't ask any more questions, just taking one of the novels and flipping it upside down, giving it a little shake. He thumbed through the pages, but nothing. Then he moved onto the next. I did the same, but still nothing.

When he tipped up a copy of one of the novels with the original French title *Le tour du monde en quatre-vingts jours,* my heart pounded when a small sheet of paper slipped out.

Find me at the Iron Nautilus.

I held the crumpled piece of paper and stared. What did that mean? I stood up, continuing to study the paper like it might reveal something more. Otto was still holding the book, though he'd tucked it under his arm so he could pull out his phone.

He frowned. "According to Google, the Iron Nautilus is a bookstore in London. Do you want to go?"

I chewed my lip. I'd known this was coming, knew that it wasn't going to be easy. Taking a deep breath, I nodded.

He smiled and shrugged. "At least I can give the travel agent some specifics now." He rested his free hand on my spine. "Come on, I'll buy you this and we can head back to tell the guys the good news."

Chapter 11
Sampson

When Otto returned with Aviva, her cheeks were flushed and her eyes were too bright. She looked wild, and now I kind of saw the appeal. Not in the fiery way she stared at Hendrick, like she was picturing ways to dismember him, or in the doe-eyed way she gazed at Otto. No, that crazed wildness where she looked like she'd run too hard, or been chased by the Wild Hunt—that version of Good Girl made my blood run hot through my veins.

She chewed her lip, and it was something I wouldn't mind doing too. I remembered the taste of her lips, but the sensation was starting to fade. I wouldn't mind refreshing my memory.

"Your room is ready." Reception had actually

called up a while ago, but I'd liked watching her tell me about what she found. Hendrick still wasn't back, and Otto thought something might've happened while he was with his dad.

When Otto had left with the girl earlier, I'd spent fifteen minutes researching how much it would cost to kill off a senator. The answer was too much, even for me.

She grabbed her jacket and purse. "Thank you." I held out the keycard to her room, letting her step forward to grab it. When she stepped closer, I grabbed her fingers and pulled her closer. She let out an adorable squeak, but I didn't kiss her. I was so close that I could feel the puff of her breath on my face as she froze up before me. I grinned down at her wide-eyed surprise, then stepped back.

"They'll have put your bags in your room. You should change into something warmer—and nicer—for dinner. We aren't in Florida anymore."

I was satisfied with her wince. I knew I was being a fucking asshole, but I liked to see those emotions on her face. Liked to snap her out of that crusty, sarcastic exterior that she seemed to propagate around Hendrick.

She turned on her heel and fled from my suite, and I watched her go with hungry eyes. I'd respect her rules, but I *knew* I'd have her on her knees, staring up at me with those pretty blue eyes soon enough.

When Otto let out an exasperated sigh, I turned in his direction and raised an eyebrow, waiting. "Am I going to have to watch you guys twenty-four seven to make sure you aren't dicks to her? Newsflash, Sam, she was in the institution because she tried to kill herself. Hendrick told me. She only just got out, so if you could not push her over the edge, that would be great."

I tilted my head at him. He was one of the few people in the world who didn't flinch away from my gaze. "Do you like her?"

He shrugged, looking back at his phone. "She's nice. She doesn't deserve whatever dastardly shit you and Hendrick will come up with to torment her."

I narrowed my eyes. "I'm not going to torment her. And you didn't answer my question."

Now it was his turn to look incredulous. "Remember that girl, Tiffany? Stephanie? Something like that—the one in our freshman year of college that you flirted with, until she was sure she was in love with you, and then you crushed her? She dropped out. Just because you were bored."

I shrugged. "And because she had a bet going that she could get me to propose by the end of college. She saw me as a meal ticket, so I treated her like garbage."

"Be serious, Sampson. Half the girls you meet have dreams of becoming your wife, though I don't really understand why they'd spend more than ten minutes in your presence."

"The zeros in my bank account help to smooth over my personality faults," I teased, giving him a crooked smirk. "Message Hendrick and tell him to meet us at Saks. Good Girl needs some clothes if we're going to London and god knows where else."

Otto was pulling out his phone and messaging the group chat even as he said, "She can't afford Saks. Maybe we should take her to a mall somewhere."

I waved a hand. "Cheap crap. Besides, this is for me. It will entertain me to dress her up how I like."

"Then get a Barbie doll, you psycho." There was no heat in his words though. I think he wanted to give the girl her Pretty Woman moment, despite what she'd said. He stuffed his phone in his pocket. "I'll go and grab her. Better she knows what she's in for now, while she's still on US soil and not trapped in Europe with you fuckers."

Such a goddamn white knight, that one.

I read the email from my assistant, who had a cushy as fuck job since I didn't really want or need an assistant, except for moments like these. When I needed someone to throw around the weight of my name and didn't want to do it myself. He'd gotten Aviva's travel documents Express Expedited, which I'm fairly sure was code for he'd paid off someone every step of the way. It was fine, I wasn't worried. Looks like he'd earned his wage this week.

I called down to Reception to make sure that they knew to expect a parcel for me, and that they'd keep it somewhere safe until I collected it. Finally, I grabbed my wallet and jacket, and stepped out into the hall. There were only four suites on this floor, and from what I knew, the only other long-term tenants were the Chinese Embassy—who kept theirs for visiting diplomats—and an aging rockstar who'd been divorced three times and still had loads of money. Airtight prenups were the key to a good marriage. The other suite was still occasionally rented out to music stars and European royals, but not often. No, I appreciated the peace of living in the St. Regis. All the services of home, without having to worry who changed my sheets.

I took the stairs down three flights to the floor where Aviva was staying. I should've had her put in the spare suite on my floor, but I imagined that if she knew I'd sunk five k on a room for her for the night, it'd make her face scrunch up in horror. I wouldn't tell her that this one wasn't much less, though to Hendrick and I, it was pennies.

As I knocked on the door, I could hear the slow rumble of Otto's voice with the softer, higher cadence of Aviva's. They'd probably make a good couple. Otto needed to be a savior, and Aviva desperately needed rescuing.

But I was a selfish fuck. I didn't mind sharing, but I wanted some too.

Otto pulled open the door and stepped into the hall, and a frowning Aviva stepped out after him. She scowled at me, so I guess Otto hadn't done a great job at selling the whole 'let's go shopping' idea. Maybe I liked Good Girl for that too. Most girls would let out an ear-piercing squeal at the idea that I was going to buy them a whole new wardrobe, so Aviva's recalcitrance was what made it so much fun. She opened her mouth, her cheeks flushing pink, and I knew she was about to argue.

"Let's go." I spun and strode down the plush carpeted hall, grinning at her angry huff. I could hear her stomping short strides behind me, and I tried to school my features back into nonchalance. "Is Hendrick coming?"

Otto nodded. "He said he needs to pick up a few things too." I frowned for real this time. What went on with Hendrick and his father that he'd bailed without his shit?

We walked down Fifth, and Aviva gawped like she'd never stepped foot in a city before. I tried to see this place as she did, the old beside the new, the shine of the city next to the homeless who hadn't been moved on yet. NYC had always had its own kind of magic appeal. It wasn't the glitzy kind like the West Coast. NYC had history in its very foundations—from the tallest building to the sewer rats—and it infected any person who stepped into it with the same magic.

But like anything new and magical, the shine eventually wore off, and you realized there was a nervous old white dude behind the curtain pulling the strings the whole time.

We dodged around the tourists taking pictures of Saks, and I ushered Otto and the girl through the front doors. Hendrick was waiting for us just inside the door, though I had no idea how he'd gotten here so fast. He was staring at his phone with a frown on his face, his foot tapping wildly. There was a small bandage on the side of his head that wasn't quite covered by the longer ends of his hair. I stared at that bandage, rage flowing through my veins.

Maybe I needed to re-evaluate if I really could afford to kill a senator. My stocks in a certain streaming service had gone up this last year, giving me a bit more liquid capital. Pretty sure I could get my accountant to cover it somewhere in my finances.

He looked up when Otto cleared his throat. We were both staring at the same thing, but Aviva seemed oblivious as she just stared open-mouthed around the department store. Hendrick cut us both a sharp look, and I didn't need to be his best friend to understand his expression was telling us *no questions*. He may as well have been shouting it.

He placed himself on the other side of Aviva, so she couldn't see the bandage if she turned to look at him. "Are we going shopping, Viva? I'm in desperate need."

I didn't know if they gave the employees here flash-cards of prominent New York families, or if we were just in the tabloids a lot, but a personal shopper appeared in front of us almost immediately.

"Mr. Rubio, Mr. Kenley. Welcome to Saks Fifth Avenue. How may we help you today?" She was blonde, coiffed to perfection, and her uniform tailored skillfully. Hendrick dragged Aviva forward, and I watched the personal shopper's eyes quickly take in her outfit, the customer service smile never dropping from her face. In that one quick expression, she'd made several snap judgements about Aviva, who she was to us, and where in the social ladder she belonged.

"She needs a wardrobe suitable for Europe."

The employee nodded. "What season?"

I grumbled low in my throat, drawing the woman's eyes. "Right now. Here's what I want…"

By the time I was done with my list, Aviva looked pale. The personal shopper directed us to the VIP dressing rooms, then scurried away with a small, busy army of other employees.

"Let's see how bad we can make you, Good Girl," I growled, and watched a shiver run over her skin. Mmm, yes. This was fun.

Chapter 12
Aviva

Well, I couldn't say the girl in the dressing room mirror was beige anymore. Sampson had dressed me up somewhere between hooker and badass bitch. He was insane of course, and seriously fucking annoying. I could hear him out there approving and rejecting outfits.

As aggravating as it was though, he had good taste. I looked beautiful. The cuts flattered my figure, the material well made and not ostentatious.

The price tags nearly gave me an aneurysm.

"Hendrick, I can't afford this shit," I hissed as I flicked back the curtain. But Hendrick apparently didn't believe in change rooms. Instead, he was standing in his boxer shorts right outside my change room, completely unfazed by the fact that his whole body was on display and the personal shoppers were eating him up with their eyes. Hell, he probably loved it.

I dragged my eyes from the V of his hips back to his damn smirking face, clearing my throat. "I draw the line. I can't take this."

Hendrick just grinned at me. "I refuse to take you to Europe looking like a fucking hobo, so suck it up, Viva."

"Go fuck yourself, Hendrick." I flicked the curtain back across.

"Rather fuck you, Viva," he said too loudly from the other side, and my face flushed. I was so glad he couldn't see it.

I managed to keep my voice even as I said, "I'm beginning to think you'd fuck anything with two legs." His laughter was like velvet brushing softly over your skin. It made my flesh feel too tight, and I pretended it was with repulsion but everyone in this room knew it was arousal.

"You definitely have two legs. Two very nice ones, as we all saw when you were in that little black Chanel number."

That dress had been gorgeous, but had way too many zeros at the end of the price tag for my mental health. I'd made Sampson tell the shop girls no more high end labels, and they'd all looked at me like I'd grown another head. Maybe they'd given me electroshock therapy back in that damn wellness center and this was all just a coma dream.

So no more Chanel or Versace or Louis Vuitton. They'd agreed, but Sampson had then told them to remove the tags of anything they brought in, so now I was standing in jeans that could cost a hundred bucks or six hundred, and I would never know.

The guys had insisted I needed a clubbing dress and a formal gown—I didn't know what the fuck for, but even Otto had agreed. I'd already accepted three pairs of jeans, two pairs of tailored shorts, an entire array of pretty dresses and a puffer jacket that cost more than my car just by itself. Plus half a dozen tops, from sheer blouses to casual yet pricey t-shirts.

A hand reached through the curtain, and I was beginning to recognize the expensive manicure of the original personal shopper we'd met. "The gentlemen informed me that you might be going to the opera or out for dinner, and needed a dress to fit these occasions." She thrust a dress at me. "This will be perfect. While it isn't an evening gown, it is well made and will suit most occasions with the right accessories. I shall pick appropriate pieces." She wasn't asking. She was telling me.

I gritted my teeth and shucked on the dress. I had to admit, it was beautiful. Short enough to hit me midthigh, it draped around my body in a way that gave me more curves than I naturally had. It was simple, understated and... Holy shit, two and a half thousand dollars?

I must have screeched, because Sampson was suddenly there, whipping open the curtain. His eyes dipped to the dress, spending a long time on my legs, and then back to my face. "Want me to zip it?"

I shook my head furiously. "Not this dress."

"Don't you like it?"

I shook my head again. "It's beautiful, but it's too much."

He had the fucking audacity to roll his eyes. "This is the dress then." Then he shut the curtain. Fucking asshole.

I put my own clothes back on—comfortably from Target—and slid into my Converse. They kept bringing me street shoes, and I'd rejected them all. I was a Converse or die kinda girl.

Stepping out from behind the curtain, I frowned at the guys all sitting there on the plush couch. "I'm done. I won't be an embarrassment anymore."

Otto looked concerned, but Hendrick laughed. "Not sure that will be possible, Aviva. You radiate basic bitch." I gave him the finger, and he just laughed harder. "It's okay, we got you a selection of yoga pants and oversized sweatshirts too. You'll still be comfortable, but now they're designer, and it's an 'aesthetic.'"

He did little finger quotations around the word aesthetic like he thought it was crap, yet they were the ones who'd dragged me here to play dress-ups.

Sampson handed the assistant his credit card. "Ring it up and have it sent to the St. Regis. Also, she needs a suitcase and a travel wallet. Plus anything else you think she'll need, I don't care."

The woman scurried off, her comrades grabbing the hanging rack and wheeling it out. There must have been ten thousand dollars worth of clothes on that rack.

All the fire left me as they rolled away and the door shut behind them. "It's too much," I whispered. "You can't buy me."

Sampson swaggered over, his mouth a cocky smirk. "I'm not buying you, Good Girl. I'm making you a fantasy." He leaned forward, getting in my personal space again, and fuck, he smelled so damn good it was distracting. "Don't you want to be a fantasy?"

I swallowed hard. "No."

He pulled back and smiled. A real one, not that cocky half-grin. "Yeah, you do. You aren't beige anymore. No, Good Girl. You're going to be so much more." He spun away from me, and I sucked in oxygen like I'd been immersed underwater. "Let's head back and get room service. I'm fucking starving."

Hendrick made some manly grunt of agreement

and came over, slinging his arm across my shoulders. "Aren't we having fun already?"

Hendrick had nearly bought one of everything from the room service menu, and then they'd all watched me eat it. Have you tried lobster and truffle mac'n'cheese? I was generally a purist; I believed that good, wholesome food was just as nice as fancy fine dining.

But combine the two? I moaned. It was heaven.

The pulled crab ravioli? Like a divine revelation.

Hendrick kept feeding me bites of different things, watching my face as I ate them. At first, it was weird, but if he wanted to watch me make an O face while eating German chocolate cheesecake, who was I to deprive him—or myself—of the experience? Finally, I was stuffed, and Sampson handed me a small glass of cognac. I sipped it warily, surprised at how smooth it was.

"You guys finished playing 'feed the country mouse?'" he asked Otto and Hendrick, and I scowled at him. He grinned at me again, and I was glad he couldn't see my heart rate. "Don't be like that, Good Girl. It's interesting watching someone who still has firsts."

"What he means is that it's been a long time since someone moaned like that when I fed something to them. Usually it's my cock, but a spoon will do," Hendrick teased.

I flushed pink. "What, like a week? Poor baby."

Hendrick laughed. "Exactly." He sighed. "We should go out. I haven't been in town for ages and if I don't go out, people will think I got a lobotomy this time."

I gasped, looking down at my food baby. "I can't fit in that dress now—I just ate half my weight in luxury foods."

Sampson sighed. "You'll be fine. We'll go some-where lowkey. Just wear the sequined shirt dress. It'll hide all your sins. Or the tabloids will think Hendrick knocked you up and you'll be on the front cover of every trash magazine by next week."

They all laughed like it was a joke but I was horri-fied. I was quickly coming to understand that Otto was the empathetic one. "Don't worry, Aviva. You can borrow my anti-flash jacket. It's like a shiny material that reflects the photographers' flashes. I like to protect my privacy too, and there's very little around these two assholes."

I was still frowning when the alarm on his phone went off. He flicked it off and gave Hendrick a pointed look.

"Going, Mom," Hendrick sighed, unfolding from the couch and heading into the bathroom.

Otto watched him go, his jaw tense, and then he turned his gaze to me. "This might sound... insensitive, but did the psychiatrist release you with any medical instructions? Prescriptions you need filled, that kind of thing?" I sucked in an offended breath, but he continued on before I could tell him it was none of his business. "I set reminders on my phone so Hendrick remembers to take his meds. Otherwise, he gets caught up in whatever he's doing and forgets. I'm, uh, happy to remind you too? No pressure though, of course. It's just easy to lose track of time and days when you're traveling."

His cheeks had gone pink, and I wasn't sure which one of us was more embarrassed. But considering I'd forgotten to take my morning meds already... "Uh, thanks. That would be helpful."

He looked relieved that I hadn't taken offense, and I couldn't help but smile. We sat there, just staring at each other until Sampson made a rude sound.

"Stop eyefucking. Good Girl, go get changed and take your meds. The dress and all the crap that goes with it are in the bags in the foyer. Might be some makeup in there too; told the rep to get you the basics." He pointed at Otto. "Go get ready too. I know it takes you twenty fucking minutes to do your hair."

Otto saluted him, then gave him the finger. I did as

I was told, but when I saw the absolute mass of designer bags in the foyer, I winced.

Maybe Sampson really was the devil, and if that was the case, I was pretty sure I'd just sold him my soul.

Chapter 13
Otto

"Hendrick! Over here!"

"Sampson, who's the girl?"

"Over here! Hendrick, what do you think of your father's campaign?"

The paparazzi were intense tonight, and I could feel Aviva shrinking away. I was glad I'd given her my flash jacket, and I pulled her closer to me. Security kept the paparazzi away from the doors but they were still full on. We'd have to wait for Hendrick or Sampson to rock up to have enough clout to get in, but they were only a few steps behind us. The bouncer pulled back the velvet rope, and the low thumping beat of techno music poured out. I pressed a hand to Aviva's spine and guided her inside.

She looked so fucking beautiful. She'd taken care

with her makeup, obviously as a giant 'fuck you' to Sampson, but I appreciated the way the heavy liner made her eyes pop, and how instead of calming her wild curls, she'd made them crazier, like she had a golden halo framing her face.

Hendrick had almost swallowed his tongue when he'd seen her, and Sampson had looked smugly satisfied. The man had taste, I'd give him that, but Aviva hadn't exactly been an ugly duckling before, either. Now she just shimmered, and it wasn't just the sequins on her dress catching the strobe lights.

Hendrick walked in front, kissing the cheeks of the society girls who threw themselves in his direction, and the guys gave him tight hugs and hearty slaps on the back like they didn't all try to trample over him to get to the top.

Fake. All this shit was as fake as the tits pressed against Hendrick's arm right now, while their owner whispered in his ear. I shot a quick look at Aviva to judge her response, but she seemed fine. Maybe she really wasn't interested in Hendrick, but I found it hard to believe.

Some women loved the asshole version of Hendrick, and they ate up his cruel words like candy. The ones who made it closer began to know the real Hendrick—who was funny and surprisingly empathetic—and those were the ones who really ended up broken. But those ones who really knew Hendrick, they knew to leave. Once you were sucked into his vortex, there was no escape. I should know.

Sampson made an impatient noise, and I looked over my shoulder to see him glaring at Hendrick. "Just take her somewhere to fuck her already! I need a drink," he shouted over the music, and Hendrick looked over his shoulder and smiled.

I felt Aviva stiffen marginally under my hand, and I knew the reaction well. Hendrick's smile was really something else. The best row of teeth money could buy, all the better to smile at his daddy's constituents with. It was a weapon, that smile. He waggled his eyebrows, and I could hear Sampson huff over the music.

Stepping around us, he grabbed Aviva's hand and dragged her through the crowd. I was kind of glad that she had her outfit paired with a pair of chunky boots rather than the sky-high heels most girls wore in the club, because the tug of Sampson's hand would have sent her flying. As it was, I grabbed her other arm to steady her and then followed along behind Sampson as he plowed through the crowd.

We were ushered through to a table, and Sampson ordered bottle service from the server bustling past with a tray full of glasses. He sank onto the couch, dragging Aviva down beside him.

She scooted away from him a little, pushing down the skirt of her dress.

"You look great," I told her, working hard to keep the lust from my voice. "I'm not sure if we told you that yet."

She flushed, but couldn't keep the pleased look from her face. "Thank you."

Hendrick finally caught up, the chick with the bolt-on tits still clinging to his arm. "You guys remember Destinee, right?"

Nope, didn't recognize her, but that didn't mean much. "Hey, nice to see you." I didn't say *again*, because that would be a lie.

"You too, Otto," she said in her high giggle. "Sampson, nice to see you again," she purred, and I mentally rolled my eyes. Aviva's lips twitched, so maybe I didn't do it mentally. Whoops.

Sampson grunted. "This is Aviva. She lives with us now."

Aviva's mouth fell open, and not gonna lie, so did mine. The fuck was he playing at? He knew how that sounded, right?

"She's your girlfriend? I thought you didn't do girlfriends," Destinee squeaked, her hand pressed to her chest like she'd received devastating news, even as she dissected Aviva to pieces with her incredulous gaze.

"I don't do commitment, Destinee, except in rare and unique circumstances. Or with special people." His tone insinuated Destinee would never be either of those things, and I had to agree. She was designed by fashion magazines, a product of the whims of people more creative—and far more clever—than she would ever be.

Destinee obviously didn't understand tone though. "Ah, that's okay. No ring, no big thing."

That didn't even make sense. Aviva must have taken pity on the girl though, because she waved a hand. "Too right. Why have one when you can have three, am I right?" She fluttered her lashes at Hendrick, and he stared back at her with feigned insouciance.

The server appeared, dropping a bottle of Belvedere in an ice bucket in the center of the table. Glasses were placed on the table on a shiny silver tray engraved with the bar's name. "This one is on the house, Mr. Rubio. Compliments of management."

Sampson gave her a tight smile, and she knew when to leave. That was what made a good server. The ability to appear when needed and disappear as soon as they were done. I hated that we dehumanised them like that, but they'd literally get fired otherwise. The owner wasn't an idiot; this might be a two-hundred dollar bottle of vodka, but people would start flooding here once Hendrick and Sampson's pictures hit the tabloids in the morning. If they were seen here enough, this place would become the new "It" place.

Pity that we were leaving for Europe tomorrow night.

I poured, lifting the bottle at Aviva. "Want some?"

She hesitated, but nodded. I'd looked up her meds, and knew that they shouldn't react too badly with alcohol. I'd keep an eye on her though, because I knew sometimes they could mess you up. I was glad she'd trusted me with her med schedule. I didn't want Hendrick and his impulsiveness to be the reason she fell back into something unhealthy.

There were several bottles of mixers on the table too, and I poured in a healthy splash of lemonade. I didn't dare do that to Sampson's though; I'd get a two-hour lecture about the process of making good vodka and the absolute sacrilege of mixing it with anything. Even now, his eye twitched, but he didn't say anything as he grabbed his glass.

"This place is nice?" Aviva said over the noise, and I snorted.

"Is that a question?"

Someone laughed loudly at another table, and I recognized a young singer and her entourage. Plus all her security, which swarmed around her. Aviva followed my gaze, and while her eyes widened a little when she noticed the singer, she didn't say anything.

She did take a giant gulp of her drink though, and leaned in close. The neck of her dress was hanging loose so I could see her cleavage, but I dragged my eyes back to her face. "Why don't you guys have security?"

Sampson grumbled, and Hendrick laughed. "Otto knows Krav Maga."

She reared back, shocked. I didn't know whether to be amused or offended by her surprise. "You do?"

I gave Hendrick the finger. "No, I don't. These guys do have security. They're just really good, so you don't notice them." I pointed to a guy at the bar. "That's Sampson's security guy, Evan. He's scary as fuck and really does know Krav Maga." I searched the walls of the room. "That one over there in the expensive suit belongs to Hendrick. More conspicuous, but still, quite good."

Her eyes had slid right past Evan, which was why he was paid so well.

"Have they been with us all day?"

I shook my head. "Not when you and I went to the bookstore. We aren't that important."

Sampson frowned. "Don't say that."

And that's why I loved Sampson. Unlike the rest of the world, he didn't see any difference between the value of my life and his. He wasn't an idiot; he knew that he would be more likely to get abducted and ransomed or some such shit. But he'd mourn my death just as much as he would Hendrick's. I wasn't worth less as a person to him, just because I was worth less monetarily. I couldn't say the same for everyone in this room though.

Tossing back the rest of my drink, I smiled at Aviva. "Want to dance?"

She chewed on her lip. "I'm not a great dancer."

I stood, holding out my hand. "Neither am I. But it's fun anyway. Let's go."

She hesitated for a moment, then put her hand in mine. "Okay."

I held her close as I dragged her down to the dance-floor, the crowd pulsing with lust, sweat and music. Putting us in the middle, I held her hands, just holding her loosely as she swayed from side to side awkwardly.

I grinned at her, grabbing her arms and putting them around my neck, then placed my hands on her hips. "Just feel it pulsing through your feet, then close your eyes and let it fill your limbs," I yelled beside her ear.

She continued to bite her lip, but closed her eyes, and I used my hands on her hips to slowly sway us to the music. She was stiff, but after a few minutes, she finally began to unwind, her body relaxing into the music and into my hands. I pulled her closer, letting her body move with mine, her head lolling back, her eyes still scrunched shut.

Her lips parted and I desperately wanted to kiss her. Instead, I let the music strip us both down until we were free.

Chapter 14
Aviva

We danced until my feet ached and my mouth was dry. Otto led me back to the VIP area, and I noticed Hendrick was gone, as was Destinee. I frowned, before slumping back down beside Sampson. I felt sweaty and disgusting, but my heart was racing and I was smiling so wide I thought my face would crack.

"Having fun, Good Girl?"

I grinned at him. "I—"

"Excuse me. You're in my spot."

I looked up, and then up a bit more, at one of the most beautiful women I'd ever seen. She looked like a Victoria's Secret runway model. Beside her was a girl who was smirking into her phone.

"Oh, I'm sorry," I said, my buzz leaving me in a rush. Of course Sampson hadn't been sitting up here alone. I looked at him, and he had his eyes narrowed at the girl. He didn't look particularly happy to see her.

"Is it your spot?" he drawled coolly, and the sound of it made all the hair on the back of my neck stand on end. He may as well have growled. "Good Girl, you aren't in your proper seat." He grabbed my waist and dragged me onto his lap. I sucked back a gasp as he settled me across his thighs. I couldn't help but look up at the beautiful woman again.

"My place is always at your side. You know after you're bored with whatever this is"—she waved a dismissive hand in my general direction, and I bristled —"you'll come back to me, Sonny. You know I'm the only one who can give you what you want." She leaned over me to purr the last part in his ear. Would it be rude to tit punch her? Would it rupture her breast implants?

Also, Sonny? Seriously? The hell kind of nickname was that? This dark, brooding man was the opposite of sunny.

Sampson held me tight, his hand wrapped almost the whole way around my thigh as he looked up at the model. "This might be a shock to you, Alexis, but the only thing you can give me is an STD. Now, fuck off."

"Just go away, Alexis," Otto groaned, rubbing a hand down his face. He knew her too? "This isn't going to end well."

Alexis shot a look at Otto. "No one was talking to you, leech."

Oh. Oh hell no, she didn't just say that. Mentally, I tore her to shreds. I threw out everything I'd ever believed about female solidarity and the feminist ideal, and told her she was a bleached blonde plastic trash bag. And that her vagina probably smelled like an old tuna sandwich and gangrene.

But I didn't. No, instead I did something stupider. Downing the drink in my hand, and holding in the cough because I realized I hadn't mixed it, I smiled sweetly at the woman in front of me.

Then I turned my head to the left and caught Sampson's lips with mine. It was a soft, sweet kiss. The type two people in love shared. Not two perfect strangers.

Sampson tasted like danger, if danger tasted like expensive vodka. As he pulled back, he nipped my bottom lip softly, like he couldn't get enough either.

He was a good actor, that was for sure. Alexis looked furious. Her cheeks were flushed, even under her perfect makeup. She looked at Otto. "I saw you out there on the dance floor with her. I thought she was with you, but still no one wants you, leech? You poor schmuck."

Nope. I twisted slightly in Sampson's arms and I crooked a finger at Otto. He leaned across the small table that held our drinks, and I grabbed the collar of his shirt, dragging him in for a kiss. I kissed him possessively, closing my eyes momentarily as I drank in the softness of Otto. Then I opened them and stared over Otto's shoulder at Alexis. A shit-eating look in my eye, I winked at her.

Well, I did until Otto slipped his tongue between my teeth, and fucked my mouth with his. Oh shit, he could kiss.

"You fucking slut," Alexis screeched, reaching for me.

Sampson's bodyguard was there almost instantly, restraining her hand and twisting it behind her back until it looked like a chicken wing. She screamed, bringing in the bouncers. The bodyguard, Evan, didn't release Alexis until security informed him that she would be removed from the VIP area. Apparently, models didn't rank quite as high as billionaires.

Alexis's friend glared at us all. "Good to see Hendrick finally took his dick from your ass and let you get some, Otto." She let out a fake gasp. Or maybe that was me. "Oh, didn't your new little whore know that you bend over and suck cock for Hendrick Kenley? Oh, what would his daddy say about that?"

She went to flounce away, but ploughed into the chest of Hendrick himself. "Probably the same thing your daddy would say when I tell him his precious daughter wanted to film herself getting railed by the both of us. Begged, even. I'm pretty sure I still have the recording somewhere. Would be a shame if it accidentally ended up in the wrong hands. Also a shame that I'm such a bad cameraman and didn't get anyone else's face in it but yours. So sorry... but hey, at least you can say you weren't in Alexis's shadow for a moment, right?"

The girl went pale, and scurried away. Destinee looked thoroughly fucked, so I guess I knew where he'd been now. She looked at the girl who was running away, and then back at Hendrick. I had a feeling they were friends.

"Fuck off, Destinee. Your friends are toxic and they've killed my night," Hendrick growled, and Destinee hesitated but stepped away.

"Call me?"

"Not in this fucking century."

She huffed, crossing her arms over her chest. "You are such a fucking asshole. Katrina was right, you fucking homo."

Sampson's growl was scary as fuck, and Destinee finally grew a brain cell, almost running out of the VIP area. We were quiet for a moment, each of them looking at me like I was supposed to be outraged or horrified or something.

In all honesty, I didn't care, not even a little bit.

What I did care about was the fact that Sampson was hard beneath my ass, and at some point his hand had slid even further up my thigh. I was still clutching Otto's shirt, and his lips were so fucking close.

Oh shit. Oh fuck. I straightened, letting go of Otto and sliding off Sampson's lap. I stood, clearing my throat.

"I think I'm kind of tired."

Otto's face shut down, and I had a sudden flash at how that must have sounded. They had no idea that my internal thoughts had cycled around from their relationship, to the uncomfortable ache between my thighs, and my lust for them, to the terribleness of that idea.

I reached out and stroked Otto's slightly wavy brown hair. "It's not that. I don't care about you and Hendrick. Though actually, you could probably do better. I'm just exhausted. It's been an insane day."

Otto nodded, though his eyes were searching my face for deceit, or my real feelings or something. I kept everything but my complete acceptance of his sexuality from my expression.

"I'm bi. We both are. That kiss..."

I waved a hand to cut him off, trying to ignore how manic it must have looked. "Was just making a point, I know. It's fine. I still have a guy to find. Nemo. That's the point of this."

Hendrick snorted. "Nemo. We are finding Nemo. The irony of this is fucking hilarious." He stood, stretching out his body. He had a hickey on his neck and stitches on his head that I hadn't noticed until now. When did he get those?

Not the hickey. I knew when he got that, and it burned a little more than I wanted to admit. I looked back at Otto. "You can definitely do better."

Hendrick waved a casual hand. "Just a warm hole, Viva. They mean nothing. The only people who mean anything are right here." He looked over his shoulder at Sampson and Otto. He looked back at me too, and grinned. "Come on, let's get some rest. Tomorrow, we skip the country for a while."

I couldn't get the way his eyes had lingered on Sampson just as much as Otto out of my head. Did they all fuck? I had so many questions that I didn't want to ask, not wanting to be rude. It was none of my business who did what. These guys were my meal ticket, literally, and nothing else.

Sampson sighed, scooping the remainder of the Belvedere from the ice bucket. "For the road. What a clusterfuck of a night."

I should apologize to Sampson for kissing him. Actually, no. It made us even now—both kiss thieves, taking what we wanted without regard.

Sampson and Hendrick's security peeled off the

walls, and now I'd seen them, I didn't think I could unsee them. The illusion of privacy was gone. By the time we got back out the front door, I was once again wrapped in the anti-flash jacket, and the car was idling by the curb in front of the club. They ushered me in first, with Otto sliding in after me. Sampson and Hendrick followed last, sitting opposite us.

The silence was tense, and I could feel the weight of unuttered words sitting heavily between us. Sampson handed me the bottle of vodka and I tipped it back, taking a gulp of smooth alcohol that didn't burn until it reached my gut.

It was a nice burn though. At this rate, I was going to get used to the finer things, and my plummet back to reality would be a painful bitch.

I didn't care. It had already been established that I liked the way it hurt.

Chapter 15
Hendrick

I was curled around Otto's back, but his shoulders were tense. Sampson's spare room was still dark, but the gray light of breaking dawn cast the room in a washed out light. I kissed his shoulder, and he sighed.

"Otto, what's wrong? I missed you."

"Not to sound like a whiny bitch, but you couldn't have missed me too badly since you fucked Destinee the first chance you got."

I rolled onto my back. "Wait, are you jealous?"

Otto rolled over, narrowing his eyes at me. "No. I know we aren't like that. But she's trash, Drix. We both know it, and if you're going to stick your dick in trash, I'd rather it didn't go in me straight afterwards."

I mean, I could see his point, but... "Technically, you had *your* dick in *me*."

Otto let out a frustrated noise and stood, uncurling his naked body. I knew it as well as my own. He'd been my best friend forever, and when I'd realized I was bisexual at fifteen, he'd once again stepped up to be what I needed. Sometimes I worried he wasn't even attracted to me, but addicted to saving me.

If he was guilt-fucking me, he did it well. I was too selfish to question it. I needed Otto like I needed oxygen; I wasn't sure how I'd survive without him. "Come on, man. Lie back down."

He paused, the waistband of his sweats just sitting below his ass. I couldn't help but notice he hadn't put on any underwear. "You can't take anything seriously, Drix. You're like a wrecking ball."

I frowned this time. "Is this about Viva finding out about us? Viva is cool, and if I'm not wrong, a little intrigued by the idea. I think eventually, we could get her to join us."

Interest flared in Otto's eyes, but it was quickly squashed. "I'm also not a gimmick for you to lure unsuspecting girls into your bed." He pinched the bridge of his nose. "I love you, Drix. But we are too old for this half-measure bullshit. I want a boyfriend, or a girlfriend, and not to be a fucktoy with feelings who just makes sure you don't do stupid shit like jump off a goddamn bridge." He stormed out of the room, and I watched him go, shocked.

Jesus, I hadn't seen that coming. I mean, for years we'd worked—I'd see other people, Otto would see other people, and if we were single, we'd see each other. It was the perfect system, and I thought we were both happy with it.

Apparently, I was wrong. I crawled from the bed, feeling the hangover this morning thumping in my temples. I wouldn't go back to sleep now, not until I was so tired that I'd sleep through most of the international flight. I slid on my own sweats—one of the new pairs I'd bought yesterday—and slipped into the main living room.

Sampson was awake, sipping coffee and watching the news report, like he was sixty-five and not twenty-four. He raised an eyebrow at me. "You fucked up? Otto just stormed through to the bathroom like someone told him that the Easter Bunny wasn't real."

I shrugged. "I think he wants commitment. Not sure with who though."

Sampson snorted. "You guys have been fucking for seven years, Drix. It's time to either jump out of the closet or let the poor guy move on to some nice girl who'll suck his dick on Sunday mornings, someone who he can dote on like she's his sun and moon. Can't all be just for you."

Fuck, was that what Otto really wanted? Domestic bliss? I couldn't give him that. I could provide him with a media storm, radical condemnation, my dad ruining his life. Nowhere in our future was a happily ever after —not for me, or Otto, or even Sampson. We were all victims of circumstance.

"He likes her, you know."

I dragged my eyes away from the scrolling stock market numbers on the TV. "What?"

Sampson muted the sound and turned to me. "Otto. He likes Aviva. She's like you, but safer. They'd probably be happy together. He'd smother her with love and she'd soak it up like an empty sponge. You should let him have her."

I frowned, my gut twisting painfully at the thought of Otto and Aviva together, but I couldn't point out which part of the equation hurt the most. Losing Otto, or the idea of Aviva being off limits. No, I did know which one hurt the most, but I was surprisingly uncomfortable with giving up chasing Viva as well.

I slid my gaze back to Sampson. "Don't fuck with me, Sam. I've seen how you look at her too. You want to dirty her up just as much as I do."

He shrugged, not denying it. "True. But I'd give that up for Otto."

I turned back to the TV, staring at it sightlessly as I thought about his words. I'd give Otto anything he wanted. He could have my whole damn fortune, my kidney, whatever the hell he asked for. Because the idea of losing Otto hurt more than I'd ever imagined.

Sampson was right—if Otto wanted to woo Aviva, I'd let him. She'd give him everything I couldn't, and probably more, you know, considering I didn't have a vagina.

I really, really wished I didn't have to though.

I looked back at Sampson. "Do you think it's greedy to want them both? Is that even possible?"

He frowned. "Anything is possible, if you want it bad enough."

Let's hope he was right.

Otto had chilled the fuck out by the time we were ready to head to the airport. It might have been because he spent the afternoon down with Aviva in the hotel's salon getting her hair done, then helping her pack. Sampson's words about him liking her came back, but I mean, he'd known her like a day. She might pick her teeth with a steak knife or chew loudly, which Otto hated. Maybe she didn't like cats or fantasy books. Pretty sure Sampson was getting ahead of himself.

We were having a summer downpour, and I stood beside Otto under the awning as the doorman loaded up the bags. Aviva stood beside Sampson while he gave orders to his assistant, her eyes wide as she took in all the luggage we had between us.

"I'm sorry," I murmured to Otto, and he looked over at me. His eyes were sad but he was smiling.

"I know, Drix."

"You know I love you, right?"

He shrugged. "I do. As much as you can love anyone who isn't your reflection in the mirror," he teased, and I punched him in the arm.

"Shut up. Like you don't spend ages in the bathroom getting ready every day."

He just chuckled, and I relaxed a little. Finally, all the bags were loaded, and the trunk on the hire car barely shut. Sampson pushed Aviva gently toward the open door, his hand lingering on the small of her back.

"He likes her, you know," Otto murmured.

I laughed. "He said the same thing about you."

Otto looked comically shocked, but I hustled him to the car. We needed to leave, and I was excited. I'd been to Europe a dozen times, but as a kid, my brain had been too wild to fully appreciate these places for the first time. They'd just looked like another city, just like *every* other fucking city really. So experiencing it through Aviva's eyes would be something new in a world where nothing was ever new.

She had on a flowing black skirt that ended just above her knee, but it had ridden up a little and was showing the long length of her pale legs. I wanted to run my tongue up the inside of those thighs and not stop until she screamed my name. Otto poked me, and I realized he was waiting for me to climb through to the back row of seats.

I flopped down in the seat right behind her and leaned forward until I could inhale the scent of her shampoo. "Excited?" I whispered in her ear, and her whole body shuddered. I wondered what she'd do if I sucked that cute little earlobe between my teeth.

"Yes," she breathed, and I almost thought she was answering my thoughts, until I realized she meant she was excited.

"Let's go!" I yelled to the driver, and he peeled out of the park. My security detail was on a change of shift, and I wanted to be in the first class lounge sipping mimosas before they realized I wasn't in my room. Hell, better yet, out of the country completely. Evan was cool; he hated my detail. Thought they were incompetent assholes.

Besides, no one would give a fuck about me in Europe. Why would they? Evan was enough for all of us.

Aviva's phone rang again and she put it on mute. Sampson watched her out of the corner of his eyes, still talking to his assistant on the phone. "Just get it done," he snapped, and then hung up. I would have hated being his assistant—Sampson could be a fucking asshole when he wanted to be. I knew he paid the guy well, probably as compensation for pain and suffering. Aviva's phone started ringing yet again, and he looked at it pointedly.

"Should you answer that?"

Aviva shook her head. "It's my parents. They've been blowing up my phone for the past day. I messaged them and told them I was fine, but I don't think they believe me." She hesitated. "Once we're in London, I'll answer their call. It'll be too late then."

Otto was frowning, but Sampson just shrugged. "Okay."

Aviva was a grown woman. She could live her life however she wanted. If that meant ignoring her parents, so be it. None of my business. I laid my head back and watched the sun fall behind the skyscrapers.

The trip to the airport was quick, and we managed to get our bags checked in and get situated in the first class lounge almost immediately. We had an hour or so until our flight, and I intended to wash down my meds with some scotch and nap on one of the plush recliners.

Sampson peeled off from the group, heading toward the bar. "Get me one too," I shouted, and he gave me the finger.

"I'm going to get some food," Otto grumbled.

Good. He was a fucking grumpy asshole when he was tired and hungry, like a damn toddler.

That just left Aviva. I looked over at her, and she seemed... tense.

"You okay?"

She darted her eyes in my direction and nodded tightly. Yeah, I didn't believe her. I grabbed her hand, dragging her down a short hallway to the bathrooms. I pushed her into one of the family rooms and locked the door.

"No, seriously? Are you okay?" I softened the natural arrogance of my tone, trying to emulate Otto. "We don't have to do this, if you don't want to. We can walk out of here and I'll buy you a ticket home. It won't matter at all."

Her lips fell open and her eyes went too wide. "No, I want this. I'm... Oh god." She started sucking in air, and you didn't have to spend half your life in rehab to know she was having an anxiety attack.

I pulled her into my arms, anchoring her to my chest. "Hey. It's okay."

She just wheezed harder. "I can't breathe."

Dammit, where was Otto when I needed him? He'd be able to talk her out of this. I didn't have his way with words. Fuck, the only thing I could do with my mouth was...

Well. That wasn't a bad idea.

Picking her up, I put her on the bathroom sink. "Viva, this is purely medicinal and definitely isn't breaking the rules," I warned. I pushed her back against the mirror and thanked the interior designer for low countertops as I dropped to my knees in front of her.

"What... Oh shit."

I kissed my way up her thighs, nipping the soft flesh between my teeth before looking up at her. "This will settle your wild emotions. Like a good dose of Percocet." I grinned from between her thighs, and I met her eyes, with their blown out pupils. "I'm still going to need that enthusiastic yes though?"

I could feel the heat of her pussy on my face, and it was the longest five seconds of my life as I watched and waited for her whispered, "Yes."

Hell motherfucking yeah. I gripped her panties and pulled them off, stuffing them in my pocket so they weren't on the dirty bathroom floor. Gross.

I pulled her toward my face and flicked my tongue against her clit. She hissed, her thighs trying to wrap around my head, but I pushed them wider. I fucking wanted to see. I darted a look up at her face, just to make sure she was still with me as I swirled my tongue around her clit this time, and her head fell back against the mirror with a moan.

Okay. Swirly it is. I sucked her clit into my mouth

and hummed my pleasure, grinning as her body rolled against my face. Then I swirled again.

Oh fuck yeah. I was going to enjoy this. Fast and intense was my forte. We had a plane to catch, after all. I ran my tongue up and down her slit before thrusting it inside her dripping core. Viva got wet fast, and I loved it. I lapped at her, nudging her clit with my nose until she had her hands buried in my hair and was riding my face.

Fuck, she tasted divine. I slid my fingers inside her and she gasped, clenching around them immediately, her greedy little pussy trying to get what it wanted. I could have told her that I would always give her what she needed—she just had to ask.

Pulling back, I looked up at her, and her lip was puffy from the way she was gnawing on it to keep her moans quiet. "Do you want to come, Viva? Want to soak my face?"

"Oh god... Yes," she moaned, and I thrust my fingers back inside her, curling them as I sucked on her clit. She screamed, before pulling a hand out of my hair and slapping it over her mouth. I couldn't help the smile on my face as she came on my fingers, soaking my hand and my face.

When her body stopped pulsing around me, I withdrew and sat back on my heels. She stared down at me from the counter, boneless and lazy, like a beatific goddess.

"Feel better?"

She blinked at me slowly, a small smile curling her lips. "Yes."

Chapter 16
Sampson

I couldn't work out if he'd fucked her in the bathrooms or what, but when Otto and I had finally found them, it had been to the sound of Good Girl's orgasm, and I wasn't sure I could ever unhear it.

We'd quickly made our way back to a set of seats so she wouldn't know we'd heard, but just looking at her was like seeing a flashing billboard for 'Just Been Fucked.' It was goddamn beautiful. Her lips were puffy and red, her cheeks pink and flushed. Her hair was wild and her eyes were a little glassy. Otto's fingers had flexed around his glass, and he'd swallowed the contents in one gulp, but no one said anything.

No, we ate and drank, Hendrick's messy hair and shit-eating grin almost a taunt. But he was infectiously happy, and when Hendrick got that way, it was hard not to get caught up in the revelry. We were talking and laughing, even Aviva getting caught up in the excitement.

Soon enough, we were boarding the plane, and I tried not to laugh at Aviva's wide-eyed wonder. "Otto! They give you pajamas!" she hissed across the aisle, and I heard Otto laugh.

"Put your belt on, Aviva," I growled from the next seat over. There was hardly anyone in the first class section, only the four of us and a solitary gentleman in the front. Just how I liked it.

The attendant came over, smiling brightly. "Would you like a hot towel, sir? Or anything else?" I eyed the flight attendant in her form-fitting suit, with the bright smile that seemed to promise something more, and pointedly ignored what she was offering. I'd joined the mile high club years ago, and besides, that shit was cliché now.

I shook my head.

"Very well, sir. Let me know if you change your mind."

Aviva was frowning at me. "That was a bit rude, Sampson."

I gave her a droll look. I forgot how naive she was, despite the fact that Hendrick had just had his dick between her thighs. "She was politely offering to blow me in the first class bathrooms, Good Girl. I can take her up on the offer, if it would make you feel more comfortable?"

She flushed that pretty pink again, and I resisted the urge to torment her more. Maybe see if she wanted to take the flight attendant's place. But it was a long ass flight and I was tired already. I got jet lagged like a bitch, even in first class. Humans weren't meant to skip across time zones like this.

As soon as we departed JFK, Aviva seemed to relax, like any other decision was impossible now, and by extension, we all relaxed. I hadn't realized how much her mood had affected us all. Airlines kept you happy by feeding you constantly, and in first class, that meant constant refills of champagne as well.

A three-course meal, two more champagnes, a turndown service, and Good Girl's enthused excitement over a set of pajamas later, she was asleep, curled in a tiny ball and snoring softly. I wasn't far behind her, but first, we needed to talk.

Unclipping my belt, I stepped into the aisle between Otto and Hendrick. "You fucked her."

Hendrick looked comically surprised by the flatness of my tone. "I did not. I ate her out." Otto scoffed, and Hendrick gave us an innocent look. "She was having a panic attack. What was I supposed to do?" he hissed.

"I don't know, how about talking her down? Your

tongue isn't just for fucking cunnilingus, Drix," Otto said sharply.

"Who the fuck still calls it cunnilingus? What are you? A 1970s sex ed teacher?"

I lifted a hand to cut them off before they really got going. "Whatever. I don't care if you fuck her into next week, Drix. What I care about is that you guys don't have another lover's quarrel over it." I dropped my voice lower. "So here's the new rule. An addendum to Aviva's rule, if you will. Do we all want her?"

Hendrick grinned and nodded, but Otto seemed more hesitant. Finally, he gave a short, sharp nod.

I sniffed. "She intrigues me too, and I'd be lying if I said I hadn't thought of her stretched out beneath me. So, this is how it's going to be. It's Aviva's choice—"

"That goes without saying," Otto interjected. Fuck, he knew I hated interruptions.

"And we aren't in competition with each other. We are family, brothers. Well, maybe not you two, because that's a fucking weird analogy when you fuck, but still. We are a unit, stronger together. As long as she's only with us, it doesn't matter which one of us it is, does it?"

Otto shook his head, and Hendrick shrugged. "Not to me."

"Her enthusiastic consent rule still applies too," Otto said, his eyes boring holes in Hendrick's head.

"Hey, I think we can all agree she was very enthusiastic in her willingness." He winked, the fucking gloating asshole, and I resisted the urge to punch him.

Rolling my eyes, I looked at Otto. "Of course." I hesitated. "And when this trip is over, we forget about her. Because a girl like that can only lead to heaven or complete and utter ruin, and I refuse to take that chance with you guys."

Hendrick shrugged again, just happy to get his dick wet. He was having a good week, but I knew those wouldn't be around forever. With Hendrick, you just had to wait for the inevitable fall back to earth.

My eyes moved to Otto. He was frowning at her sleeping form, her hair spread around her face like a chaotic cloud. He looked back at Hendrick, then nodded. Self-sacrificing bastard. Today, it worked in my favor though.

Good. We could fuck her, have fun with her, but eventually we'd have to forget her. Hell, maybe she'll actually track down this mysterious book guy, though I doubted it. This was like a modern day wild goose chase. All pretty lies and tantalizing promises. I doubted this guy even existed. I really doubted he'd made it to Europe and was just waiting around in a bookstore for some depressed little Good Girl to come and find him.

However, I knew desperation when I saw it—a need to escape—so I was happy to humor her for now, and maybe get a taste along the way. She let out a little snore, and I held back a chuckle. I was Sampson fucking Rubio; I couldn't afford to love anyone.

"She is cute though," Hendrick said softly, and I couldn't disagree. Cute and sweet.

I wanted to ruin her completely.

I slept for most of the flight, the attendant touching my shoulder lightly to tell me that they'd be serving breakfast soon and then preparing for descent. I stood, heading to the bathroom to change out of the pajamas and into fresh clothes.

I was stopped by the same attendant near the front of the plane. "Do you require any assistance, sir?" Yep, there was that purr again. Fuck, she definitely knew who I was.

It happened too often. Everyone wanted that fairytale, where the rich billionaire swept them off their feet and away from their mundane job, and made them a princess. I didn't want to burst her bubble, but this wasn't a fairytale.

Most rich people married other rich people. It was the only way you knew they were marrying you for you and not your money. But even then, you couldn't be sure.

"No."

I slammed into the bathroom. While it wasn't as small as the bathrooms in economy, it wasn't huge either. Throwing on my clothes, I brushed my teeth and wet my hair, combing it back into something that resembled a style. I didn't look too bad, considering I'd barely slept before this flight.

By the time I emerged from the bathroom, a sleep-tousled Aviva was standing outside, her clothes clutched to her chest. She was frowning, and I paused in the doorway.

"What's wrong?"

She screwed up her nose. "I didn't bring fresh clothes on the plane with me."

I shrugged. "Just wear yesterday's. We're going straight from the airport to the hotel."

She sucked her lip between her teeth. "I don't have any clean underwear."

She'd been wearing an adorable skate skirt yesterday, and I desperately wanted to see her in a pair of lace thigh highs, legs wrapped around my hips as I buried myself deep in her—

"I don't actually have *any* underwear. Hendrick didn't give them back yesterday. After..." She trailed off, her cheeks so red I thought they'd catch on fire.

Which meant I couldn't help but needle her a little. "After Drix ate you out on the bathroom counter like you *were* the breakfast buffet?"

Her lips parted, and she gave me a short nod. I grinned. I could ask Drix to give them back to her, but I kind of liked the idea of her sitting across from me, her bare ass on the plush leather seat.

"Well, looks like you're shit out of luck because there's no way he's giving them back. I'd be surprised if he didn't hug them to his chest like a teddy bear while he slept last night."

"That's gross," she huffed, and pushed past me into the bathroom. I stepped to the side, but didn't move out of the way, so she had to squeeze that delicious, panty-free ass against me before she could slam the door shut.

Otto looked at me suspiciously as I sat down opposite him. "What are you so happy about?"

As the attendant wheeled breakfast down on a polished silver trolley, the red Occupied light above the bathroom caught my eye. I slid him a grin. "I'll tell you all about it later. Let's eat."

Chapter 17
Aviva

"Why is there always so much marble?" I whispered, and Otto stifled a laugh.

Hendrick waved a hand. "It's usually because these places are old as fuck."

Men in red uniforms gathered our bags onto gold luggage trolleys, and Hendrick swaggered up to the reception desk, giving a broad, good ol' American boy next door grin to the receptionist, who had an honest-to-goodness chignon.

I stood sandwiched between Otto and Sampson, both of whom looked bored. Well, maybe not bored, but like they'd done all this before. It wasn't new and exciting.

I was in fucking London. England. Holy shit. My whole body felt tingly and electric, and I felt giddy.

Otto's phone chimed and he stared down at it, before stuffing it back in his pocket. "I hope Hendrick got us a suite. I want Aviva with us." He looked down at me, a soft smile curling his lips. "You'll be better company than these two assholes. You definitely smell prettier."

I snorted. Doubtful. These guys smelled like six-hundred-dollar cologne and sex. If there was a better scent than that, I was yet to find it.

Hendrick tilted his head at us, and Otto placed a hand on my spine, gently guiding me to the elevators. Or lifts, as the sign said. All my awareness narrowed to that one spot, to the touch of each fingertip through my dress.

It didn't help that someone opened the front doors right then, allowing that London breeze to sweep up my skirt. I'd made a grave error letting Hendrick Kenley between my thighs, and I didn't think it was something that could be undone. I wasn't even sure if I wanted to undo it.

Being crowded into the elevator together felt different this time. The energy around us felt fraught with tension, and I didn't know if it was just me and Hendrick, or Otto as well. I turned my head and caught Sampson looking down at me. It was definitely Sampson too.

We were going to have to talk about Rule No. 1

again. This time, I was going to have to follow my own rules though.

The elevator doors slid open and Hendrix strode forward, flinging open the hotel room door. I stepped through and gasped. We were in the goddamn penthouse.

"Holy shit." My eyes flew to Hendrick. "This is too much."

He shrugged. "Two rooms would have cost more. This is better."

No. No, no, no. "How much does this place cost per night?"

He was saved from answering by a knock at the door. A young man in a finely tailored suit stood there smiling. "Good afternoon, sirs, miss. My name is Jonathan, and I'll be your butler for the duration of your stay."

Hendrick let the man in, while I continued to gape. Behind Jonathan the Butler were more of the red-suited bellhops, who carried in our bags and distributed them to the different bedrooms. A maid appeared behind them, apparently to unpack the clothes from the suitcases and into the fancy walk-in wardrobes.

I grabbed Hendrick's hand and dragged him out onto the balcony. The view of Hyde Park was amazing, but I didn't let it distract me. Both Otto and Sampson slipped through the door as well, and Otto shut it softly behind him.

"Seriously, Hendrick, how much did this cost? Two thousand bucks a night?" Sampson snorted, and my jaw unhinged. *"More?"* I looked between them all, and while Sampson and Hendrick gave me blank looks, Otto relented under my stare and nodded once. "Holy shit. No. New rule. No more hotels that cost more per night than my family's monthly mortgage repayment. We stay in normal hotels, in normal rooms." I paused and sucked in a deep breath. "I can't pay this back in a million years. Not this level of luxury. I want to be able to pay you back. This is insane."

"Good Girl, don't be fucking ridiculous. No one expects you to pay back the cost of a fucking week at the Mandarin Oriental. It costs more than your college education."

"Not helping," Otto muttered after I gasped.

"It's a waste of money," I argued, spinning to face Hendrick.

He looked aggravatingly chilled out. "It's my money to waste."

I huffed, storming back into the suite and then into the closest bedroom before slamming the door. It was too much. How much could you accept from strangers without giving anything back?

I stared at myself in the full-length mirror. "Am I

about to be human trafficked?" I asked the stupid girl staring back at me. "Let's look at the evidence, shall we?" The girl in the mirror quirked a brow.

"Rich guy with connections plucks you from a mental institution, and flies you *out of the goddamn country*. That should be red flag number one." My reflection seemed unconvinced. "Then, they completely makeover your entire wardrobe, so you look like pretty cattle for the rich mafia dude who's going to keep you in the basement of his stone mansion, where no one can hear you scream. That shit is hot in fiction but I don't wanna be someone's chained-to-the-wall fuck-doll." I pointed at my reflection, and she pointed back. "They put you up in a fancy hotel so you feel like you owe them something and boom, you're a high price escort being trafficked across international borders. Plus, your parents think you've run away so you don't even get your damn face on a milk carton. You're an idiot, Aviva."

"Do they even put missing kids on milk cartons anymore?"

I whirled around to see Sampson leaning against the doorjamb. "That was a private conversation."

"With yourself?" His lip quirked but he was trying to keep a straight face.

I crossed my arms and glared. "Yes."

"I'm gonna be real with you, Aviva. You're right. We are here to sell you to the Russian Bratva."

My heart plummeted to my gut, at least until he burst out laughing. I took two steps toward him and punched him in the chest. "You fucking asshole. Don't say shit like that." I punched him in the tit again. "God, you guys are about as sensitive as a fucking freight train."

Sampson caught my hand as I went back for a third punch. He held my fist easily, staring down at me. "You want the actual truth?"

I nodded. Yes. I needed the actual truth, because this shit didn't happen. I hadn't wanted to look at the truth back in the States, but there was no safety net here; I couldn't blindly follow my delusions with no thought for my safety.

"Truth is, Hendrick wants to fuck you. Ever since you said no, that you had no interest in him, you've become a bit of an obsession. You're prey to him, a challenge that he's been missing for a while." I went to open my mouth to say fat fucking chance, but then I remembered he'd already been nose to clit with my body, and I'd left my high horse parked in the first class lounge at JFK. Using my fist, Sampson dragged me closer. "The truth is, Good Girl, he's not the only one. Otto out there? He's basically coming in his pants at the thought of you, him and Hendrick alone in a room together, skin to skin, fucking each other until you can't breathe air that doesn't smell of sex."

I dropped my eyes to the floor, trying to get myself back under control. My whole body shuddered, partly from his words, and partly from the fact that he was so close I could feel the warmth of his chest against mine, the rumble of his words against my nipples that were already hard.

"And you?" I whispered, not looking at him or those dark eyes that threatened to drag me down into madness.

"Oh, Good Girl, you can't fathom the bad things I want to do to you." He leaned down until his lips were close to mine. "I want to make you beg for me. I want to be your whole fucking world." His lips brushed mine ever so softly as he whispered, "I want to consume you."

My whole body began to tremble as I arched toward him, reaching for its inevitable doom. He turned his head slightly and nipped my lower lip at the very corner of my mouth, hard.

Then he stepped away. "Get changed. I'll take you to find your Iron Nautilus."

As he left, I stumbled on shaky legs to the bed and collapsed down on it. Well, I'd wanted the truth and I'd gotten it. I was going to be a sex slave alright, and I had a feeling I would be down on my knees, begging for the privilege before the week was out.

Just like the good girl Sampson had accused me of being, I picked out an outfit that had been chosen for me, went into the ensuite and showered.

Did I touch myself to relieve the ache? Yes.

Did I think about Sampson's dark voice, Otto's sweet touch and Hendrick's filthy mouth? Absolutely.

Did I regret it? Not the shower rub, but this whole fucking circus? No. And that was the scariest part of all.

Self destruction could be such a fucking beautiful way to go.

Chapter 18
Otto

Aviva still wasn't speaking to Hendrick when she emerged from the bedroom she'd chosen. Sampson gave us a confident look, but she looked flushed. He'd taken her to the London bookstore, this Iron Nautilus, and I guess she wanted to get it out of the way. I hoped she wanted to stay in London for a couple of days at least, because I hadn't been here in years.

Maybe she just wanted to find this guy, this Nemo, and get away from us as fast as possible.

That kind of hurt but I didn't blame her.

Hendrick was tapping his finger on the glass dining table that seated twelve. Jonathan the Butler had left for the moment to get our evening meal organized. It was just me and Hendrick left in this big, empty penthouse, and the silence was going to kill me.

"We should talk about what we're going to do after this. It's obvious that these grand shows of wealth are making her uncomfortable."

"I don't want to sleep in a bed bug-infested shithole either."

I gave him a droll look. "Drix, there's a huge leap between six thousand pounds a night and a charge-by-the-hour brothel." Hendrick just shrugged, his mind obviously elsewhere. I'd known him long enough to know what was at the end of this spiral. "Take your meds, Drix."

He narrowed his eyes at me, but stood up and went to the bathroom. I heard the rattle of a pill bottle and the running of the tap. Hendrick might be stubborn as fuck about a lot of things, but he knew the meds made him better. Returning, he stared down at me, and I knew that wild energy in his eyes. It meant we were about to fight or fuck. Sometimes, if we didn't do either, shit went bad. It wasn't a hardship; my dick was already hard at the thought of that crazy fucking.

He continued to stare down at me. "Why doesn't she like me? Most girls would be crawling all over my dick by now."

"Because you're an asshole and she has more brain cells than your usual conquests," I quipped back, and laughed as he launched himself at me. The couch gave an ominous creak but held. He threw a soft punch at my ribs, and I wiggled out from underneath him.

However, Hendrick was quick, and he had his thighs locked tight around my hips and his forearm across my throat before we could make it to the ground. I tapped his arm and he pressed a little tighter, making my dick harder, before releasing pressure.

"Seriously, Otto? Why?"

"You're everything that nice, middle class girls are trained to resent. You're rich. You're entitled—"

"My father has beaten me within an inch of my life several times over the years."

I shrug. "She doesn't know that. She just sees you drop a small fortune on a hotel room, basically confirming all the shit drummed into her by the media since she could walk." I paused. "Do you want her to like you? I mean, like you for more than your dick?"

This was new. Hendrick had been obsessed with girls before, but they were always just a game to him. He didn't really care about their feelings. Once the challenge was over, he moved on. It was what I assumed he'd do with Aviva too.

He shrugged again and gripped my chin. Then he launched himself at me, kissing me hard and wild. It was always like this, right before he crashed. It might be in a month, or days, or even hours. Sampson had taunted me once, said I was acting as a bandaid for all the gaping, festering damage that was hiding away inside Hendrick. As a way for him to fuck out his demons before he self-destructed.

I was surprisingly okay with that.

He was still straddling my hips, but as he leaned forward to kiss me, I could feel the hard line of his cock pressing against my stomach.

"What, are you topping me today?" I teased. I mean, it did happen, but most of the time I was top. He liked to be out of control, liked to feel punished, and while logically I knew that was a little fucked up given his childhood, we were all a little fucked up. So who was I to judge?

He ground his dick into me and grinned. "I think I might. You have a problem with that?"

As an answer to his question, I grabbed the back of his head and dragged him down for another kiss. No, a kiss made it sound like something sweet and soft. In reality, Hendrick fucked my mouth with his, and I loved it.

I moved my hands down to his waist, unbuckling and unbuttoning his jeans quickly so I could pull them out of the way. Hendrick was fucking beautiful, and he knew it. He worked out a lot, running every morning in the gym until he was exhausted. Maybe tomorrow we could run on the streets of London, since he wouldn't have to worry about his security detail for now.

All thoughts of running fled my brain when I circled my hand around his cock and he thrust into it, his mouth not relenting for a minute. It was like he didn't need to breathe, but I definitely did. I broke off the kiss so I could peel his shirt up over his head.

And then he was naked, and I could only stare at the beauty of him. It was like this every time, really. I knew I loved him, and it was hard to deny when I held his cock in my hand. When he'd taken my virginity, I'd taken his too. I knew just as much about what pleased him as I did about myself.

Drix moved his lips down my throat, scrunching my shirt up around my neck so he could suck at the skin of my chest, stopping to bite the flat of my nipple.

"Motherfucker," I growled, thrusting up against him as I shuddered with pleasure. "We should take this to the bedroom in case Sampson and Aviva come back."

He paused to look back up at me from beneath thick brown lashes, a grin on his face. "So what? Wouldn't be the first time Sampson has caught an eyeful."

"And Aviva?"

"She'd like it," he grunted, as he struggled with my belt and jeans. I lifted my ass so he could pull them down, underwear and all. He crumpled the back pocket of my jeans and grinned. "Fuck me, Otto. Is there a condom and lube back here? You really are a boy scout."

"Shut the fuck up and put it on already," I growled, and he laughed. He slid the condom onto my cock, making me raise an eyebrow. "If you're topping, Drix, it's meant to go on you."

He shook his head. "I want you to fuck me against these stupidly expensive windows." Oh yeah.

I curled up, capturing his mouth again so I could kiss him softly. Hendrick might kiss like he fucked, but I tried to tell him I loved him with my lips.

He climbed off my lap and I stood up, still kissing him as I walked him backwards toward the floor-to-ceiling windows. He reached out and stroked my cock, and I groaned. I was already fucking hard as a rock.

"Keep that up and it's going to be a short fuck," I muttered, and his laugh made my own lips curl.

He tossed me one of the tiny lube packets I usually kept with me. I always liked to be prepared because Hendrick was unpredictable. Maybe even more so, now that Aviva was around. She made me feel wild too, but I had more care for consequences than Hendrick.

Which was why we still used condoms when we had sex, because I didn't trust that Drix wouldn't stick his dick in some diseased gold digger, causing us both to end up with antibiotic-resistant super gonorrhea. He swore he was always safe though, because the quickest way to get pinned down was a paternity suit, especially when you were a senator's son.

I lubed up my dick and his ass, and pressed two fingers inside the hard ring of muscle. His head fell forward onto the glass. "Quit with the foreplay, Otto. Fuck me already," he ordered, and while most people would think that meant he was desperate for me, I knew it was because Hendrick wanted it to hurt.

I hated when he was like this. Still, he pressed his body against the tinted glass, and I hoped it was nice and dark, or the lovely people walking their dogs in Hyde Park were going to get a good eyeful of Hendrick's cock. I curled one hand in his hair and held his hip with the other, and slammed my cock inside him. He clenched tight around the base of me, and we both grunted loudly. I drew back gently, not pulling all the way out, and then slammed home again.

I tilted his head to the side so I could suck at his throat, snapping my hips into his. "Stroke your cock. I want you to come all over the glass." I paused, nipping at his ear. "We'll leave the cleaning staff a huge tip."

He laughed, but it turned into a moan as I fucked him harder, his hand on his dick moving at the same speed as my thrusts. Fuck, he felt so goddamn good. I'd missed him more during this stint in rehab, and not just the sex. I turned his head to the side so I could kiss him, fucking him with my tongue, wrapped around each other so tightly that our sweat-coated bodies were sticking together.

Hendrick tore his mouth away. "Fuck, I'm gonna come," he groaned, before his body clamped around mine and thick ropes of cum painted the glass. A few more strokes and I couldn't hold off any longer, tugging on his hips so I was pressed so tightly to him as I blew that we could've been one person.

A soft squeak from behind us and Hendrick's silent chuckle vibrating against my chest let me know that he'd gotten exactly what he wanted. I glanced over my shoulder at a stunned Aviva and an unimpressed-looking Sampson.

"Seriously? Three goddamn bedrooms and you guys have to fuck in the living room?" He rolled his eyes, dragging Aviva back out of the door and slamming it shut. Hendrick's laughter bubbled from his lips, until it was echoing around the room.

I kissed between his shoulder blades, and shook my head. "You are one crazy fucker, Hendrick Kenley. Go shower and I'll clean up this mess, at least a little."

He spun in my arms and pressed his lips to mine, hard. "Leave the handprints," he murmured, before cupping his dick and swaggering away to the bathroom like I hadn't just fucked him stupid.

God, I loved that man. I was so screwed.

Chapter 19
Aviva

The ride to the Iron Nautilus in St. Giles had been silent as I contemplated Sampson's words. Evan, Sampson's bodyguard, had organised a hire car that had blacked out windows, and if I wasn't mistaken, it was also shielded by bulletproof glass.

My heart didn't start to pound until we pulled up outside the bookstore. The lights were all off, and a closing down sale sign was stuck to the window.

No.

"It can't be over already," I whispered, and Sampson scoffed.

"Relax, Good Girl. Stay here." He slid from the car, while Evan watched him and the surrounding area like a hawk.

"What's the chance of me accidentally getting

caught in the crossfire of someone trying to take him out?" I asked the guy. I wondered if he even spoke.

"Unlikely," he grunted back. His voice was deeper than I'd imagined, low and rumbly like distant thunder.

"But not impossible?"

Evan just gave me a dead-eyed stare and went back to scouring the surrounding streets, as Sampson came over and slid back into the car. He was typing something into his phone, and waved his fingers to Evan, indicating we should go.

"So?" Jesus, way to draw out the suspense. "Enough with the cliffhanger already."

He raised an eyebrow at me. "It closed three months ago. I'll have my assistant track down the owner to get us in there. Stop stressing. Let's go back to the hotel, get the guys up to speed on everything, and then sleep off this fucking jet lag."

He went back to his phone and I tried not to pout. He was such an asshole, but I trusted him when he said he'd take care of it. And I was kind of tired, despite the fact I'd slept nearly the whole flight. The last couple of days had been a lot, physically and emotionally.

The traffic was unusually light on the way back to the hotel, so in barely any time at all, Sampson was guiding me to the private elevator that led to the penthouse, his hand resting possessively on the curve of my spine.

"You seem like an honest kind of guy, Sampson. Do you think what I'm doing is crazy?"

He looked down at me, and snared me in his irises. His dark eyes were actually hazel, the outer rim of his iris dark brown and the inner rim vibrant green. They were mesmerizing, and I tried to avoid meeting his gaze for that very reason.

"Yes."

My body sagged. He was only confirming the little nagging voice in the back of my mind, but Hendrick hadn't cared, and Otto was a classic enabler. Sampson wasn't the kind of person to sugar-coat things—I'd only known him for days and I knew that with absolute certainty.

"I don't think it matters though. I think going back to college and pretending the last three months had just been a phase would also be crazy. At least you have a purpose, something to inspire passion. People have done shit for stupider reasons."

We stepped out of the elevator and Sampson opened the penthouse door. I stepped through and my feet immediately locked like I was stuck in quicksand.

Otto was fucking Hendrick against the windows.

My brain scrambled to comprehend what I should do as I watched the snap of Otto's hips and Hendrick's low moan as he came all over the glass.

Sampson plowed into my back and cursed. "Seriously? Three goddamn bedrooms and you guys have to fuck in the living room?"

Otto looked over at me, his eyes flared in panic, while Hendrick laughed. Sampson grabbed my hand, dragging me out of the suite and back toward the elevator, slamming the door with an unnecessary bang. He stabbed the ground floor button, while I blinked dazedly.

Sampson frowned at me. "What? You knew they fucked."

I did. I did know that. I just don't think I was prepared for how I'd feel if I saw it.

Sampson went rigid beside me, and I realized I'd spoken out loud. "How do you feel?"

His tone was short and terse, like he was waiting for me to say disgusted or appalled. But I felt neither of those things. I felt...

I looked up at him, and his face morphed. A smirk curled his lips. "Oh." He ran a hand down my spine, and I shivered. "It made you feel... hot?" He leaned closer. "Did it make you feel wet and needy, Good Girl, watching Otto fuck Hendrick?" He hit the stop button on the elevator. "If I reach under this skirt, will your panties be soaked from seeing them fuck?"

"Yes." The answer was yes. I was soaked, my gut was churning with lust, and I wanted Sampson to find out for himself if I was wet.

He slid his hand further down my spine and over my ass. His other hand bent me over a little so he could stroke his fingertips over my core to see for himself.

"Mmm, yes you are."

Then he pressed the emergency stop button again and the elevator jolted back to life, the doors opening all too soon onto a busy lobby. "Want to do some touristy shit?"

No. I wanted to find a dark corner and get him to fuck me into next week. I wanted to climb back into that elevator, walk back into that suite, and insist Otto and Hendrick go for round two.

Instead, I said, "I'd like to see Buckingham Palace."

We waited for Evan in the lobby, and he looked a little pissed to be back on the job so soon, but if he was, he kept it to himself. He got the hire car and we pulled away from the curb. Really, all I wanted was a long shower and a nap, but if I couldn't do that, I was happy to see London too. I was in London! I still couldn't believe it.

"Hendrick arranged us a table at Nobu for tonight, so we won't be able to do much sightseeing," Sampson said, not looking up from his phone. You wouldn't know that those same fingers tapping his phone had been between my thighs ten minutes ago. My face flushed at the memory, and once again, I tried to get my head back in the game.

Nemo was the endgame. Not these guys. Though, would there be any harm in tasting them?

I internally snorted at myself. I was such a fucking idiot. It would be like voluntarily putting my heart in a blender.

Finally, Evan parked, and we all climbed out. It was a short walk to Buckingham Palace, but it wasn't a bad day. A little cool and gray, but not raining. I pulled my coat tighter around me as we walked toward the giant gates.

It was packed with tourists, each trying to take a selfie while getting the giant building in the picture. I thought I'd feel something being here, seeing a place that I'd only ever seen on television, but I wasn't overly enthused. I was living someone's dream right now, but it just wasn't mine apparently.

"Underwhelmed?"

I looked at Sampson, and tried to find a way to say yes without seeming ungrateful. "No, it's wonderful."

He shrugged. "I've seen bigger."

I grinned at him. "Hear that a lot?"

He gave me a heated look, and I listened to my hindbrain and scuttled away before he whipped it out to show me. I wandered over to one of the iconic guards in their red livery. Sampson was a step behind me, finally off his phone. When a tourist trying to somehow get the whole building in his viewfinder stepped back into me, I tried to move backwards, trip-ping over my feet. Only Sampson's reflexes kept me from falling on my ass.

"Watch where the fuck you're going," he growled at the old man, who honestly must have been eighty, and the old guy sneered at us both. Sampson went to step toward him, but I grabbed his hand and dragged him away before Evan had to put down an old man.

"Come on, Sam. Leave the geriatrics alone," I mock-whispered, side-stepping around more people. Too many people. The feeling of them around me was like ants on my skin until I just wanted to flee.

I looked over at Evan. He seemed bored by the whole experience, but I watched the way his eyes roamed the crowd and he held his body tight. "Do you run?"

The answer was obviously yes, because the guy was fit as hell, probably had to be to keep up with Sampson. He just gave a grunt and a nod, and I smiled brightly at him, enjoying the slight widening of his eyes. When my ex was drunk, he used to say I was as interesting as bran flakes, except when I smiled.

I turned back to Sampson. "What about you, rich boy? Do you run?" I'd felt Sampson's body against mine, so I knew he was fit too. But that didn't mean he could run. You could lift weights every day, and then drop dead if you had to run more than twenty feet.

"I've been known to jog."

I looked down at my Converse. This was why they were the superior footwear—they were always ready for anything.

"Let's run then, Bad Boy," I said, a play on his nickname for me.

"Why... Hey, wait!"

I took off, dodging around the people snapping photos, turning my head and throwing up bunny ears when I got in their shots. I just ran. I ran down alongside the high fence that enclosed the palace gardens, pushing myself harder and faster until my lungs felt like they were on fire. I could hear Sampson and Evan's heavy footfalls behind me.

I'd always been fast, mostly because I was small and light, and being a swimmer had given me good endurance. The wind on my face felt good, and I tried to remember the last time I just ran. It had been too long. Before driving into that tree. Before the drinking and meaningless sex. Maybe before I even went away to college and realized I didn't have a personality.

I swerved around the people walking their dogs, the leisurely strollers and the guided tour groups. I smiled, uncaring if I got bugs in my teeth or hair; I was just happy to be free. Free to do whatever I liked. There was no one to disappoint here. I watched a double-decker bus with a morbid kind of fascination as it came lumbering down the road. One quick burst of speed, and we'd collide.

I didn't realize I was laughing until we hit an intersection and a hand wrapped around my forearm. I looked up at Sampson, who was lightly puffing, his eyes taking in my face. "You okay, Good Girl?"

I grinned at him. "Don't you ever feel like just running?" I looked between him and Evan, who was watching the crowd like someone was about to pull a gun and shoot us both. Sampson just continued to stare, but Evan winked at me, his chest heaving slightly.

My expression probably bordered on manic as Sampson held my hand, pulling me close to his side as we crossed the road, walking toward the Wellington Arch. It was pretty, and also kind of terrifying. Walking through it, I ran my fingers along the stone of the giant arch, appreciating the grandeur of it. Old and grand—that was London in a nutshell, wasn't it?

Suddenly, Sampson dragged me into his body and pressed me tight against the wall of the arch. He captured my lips with his, kissing me hard. A dominating, oxygen-stealing kiss. His tongue plunged into my mouth, stroking mine like it was trying to lure it to the dark side. His hand dropped to my ass and he squeezed it tight with a groan. I gripped his hair, threading my fingers through the dark strands and held on for dear life as he dominated my body.

Someone made a disgusted noise and Sampson slid his hand higher, baring the side of my ass to the world. When someone nearby muttered something about children being present, he finally drew back, and I was panting harder than I had after I'd sprinted for a mile. Sampson stepped back, but kept a hand on my hip.

"Your madness is the worst kind, Aviva. It's the kind that infects those around you."

With that, he turned and walked away. I watched his heaving shoulders as he emerged out the other side of the arch, the sun hitting his mahogany hair and making it shine.

I stood there, looking back at Evan, who was watching me with a guarded expression. My cheeks flushed and I shrugged. If he was disgusted with me, he didn't say anything. "Let's go."

He ushered me in front of him until we caught up with Sampson. Just when I thought Sampson was going to ignore me, he reached out and gripped my fingers. He didn't look at me, or say anything, but that small connection meant something.

I just didn't know what.

Chapter 20
Hendrick

Aviva was still avoiding me, but it was harder to do in a small suite than it had been in a large facility. I'd been asleep when she and Sampson had returned home again, but Otto had said she'd basically gone straight to her room. He also said that she'd looked flushed and disheveled, and I briefly wondered if Sampson had fucked her in the back of the SUV.

I was surprisingly okay with the idea. I kind of wished I'd been there to watch, but that was it.

I was almost finished dressing for dinner at Nobu, and she still hadn't emerged. Otto was playing with his hair in the bathroom, looking fine as fuck.

"Should I go and talk to her? Maybe she wasn't as cool with us as I thought."

Otto looked at me in the reflection of the mirror. "I

don't think that was it. She's probably just embarrassed."

I screwed up my face. "Why? It wasn't her that got caught with their dick in their hand."

He shrugged, and went back to making his hair look like he just ran his fingers through it rather than styled it for twenty minutes. It was an artform, apparently.

I knew I should just leave it alone, but leaving it alone wasn't really my style. I liked to poke at things until they bled.

I didn't knock on her door, just entered, kinda hoping she'd be naked. Instead, she was applying her makeup in the bathroom.

"Ever heard of knocking, Hendrick?" she snarked as she attempted to apply her mascara.

"Why? Whatever you've got, I've seen a hundred times over."

She speared me with a look. "I don't want to hear about your body count."

I snorted. "As if my body count is a hundred." It was more like twice that. I'd lost count after a while. Her expression said she definitely didn't think it was lower.

I cleared my throat. "Should I apologize for what you saw this afternoon?"

"Not to me. Maybe to Sampson though."

I frowned again. Had Sampson said something? "I don't think Sam minds. He's seen it before. Sometimes when we all fuck one girl, he watches me fuck Otto. Or vice versa."

"Fuck." There was a loud clatter as she dropped the mascara wand, her left eye all scrunched up. "Fucking hell, Hendrick. You can't say that shit while I'm waving something that close to my goddamn eyeball. Jesus. Dammit, that stings."

I walked further into the bathroom, grabbing a cotton pad from the vanity. Pouring some makeup remover over it, I held it up to her eye, batting away her fingers. I stroked away her carefully applied eye makeup, and she sighed.

"Now I have to start again."

I grabbed the makeup remover, pouring some on another cotton pad. "You don't need it anyway." I carefully wiped off the eye makeup on the other side, stroking off the foundation until she was barefaced again.

"Maybe I like to wear it. Men always think we wear makeup for them. Maybe I just enjoy using my face as a canvas?"

I met her pretty blue eyes. "Do you like it?"

She shrugged. "I just don't want to look like I haven't made an effort."

I looked down at the pretty silk shirt and tight

black jeans she was wearing. Everything hugged her tightly, and her hair was tamed into soft ringlets today.

"You look beautiful."

She shoved at my shoulder. "Stop being sweet, butthead." But I noticed the pink on her cheeks. "You take makeup off like a pro. Are you a drag queen in your spare time?"

I gave her a shit-eating grin. "Worried about me wearing your pretty lace panties?"

She flushed even redder, but gave me the stink eye. "Now I've seen your dick, I'm pretty sure the thongs that Sampson chose for me aren't going to keep that shit in."

I laughed, climbing up to sit on the vanity beside her. "My mom would get blackout drunk and I'd take off her makeup for her while she slept. If she woke up in ruined makeup, my dad would hit her. I like to think I was saving her a little."

Viva's hand stilled from where she was applying a nude lipstick. "I'm sorry, Hendrick."

"Sorry for what? You didn't beat her."

She chewed her lip, already ruining her lipstick. "Sorry for thinking your life was all gold bullion and roses."

I lifted a shoulder. "You aren't entirely wrong."

She swiped on the mascara again, blending some pink cream onto her cheekbones, and that was it. She gazed at herself skeptically, but I thought she looked beautiful.

"So we're okay? Otto said you might be embarrassed." She stood, uncurling from the vanity. She was wearing chunky high heels and it made her legs go on and on. "Fuck, you are so goddamn hot."

She waved me away. "No, I'm not embarrassed. Well, maybe a little, but no more than if I'd seen a private moment between two other people." She picked up a small clutch, looking over her shoulder at me. "Maybe a little jealous."

I swaggered over to her, a smirk on my face. "Wish it was you fucking me?"

She grinned. "Well, I have always wanted to peg a guy. But no."

I frowned. "Wished Otto was fucking you?"

She shook her head again, and my heart unclenched. I stepped closer so my lips were close to her ear. "Wished we were both fucking you?"

She paused, and looked up at me under those long, long lashes. "Yes."

I grinned, racing for the door. "Dinner's off. We're staying home to have an orgy," I shouted out to the living room, and she gasped.

"Like fuck! Get your ass out here—it's nearly time for our reservation," Sampson yelled back, and I laughed. Viva was gazing up at me with that sneer again, the one that made me hard as fuck.

"Not funny, Hendrick," she hissed.

I leaned forward and kissed her hard. "I wasn't making a joke, Viva." I spun her around and slapped her ass. "Let's go before Sampson gets his balls in a twist. He hates being late for things."

She squeaked but strode out of the room, shooting daggers at me over her shoulder. She met Otto in the hall, and he looked hot as hell. She gazed up at him, and I could see him melt into a puddle. They really would be perfect together.

"You look very handsome, Otto," she murmured.

"You look beautiful too, Aviva."

She leaned in close, whispering something in his ear. His eyes widened slightly and his cheeks flushed. Dammit, I wanted to know what she said. As she pulled away, he looked over her shoulder at me and yelled, "Dinner's cancelled. Staying home for an orgy!"

Sampson appeared at the other end of the hall, a frown already on his face. "One, I'm hungry. Two, you bastards fucked this afternoon. So keep it in your goddamn pants."

"Three, I spent hours getting ready, even though Hendrick ruined it," Aviva added, and gave me that disgruntled look again. "And I really feel like sushi."

"Mmm, I could eat too," I purred, but no one thought I was talking about sushi.

Sampson's phone chirped, and he looked at us, still scrunched up in the foyer, Viva happily surrounded. He put on his stern face and pointed at the door. "The car is downstairs. Go."

I grinned at him as I walked past, and winked. I hadn't been this excited for the future in months. We were definitely going to have to leave the cleaning crew a tip.

Chapter 21
Aviva

Despite all the talk of an orgy, I drank way too much wine with dinner. On top of my meds, I'd been drunk as hell by the time we walked back through the door of the suite. Otto had put his foot down, taken me to bed, helped me strip down to my underwear and tucked me in like the true gentleman he was. I had a vague memory of telling him how hot he was, and how sweet, and goodness knows what else, but then I'd passed the hell out.

Thank fuck for that. I felt like I was bipolar around these guys.

In the morning, I woke up clear-headed, determined to get through this trip without succumbing to the insane sexual attraction I felt for them. But the longer I was in their presence, the more I wanted to throw caution to the wind and bang them all into next week.

Not one of them was safe. It should be illegal to have three hot friends.

The smell of coffee dragged me from the bed, and I threw on my oversized hoodie. Despite not being a designer brand, I loved it. It was roomy and comfortable. I felt like me in it.

Jonathan the butler was in the kitchen when I emerged. "Good morning, miss. Would you like a coffee or tea? Some pastries?"

My hangover made me squint at his loud voice. "Yes. Please. Coffee."

Jonathan managed to contain his mirth and whispered, "Your companions are on the East Terrace. I shall bring you out your beverage momentarily."

Now I kind of wished I'd put on pants, but at least this hoodie hit me mid-thigh. I walked through to the furthest door that opened onto the terrace. The guys were all sitting out there, drinking coffee and talking quietly.

Otto noticed me first. "Morning, Viva."

I smiled as much as I could without giving myself a pounding headache. "Morning."

He pushed a glass of water toward me, with cucumber and lemon slices floating in it, and I drank it down gratefully. They all watched me like predators, and I knew something had shifted in our dynamic.

Jonathan hustled out, breaking the tension, placing a coffee and some pastries in front of me. The first sip of coffee was like an orgasm. So freaking good.

Sampson cleared his throat. "The former owner of the bookstore has agreed to meet us there at eleven. You have fifty-seven minutes to be ready."

Hendrick had insinuated that Sampson had a 'thing' about being on time. I guess he hadn't been exaggerating.

"Okay." I tried a scone with strawberry jam and cream, and moaned. Delicious.

The guys fell into easy conversation, while I looked out over Hyde Park. It was weird being up here, seeing such an iconic part of London spread out before me like it was my backyard.

Taking another sip of coffee, I turned back to them. "Sorry I was so weird about the hotel yesterday."

Hendrick waved a hand. "Don't worry about it. We're used to you being weird now."

Otto elbowed him but I couldn't keep the grin from my face. "Asshole," I teased back. "But, I'd appreciate it if we didn't, um, stay anywhere this..." I gestured around the suite, trying to describe everything without words.

"Ostentatious? Over the top? Ridiculous?" Otto supplied helpfully, and Sampson snorted.

I nodded. "Yes. I appreciate it, but it makes me feel wrong."

Hendrick rolled his eyes. "Otto explained about your middle class guilt, Viva. Don't worry, the next place we stay will be the size of a cardboard box and only have one bed." He grinned. "Just to keep you happy. I don't have an ulterior motive or anything." He wiggled his eyebrows, and I laughed.

"Sure."

Otto popped a strawberry into his mouth. "I'm in charge of accommodation now. It'll be fine, Aviva. I'll balance us all."

Once my stomach had settled from full-on revolt to mere grumblings of discontent, I hurried through my routine, not only to meet Sampson's deadline, but because I wanted to see the bookstore. Wanted to see if Nemo had left me another note.

I pulled out my copy of *Twenty Thousand Leagues* from beneath my pillow. It was beginning to look well thumbed and a little tatty already. I let my eyes wander over the cursive strokes of Nemo's handwriting.

. . .

Love, it's a wild force. Ferocious and cruel, or a soothing savior. It's always a gamble, but it's a wager between God and the Devil to which side the coin will land.

What had Nemo been through? Was he like me, just desperately searching for something to give his life meaning, to draw him out of the numbness of existing?

"Let's go, Good Girl," came Sampson's voice, and I slipped on my sneakers, pushing the book back under my pillow. I knew that Nemo wouldn't be at the Iron Nautilus now, but what if he had arrived at the Iron Nautilus and it had been closed? How would I find where he went next?

So many fucking questions.

"Aviva!"

"Fucking hell, Sampson. I'm coming." I stepped into the hall and found Hendrick leaning across from the door.

"Not yet, Viva, but it can be arranged."

I rolled my eyes at him and strode down the hallway. Stopping in front of Sampson, I gave him a jaunty salute. "I'm ready, sir."

His eyes hooded with lust and he growled low in his throat. Whoops. Should've thought that one through. It wasn't quite the effect I'd intended, but apparently I'd unlocked a kink I didn't realize I had until right now.

Hendrick was laughing behind me. "You're in trouble now, Viva. I'd run if I was you."

Sampson flicked his eyes at Hendrick. "You are both lucky we have an appointment right now." Turning on his heel, he walked toward the door.

Otto came up behind me, looking between us all with amusement. He held out his elbow and I slipped my hand into the crook. No one spoke as we left the hotel and climbed into the car. Evan appeared from nowhere, sliding into the driver's seat.

I leaned between the seats. "Morning, Evan."

He looked at me, his face giving away nothing. "Morning, miss."

"Call me Aviva." If we were going to be on a round the world tour together, he should call me by my name.

I could feel the tension in the car again, and I looked back over my shoulder. All the guys were watching the interaction with wary expressions. For fuck's sake.

"Put your seatbelt on, Aviva."

Did I imagine the emphasis Sampson put on my name? Probably. But like the good girl he always taunted me for being, I belted myself in. "So, how'd you track down the former owner?"

"My assistant is adequate at finding public records."

"And how did you get him to agree to open the store for us?"

Sampson looked out the window. "I bought the store."

There was a giant tire screech in my brain. "You *what?*"

He slid his eyes back to mine, his chin tilted stubbornly. "I bought it."

"Pull over," I said to Evan. When he didn't move, I got slightly more hysterical. "Pull the fuck over!" I screeched.

"Aviva," Otto started, but when the car slowed to a stop, I climbed out.

"Do not follow me. Any of you."

I slammed the door. I could hear Sampson yelling, but ignored him as I ran down the sidewalk. A door slammed, and there was the pounding of feet behind, letting me know someone was chasing me. Finally, a hand reached out and grabbed mine.

"Fuck off, Sam, I told you I didn't want any..." It wasn't Sampson, but Evan. I frowned because I guess they'd followed my wishes, kind of. "What are you doing here?"

Evan's jaw tensed. He was younger than I thought, but still easily in his thirties. He was average looking, but not in an unattractive way. The perfect kind of bodyguard. He'd blend into the crowd unless you were looking for him. But the lines at the corners of his eyes said he smiled often, and I had a feeling that when he did, it lit up his whole face.

"I was ordered to be here."

I shook my head. "You're Sampson's bodyguard. Go back and do your job."

He raised a single eyebrow. "You definitely aren't my boss, so no." He looked around, and still holding my arm, dragged me across the road and into a pub. The inside was dark and smelled of old cigarettes, but Evan herded me to the bar.

"Two scotches. The good stuff. Neat," he told the bartender, who had the most impressive sideburns I'd seen since Elvis. The guy didn't say anything about us drinking before lunch, just pouring us both a couple of fingers of scotch. Didn't ask to see my ID or anything.

Evan threw a bill on the bar, and looked pointedly at the glass in front of me. "Drink." I frowned at him but being drunk did seem like a pretty good idea right now. I threw it back, and then he pushed the second one in front of me. "This one too."

Whatever. Down it went too.

"Feel better?"

I shook my head. "No. I feel like a high-priced hooker."

The bartender raised an eyebrow until Evan gave him a pointed look. The man moved away to wipe down the bar at the other end. "So what?"

"Pardon?"

"So what if they're dropping cash? Do you not want them too? Are they pressuring you for sex? If that's the case, I'll put you on a plane home myself right now."

I shook my head. "That's not it. I do want them. All of them. But..." I looked up into his eyes. "Don't you think it's kind of wrong? Morally, I mean?"

Evan's lips twisted. "If you're worried about morality, you picked the wrong group of people to go on this trip with." He shook his head, but he was amused more than disdainful of his charge's apparent lack of morals. "Look, I get it. Their flashy shows of wealth make you feel like shit. Like you aren't worth the four hundred thousand pounds that Sampson just sunk on your bookstore."

Holy shit, I hoped that scotch tasted as good coming back up because I was going to throw up. "*How much?*"

"It's a business in the heart of London. How much did you think a bookstore would cost?"

Oh, shit. My heart was thundering in my ears. "Why?"

Evan shrugged. "He likes you. I've been guarding

that little fuck since he was fifteen, and he doesn't like anyone. That amount of money is nothing to a man like Sampson. And he's just bought a prime piece of London real estate, so don't let it stress you, kid. They aren't getting swindled in this deal. They are like vampires, sucking the innocence from you one experience at a time. You shouldn't feel bad about that; it's a fair trade."

I frowned. "You sound like you hate them."

Evan shook his head. "No. I'm fond as hell of them. All of them. But the world they live in? It isn't meant for the sweet and the innocent. It isn't meant for nice boys with good hearts. Even Otto isn't the boy he once was." He tapped the bar, and the bartender poured another two glasses of scotch.

This time, Evan pushed one at me and gripped the other. "When Sampson was fifteen, one of his grandfather's competitors had him abducted while he waited for his driver outside of school. They held him for twelve days while his grandfather negotiated his release. In the end, the kidnappers kept raising the price higher and higher because they knew that his grandfather would give anything to get his heir back. I was part of the private task force sent in to rescue him. Kid was so dehydrated I thought he'd die in my arms. He looked at me and begged me not to leave him down in the dark. What kind of world tortures a fucking kid like that for business contracts?"

Fuck. Poor Sampson.

"After that, I was hired as Sampson's permanent bodyguard. I was there when his grandfather passed away, and he was shipped to the East Coast. Not once did his father ask his son if he was okay, or suggest therapy. He did nothing to show that he cared about Sampson in any way." Evan sighed. "What I'm trying to say is that money is not a rare commodity to people like Hendrick Kenley and Sampson Rubio. Love is. Friendship. Human connection that doesn't come with strings."

I sipped the scotch. "But it does come with strings," I whispered.

"Does it?"

I was so fucking confused. Evan tapped my glass with his finger. "Relax, Aviva. I'll message the guys and tell them we'll meet them back at the hotel soon. Take a moment to breathe." He looked over my shoulder and grinned. It lit up his face, making his eyes sparkle and a dimple form in one cheek. "Do you play pool?"

I'd been right. He was really something when he smiled.

Chapter 22
Otto

Evan and Aviva returned to the hotel six hours after Aviva had stormed out of the car. No one had breathed until Evan called to say she was okay, that they were just going to take a moment and he'd make sure she was safe. That we should do what we needed to do at the Iron Nautilus and they'd meet us back at the hotel.

We'd gone to the bookstore, met with the owner and scoured every single Verne book until we found the one. I almost wished we could throw it out and go home. We were causing harm to Aviva, even if we were doing it with good intentions. Fucking road to Hell and all that. But Hendrick wouldn't let me toss it, taking it off me and holding it close, like Aviva did to that damn copy of *Twenty Thousand Leagues Under the Sea*.

He'd been sitting out on the balcony, silent, for the

last three hours. Sampson had paced up and down the hall of our suite, and I'd just sat here. Waiting uselessly.

When Evan finally knocked on the door, Sampson sprinted to open it. Evan stepped into the room, holding a drunk as fuck Aviva. She was singing Beatles songs under her breath, and smiling up at Evan like he was her hero or something..

"Evan, I can walk," she mumbled, and he shook his head.

"I told you to stop after that third Flaming Sambuca, Chaos," he teased. I'd never heard Evan tease anyone. Not even Sampson, who he'd known for nearly a decade. Sam frowned, and held out his arms. Evan locked eyes with him, but handed over Aviva. She looked truly tiny in his arms. "I swear, she only had like six drinks. She's small, and a bit of a lightweight."

I shook my head. "It's the meds." She'd missed her meds tonight, and I didn't know if she should take them on a belly filled with booze.

She looked up at Sampson. "I'm mad at you." Well, it came out like *I'm smaad at youse* but I got the general gist.

"Why are you mad at me, Good Girl?" Sampson asked softly.

"You bought me a bookstore."

He moved toward her room and I moved with him. Evan remained in the door, as if he was unsure what to do. He'd figure it out.

"No, I didn't. I bought myself a bookstore. How do you know that it wasn't my lifelong dream to own a bookstore in London, hmm?" Sampson murmured back to her.

"Is it?" she asked hopefully.

He laughed low, standing with her in the middle of her room. "No, Good Girl. It isn't."

"I don't deserve good things. Evan says that you guys are taking more than you're giving and I shouldn't feel guilty, but what does he know? He doesn't know that I would happily fuck you for free—you don't have to buy me off. Does that make me sound like a whore?"

Sampson looked up at me, an eyebrow raised. I stepped toward her, stroking her face. "No one thinks of you like that, Viva. I'm sorry if we made you think we are trying to buy you for sex."

She shook her head and snuggled into Sampson's chest. "Why do you smell so pretty? No, Evan says you're buying me for human affection, which made me sad, which made me have three shots of sambuca against a guy with only one eye called Ned. His moustache caught on fire."

"You give it so freely," Sampson said, holding her a

little tighter even though he was standing right over her bed.

"The sambuca?"

I snorted. "No, Viva. The affection."

"Oh. Whatever. No more bookstores," she said stubbornly. "No more buying."

We both nodded, and I wished Hendrick was here. "No more, Aviva. I promise. Just don't run off again. You scared me," I chastised gently, and she turned from Sampson's chest to smile at me.

"I'm sorry, Otto. We should have a drink!"

I walked to the kitchen and grabbed a bottle of water, some painkillers and her meds. "Take your meds, Aviva, or you're going to feel like crap tomorrow." I handed her the pills and she threw them back without looking at them. Ah, Aviva. No regard for herself at all. How had she survived this long in a world filled with piranhas? "Put her down, Sampson. She needs to sleep this off."

Sampson slid her to her feet, and she weaved dangerously before slumping back onto the bed. "Someone needs to turn off the bed vibration. It's spinning like hell."

"This isn't a rent-by-the-hour motel with vibrating beds," Sampson said with a laugh. "Sleep tight. I have to go talk to Evan." He leaned down and kissed the top of her head, which was more affection than I'd ever seen him give anyone, other than me and Hendrick.

When he left, I took off her beloved shoes then swung her legs onto the bed. She was like Elastigirl, she was that bendy when drunk. I pulled up the blankets and tucked them around her.

"Are you sure I'm worth this much effort?" she whispered.

I kissed her forehead. "I've never been more sure of anything, ever."

She was already out like a light though. I turned her onto her side, just in case, and partially closed the door to her room. When I made it to the lounge room, Evan was gone, and Hendrick had come in from the balcony, still clutching the damn book.

"She okay?" he asked, and I smiled.

"Merry as hell. Ask her in the morning though—I think you'll have a different answer."

We were all silent for a while, relief consuming all of us until Hendrick went to the minibar and pulled out three bottles of beer. We went back out onto the balcony and watched the never-ending London traffic.

"What's with Evan?" I finally asked, and Sampson's jaw tightened.

"He warned me to stop fucking with her emotions. He's worried we'll send her over the edge." He shook his head. "I don't know what magic she possesses, but Evan feels protective of her too."

Hendrick shrugged. "She gets under your skin like that."

I watched Drix warily. I knew him, and I knew what would come next. I just wasn't sure that Aviva would withstand it.

"We stop dallying. The longer she's with us, the greater the chance she becomes something more," Sampson said firmly. I nodded, even though it hurt my heart. Hendrick was the last to agree, sliding the book onto the table. *Journey to the Center of the Earth.*

"Tomorrow, we head to Paris."

I'd forgotten to close the curtains before I fell asleep, and the blinding morning sun pierced my eyes. Rolling to the side, I reached for Drix, but he wasn't there. Just like every time I woke up without him, I had a moment of panic.

"Hendrick?" I climbed out of bed, pulling on some sweats. The door to the bedroom was open but I couldn't smell coffee or anything. "Drix?"

The doors to the balcony were open, and I told my racing heart that it was fine. If he'd jumped off, I'd know. But still, I went outside and held my breath as I looked over the edge. The relief I felt was just as irrational as the fear. Walking back into the suite, I checked the bathrooms. He could be sleeping with Sampson—he did that sometimes—but I didn't think so. Not today.

I opened the door to Aviva's room, and sure enough, there was Hendrick, lying on top of the blankets beside her, yet still somehow draped over the top of her like a limpet. I wanted to leave him there, but I wasn't sure that Aviva wouldn't freak out after last night. I didn't think any of us could handle any more conflict.

I squatted down beside the bed and tapped Hendrick's shoulder. He slept heavily when he actually rested, which wasn't often. I pushed his arm lightly, and he finally woke. I crooked my finger at him, pointing back to the hallway, and he carefully disentangled himself.

I walked back to the kitchen to make coffee and calm my heart. Hendrick came out after me, shirtless. He was fucking beautiful, but he knew it. He worked hard to stay a social media version of perfect.

"You okay?"

I asked it in a particular way, like I cared, but not too much. If I cared too much, he spiralled into a pit of self-loathing for making me worry. If I didn't care at all, he decided I was tired of him, and then again with the self-loathing. Over the years, I'd learned to develop the correct tone when he got in these moods.

He'd seemed better after this stint at the Wellness Center though. The doctor there was pretty respected in his field, so I had high hopes.

"I'm okay, Otto. Really." I slid his coffee toward him, and he gave me that soft smile that did crazy shit to my heart. "Do you think we're ruining her, like Evan said?"

I pressed the preset buttons on the coffee machine, mulling over the question. You couldn't ruin someone in a week, accidentally. If I was being honest, I was surprised how gentle the guys were with her, despite their general high-handedness. "I think she was already ruined, Drix. But I don't think we're making it worse, if that's what you mean. She's got her own monsters to fight, just like all of us."

He nodded, taking his coffee out onto the balcony, with me following along behind him. He stopped in the doorway, leaning in to kiss me gently, our coffee cups still clutched between our bodies. "Am I ruining you?"

Yes. Hendrick ruined me every single day.

I lifted my hand and cupped his cheek. "No more than I want to be ruined."

Chapter 23
Aviva

My headache was intense, and the bright sunshiny yellow of the Channel Tunnel was equally as searing. When I rolled out of bed, I had about thirty minutes to shower and dress while a maid packed my belongings and we were shipping off to Paris.

I'd woken up to find a copy of *Journey to the Center of the Earth* on the pillow beside my face, and I flicked to the back to find the message on the rear page. Like *Twenty Thousand Leagues*, this book had Nemo's annotations right through it, and I could understand why. It was exactly what I was doing, right? Following clues from a book that could lead me nowhere. Or somewhere. To the greatest discovery of my life or to a maelstrom that would drag me under forever.

. . .

To quest when others think you are crazy is the mark of a true visionary. Meet me at Librairie Jules Verne in Paris. You're almost there. Don't lose faith yet.

Everyone was quiet on the trip, Evan driving and Otto in the front seat beside him. I was squashed between Sampson and Hendrick in the back, their bodies pressed too close for rational thought.

They were definitely giving me the silent treatment. Sampson was answering emails, while Hendrick was answering DMs from pretty girls. One of those things burned worse than the other, that was for sure, but I buried it down.

Finally, Sampson put his phone down and turned toward me. "We need to talk about you running off yesterday."

I stiffened, and Hendrick did too. "Sam..."

Sampson didn't want to hear it though. "No, Drix. She worried us, because why? She didn't like our methods? So fucking what—you don't get to put yourself in danger just because you're throwing a tantrum. What if you'd gotten lost? You left your purse in the car, with your phone and passport. What if you'd run in front of a car? How would anyone know where you were?"

He looked furious, but I was tired, hungover, and

just as pissed. "I'm sorry, but fuck you too. You don't get to make unilateral decisions about my life either."

"What part of me buying a bookstore had anything to do with you? Or Hendrick getting a decent hotel? You are so self-obsessed that you think everything is about you, and I'm sorry, *Aviva*"—he dragged out my name like it was a curse—"we already have one narcissistic asshole in the group. That position is filled. Pick another."

Hendrick flipped him the finger, and stared out the window.

"You don't get to disregard my wishes either," I said through gritted teeth. "Don't buy me things was rule number fucking two. Actually, you guys haven't followed any of my rules. Do rules just not apply to you?"

I could almost see his teeth grinding. "Oh, that would absolve you of all your responsibility, wouldn't it, Good Girl? Well, we both know that's bullshit. You want to fuck me so bad it's an ache. So not just me, is it? You're the one not following your own goddamn rules."

He slid his hand up my thigh and under my dress. I'd thrown it on because it was the only thing left unpacked, but now I had regrets, because his strong hand felt too damn good. He leaned close, his hand sliding up until his pinky finger brushed the crotch of my panties.

He leaned closer. "It's got nothing to do with the money or the bookstore, or any of that shit. You hate that you want us. Hate that you're the one thinking about me driving my fingers inside you right now, stroking you until you come."

Someone up the front made a choked noise, and I drew my eyes from Sampson's to look to the front seats. Both Evan and Otto looked tense, and when I slid my eyes to Hendrick, he was watching Sampson and I with an intense expression, filled with heat.

"Take what you want, Good Girl. Forget about what you *think* you need, or what you believe you deserve. Take what you fucking want, for once."

I grabbed his wrist and dragged his hand where I wanted it, my breaths coming short and sharp. Sampson didn't tease this time, his fingers slipping beneath my underwear to stroke along my folds. His finger flicked my clit, and I moaned. The driver's side door opened and closed softly, and I watched Evan's sandy blond hair disappear.

Sampson grabbed my chin. "Want me to make everyone else leave too?"

I stilled, and Hendrick leaned close to my ear. "Take what you want," he whispered, echoing Sampson's words. I shuddered.

"No, I want them to stay."

Otto groaned from the front seat, rustling around until he found a sunshade that popped along the windshield, essentially blocking out the view for anyone walking along. Sampson's fingers continued to tease.

"Tell me what happens next," he commanded.

I rolled my hips against his hand, the brushing of his fingers too gentle, too teasing. "I want you to make me come on your fingers." I looked over my shoulder. "And I want Hendrick to kiss me."

I looked up and met Otto's gaze in the rearview mirror, and my eyes fell to where he was unbuckling his jeans. I watched as he pulled out his cock, stroking it with his hand, but then Hendrick became impatient, turning my head so he could capture my lips.

"Let's push this up so Otto can see me fuck you," Sampson purred as he dragged my skirt up over my waist.

As Hendrick's tongue slipped into my mouth, Sampson's fingers thrust into my core, and I moaned so loud that I knew the people in the car in front of us must be able to hear. Sampson continued to stroke in a rhythm that was so good and not enough all at once, and Hendrick was moving his hand down to cup my breast.

I wanted more. I wanted everything. I tore my mouth away from Hendrick, who happily started to kiss my neck. "Please," I gasped, rolling into Sampson's hand, seeking more friction.

"What do you want, Good Girl? Tell me."

I let my head loll back onto the headrest, as my orgasm built. "I want you inside me."

His low chuckle sounded like sin. "I am inside you." He curled his fingers more, tapping my clit as if to remind me where his hand was. Like I could forget.

"I want you to fuck me," I whispered, and I felt his low rumbling purr deep in my core. He dropped his hands to his lap, unbuttoning his pants and pulling out his hard cock. He was thick and long, and my mouth went dry.

He pulled me onto his lap, reverse cowgirl, and I gripped the driver's seat. I braced myself as he held my hips and thrust into me. We both groaned, or hell, maybe we all did, but suddenly he was stretching me so fucking deliciously.

A tap at the window made me groan, but Sampson didn't stop, sliding back out and slamming me back down again, and everything disappeared. Everything except for the feel of Sampson inside me. "Oh, god," I moaned, and Sampson slid his hand up over my chest, gripping my throat and my hip as he pounded into me.

The front door opened, and my eyes went wide as Evan stuck his head in. My gaze flew to his, and his brown eyes widened, before he blanked his face, looking over my shoulder at Sampson. "Train arrived, and we have to go through customs. I advise you all to get back in your own seats. You have thirty seconds." He shut the door again softly. I'd been so close.

But instead of pulling me off his lap, Sampson gripped both my hips and thrust up hard. "Hendrick, get her clit. We're in a time crunch."

Hendrick grinned, gripping my face and kissing me again, his other hand finding my clit like he knew my body better than I did. Sampson bent me forward until my forehead was leaning against the headrest of the seat in front of me, and then he slammed inside of me, his pace punishing until, between the two of them, I had no choice but to come. I bit the headrest to muffle my scream as I pulsed around Sampson's cock over and over.

With seconds to spare, Evan slid back into the car, and we rolled off the train as an announcement was made that cars were to move forward. Evan kept his eyes forward as Sampson slid me off his cock, and I bit my lip so I didn't make an embarrassing moan. Sampson was still hard as a rock, but he put me back in my seat and belted me back in, and Hendrick smoothed down my skirt. I watched as Sampson put away his still rigid dick, and felt mildly guilty that I got off and he didn't.

"Looking a little rough there, Viva," Hendrick

teased. He leaned forward until his lips were beside my ear. "*That* should give you some pointers on how to masturbate."

I shot him an exasperated look. "This is one hell of a way to prove a point, Hendrick."

The tension in the car was electric, and I knew I must look like a mess. We were the third car through Border Control, and the border agent gave us all a narrow-eyed look. Did the car smell like sex?

"Business or pleasure?"

Evan cleared his throat. "Pleasure." Hendrick was basically vibrating with laughter beside me.

"Duration of your stay?"

"Twenty-four hours. We are just passing through on our way across Europe."

We were only staying for a day? This was news to me.

Were they so eager to be done with me already?

Chapter 24
Sampson

Otto had found us a place to stay on one of those online room-letting sites, hiring us an entire apartment so close to the Eiffel Tower that it felt like you could almost reach out and touch it with your hand.

It had been worth forgoing some of the services I was used to just to see the look of wide-eyed wonder on Aviva's face when she stepped out onto the balcony and stared at one of the world's most recognizable landmarks. Otto looked smug, and Hendrick elbowed him.

"Show-off."

Evan looked a little displeased, the lack of security here obviously a problem, but who the hell knew we were here? I hadn't even known we were going to be here.

"Relax, Evan. It's fine, and it's only for a night, two at most."

Checking entry and exit points, he let out a disgruntled noise in my direction. "This whole thing is a security nightmare, Sam."

"It's fun though." My balls ached but I still couldn't wipe the smile off my face. Evan grunted something, but didn't meet my eyes as he continued his scan of the room. The apartment only had two bedrooms, each with a king-size bed, though the couch also pulled out for Evan. If Aviva wanted space, well, it wouldn't be the first time Otto, Hendrick and I had all slept in one bed.

But if she wanted to finish what she'd started on the way through the tunnel? Well, I was fairly sure one of us would warm the other side of the bed for her.

"Are you assured that this place is safe enough?" I asked Evan, and he gave a begrudging nod. I grinned. "Take three hours to go and enjoy the sights of Paris. Actually, make it four. I promise none of us will leave this apartment."

Evan's face could've been a mask with how much he was giving me. He looked at me for a long moment, his eyes taking in my whole face like he could read my every thought. Eventually, he nodded, moving to pick up his jacket and wallet, slipping out the door like a ghost.

A frowning Good Girl watched him go. "Where's Evan off to?"

"Sightseeing."

She pouted a little. "He should have said. I would've liked to see some of Paris before we have to leave."

I swaggered across the room, my eyes catching on the small, red bruise on her throat. Hendrick and his fucking hickies. "Good Girl, I will take you on a tour of every cheesy destination in this city. Shut down the tower itself so you can stand up there like you own it." When I was close enough, I reached out and grabbed her hips, dragging her toward me. "But first, I need to finish what we started in the car."

"Need?" she whispered.

I groaned. "Want. Very, very much desire."

She searched my face for a moment, much the way Evan had only minutes earlier, before giving me a small, seductive smile. "Otto?" she called, and Otto appeared behind her like a faithful hound.

Oh, this girl knew. She knew she had us now. Tricky bitch.

But you know what? I didn't fucking care. Not even a little bit. I wanted her, on her knees, on her back, with her legs wrapped around my head.

I just wanted her.

Otto skimmed his hands down her shoulders. "Viva?"

"Can you unzip my dress?"

Otto's eyes met mine over Aviva's head, and where Evan kept his face blank, Otto always had a notoriously shit poker face. There was wonder, lust, and if I wasn't wrong, a touch of trepidation in his eyes, like he knew that this moment might mean something more than just an easy holiday fuck.

Still, he reached out and unzipped her dress, and it fell into a pile around her feet soundlessly. She was wearing some of the lingerie I'd picked out, soft blush-colored lace that complemented her skin. She looked like a damn wet dream.

I leaned forward and gripped her chin. "What do you *want,* Good Girl?"

"You. All of you."

Hendrick groaned somewhere behind me, and my dick was harder than it had any right to be, as the pleasure of her words coursed through my body. I wasn't going to overthink this. I'd been friends with Hendrick and Otto forever; I knew if I led, they'd follow. I'd do the same for them.

"Lay her down."

Otto spun her around, lifting her into his arms and kissing her. She wrapped her legs around his waist and kissed him back, like he was giving her life. He walked her toward one of the bedrooms, with me following behind them. Hendrick was beside me, his eyes hooded and his body vibrating with excitement. Like a terrier before you threw the damn ball.

"Slow and steady, Drix. We've got all night."

Hendrick threw me a cocky look. "If there's one area of my life where I don't need pointers, it's fucking. I could fuck her, Otto, and you, and you'd all be begging me for more."

Yeah, I'd heard the rumours of Hendrick's skills, and honestly? With the amount of women he'd fucked, I wasn't surprised he'd learned a thing or two.

"Keep your cock to yourself, dickhead. Or at least in people who want it."

Hendrick just gave me a smoldering look, and for a moment, I could see the appeal of the guy. He was classically good looking and moved like a big cat, with power and grace and just a little bit of feral energy. I wasn't a guy who said 'never' to many things, though I'd have to be pretty drunk or extremely horny to be lured away from the soft curves and the hot clench of a woman.

Otto lowered Aviva down onto the bed softly, before following her down, continuing to kiss her. I stripped off my clothes so I was standing there naked, gripping my aching balls before stroking my cock. I needed to be back inside her before I exploded.

"What do you need, Good Girl?" I whispered, and she tore her mouth away from Otto. She still had her hands buried in his hair, and she tugged at it softly, making him moan.

"I want someone to kiss away this ache," she panted, and Hendrick was diving between her thighs before she'd even finished her sentence. How a guy who'd fucked so many girls who would literally ask for nothing in bed—let alone foreplay—could enjoy eating pussy so much, was a miracle of life.

The truth was that Hendrick could fuck a girl's face, blow in her eye, and the girl would still thank him for a great night. Like his presence was enough. I knew it was the same with a lot of my ex-lovers. They gave too much, and it was almost permission for me to be selfish. I mean, I had a reputation to uphold, so girls always came twice before I came, but still, that was a point of pride more than any request a woman had ever made.

I hated feeling like a conquest, and apparently, so did Drix because that fucker ate cat like he was coming off a famine.

I watched her face as Otto kissed and bit down her neck, taking her lace-covered nipple between his lips and sucking hard. Watched her clamp her thighs around Drix's head so tightly it would probably make his skull a peanut shape. Watched as the two of them brought her to an orgasm so strong, there was no way the apartment three balconies over didn't need a drink and a cigarette.

Precum leaked out of my cock, and I took a moment to grab the box of condoms from my bag. Fishing out three, I threw them on the bed.

Hendrick sat back on his haunches, and I grabbed Aviva's ankle. "Did you like that?" I purred, and the goosebumps that spread across her skin were my reward. I dragged her toward me. "I asked you a question, Good Girl."

"Yes," she moaned. Fuck, I loved the husky sound of her voice when it was roughened by pleasure.

I opened the foil packet of my condom and slid it on. "I'm going to fuck you now, and Otto is going to lie back and let you suck his cock at the same time. Would you like that?" She nodded, but that wasn't good enough. "Enthusiastically now, Aviva. Gotta follow the rules."

Hendrick threw me a sharp look at the mention of the rules, like Aviva was suddenly going to remember she'd said no fucking. But I didn't want her to have any excuses in a few hours, or tomorrow, or in a month. Didn't want her to think we had her dick-dazed, causing her to agree to whatever we asked.

"Yes... Fuck me, Sampson."

I groaned, flipping her onto her stomach and then

dragging her up onto her hands and knees. She crawled toward Otto, who'd managed to get naked in record time. He lay back on the pillows like a lazy prince, and as she licked up his shaft, he shuddered with pleasure. I crawled up behind her, and the moment she sucked his cock inside her mouth, I slammed inside her.

He may be a lazy prince, but in this moment, I was the fucking king.

She moaned around his cock as I stretched her, her cunt slippery from her release. Hendrick came to stand beside Otto, who reached out to grip Drix's dick in his hand. I wasn't bi like those two, but there was something insanely erotic about being all connected like this.

Gripping Aviva's hips, I slammed into her over and over, and her second orgasm had me gritting my teeth as she pulsed around me. Letting her ride it out with short, shallow thrusts, I slapped her ass hard.

She squealed around Otto's cock, making him groan with pleasure. "Fuck, Viva. Jesus." One of his hands gripped her hair softly, guiding her up and down his cock. Deciding they'd both recovered enough, I ground into her again, and she mewled with every thrust.

"Make him come, Aviva. Show me just how good you can be. Then I'll let you come again." To punctuate my words, I thrust hard, and she screamed. Her head started moving faster up and down on Otto's cock, who was cursing beneath his breath, his own hand sliding up and down Hendrick's dick with lighting speed.

"Oh, fuck, Viva... I'm going to come. I want her to come with me," he gasped, looking up at me over the round globes of Aviva's ass.

I slid my hand up her spine and gripped some of that glorious hair. I pulled her head back by her hair gently, gripping her hip and slamming into her until she was coming around me again.

A grunt from Otto let me know he was covering her tits with his cum. I kept thrusting through her orgasm, chasing my own release. Hendrick grabbed his own cock, stroking hard and fast until he was unloading all over her back.

My handprint on her ass, coated in their release, was too much and I buried myself balls deep inside her, coming on a curse. For a moment, all I could hear was the thundering of my own heart and the whoosh of panted breaths.

I pulled out and flopped down on the bed, trying to drag in oxygen. A towel appeared from nowhere, and Otto cleaned her up, gently whispering things into her hair as she collapsed against his chest.

"Get under the blankets, Sam," Hendrick whispered, and I did what I was told for once, climbing in beside Otto. Hendrick got in the other side, dragging the blankets up over us. I realized Aviva was passed out on Otto's chest, and for a second, I leaned up on one arm and looked at the only two people I'd ever loved. Something passed between us, and then Drix grinned.

"Get some sleep. I wanna do that again, but I get to ride in the backseat this time," he said, waggling his eyebrows.

"Fuck off, Hendrick," Aviva mumbled against Otto's chest, and I laughed.

This felt almost perfect.

Chapter 25
Aviva

The sound of the apartment door opening and closing had Sampson sitting up in bed. He peeled away from me silently, until a voice in the other room yelled, "Just me."

Evan was back.

I couldn't get the memory out of my mind of Evan's face when he opened the car door and saw me riding Sampson's cock. Every time I thought about it though, I imagined a different expression on his face. Was the twist of his lips disgust? Or the hooding of his eyes desire? Or was it all just shock, and I was overthinking the hell out of it?

Yeah, it was probably the latter.

"We're just napping," Sampson yelled back, his grin in my direction making my heart flip-flop.

Hendrick still snored gently despite the yelling, and I turned my face to look at him.

"He sleeps heavily when he actually sleeps." Otto's voice was a calming rumble beneath my cheek. I tilted my head up so I could look at him. I couldn't believe I'd fallen asleep on his chest. I tried to push myself up, and he hissed.

"I think I missed a cum spot. You seem to have, uh, crusted to my chest hair."

There was a choking noise beside us, as Sampson tried to hold in his laugh. "It's not funny, Sampson," I said primly, which sent him over the edge.

He bent over, still naked and glorious, and let out a hissing laugh that shook his body. Sampson lurched toward me, gripping my hips. "Come here, Good Girl. Let's give Otto a wax."

Otto batted his hand away, holding me tightly. "Fuck off," he growled, scooting toward the end of the bed, swiping out with his feet so Sampson had to jump away. "Hold on, Viva. We're making a run for the shower."

I gripped his neck as he kicked Sampson in the knee, sending him toppling, and then he was up and sprinting toward the bathroom while I held on like a baby koala. I saw a brief flash of Evan's face, his mouth hanging open, before we reached the only bathroom in the apartment. I didn't realize I was laughing so hard until my face began to ache.

How long had it been since I'd laughed like this? Years?

Otto continued to hold me as he reached into the shower and turned it on. He kissed my shoulder while he made sure the water was the perfect temperature. "I made it melt-your-balls-in-Mordor hot, because that's how girls like it, right?" he teased, stepping into the shower. Luckily, it was one of those spacious ones where you could just walk straight in without any difficulty.

"You can put me down, you know?" I said softly, and he just nuzzled my neck as he moved us both under the water. It poured down my back, and I swear, I never wanted to take a shower any other way again. But eventually he let me slide down his body, and I tried not to gasp as I felt the hard press of his cock on my core and then up my stomach. I let my hands run up over his chest and shoulders, laying my head between his pecs.

"Are you okay, Viva?"

"Um, in case you weren't paying attention, I just had a four-way. Do you call it a four-way? Or is like, anything over three an orgy? I'll look that up in the dictionary later."

I could feel him laughing, and the warmth that

flowed through me at the sound was new. Fuck, those big O hormones really did a number on a girl.

"I'm serious. Are you okay? Turn, I'll wash your hair."

I spun and he ran a hand down my front, squeezing my breast. "Uh, Otto. Last time I checked, I didn't have hairy boobs."

Otto pinched my nipple. "Shh, I'm double checking. And answer the question."

"I'm surprisingly okay, considering. I know you want to think that I'm some innocent little virgin, but I promise, I'm not."

He rubbed shampoo into my hair, his hands more gentle than mine ever were. "Have many orgies?"

I tensed. Did he think less of me now? Like I was a slut? "Would it matter?"

Otto snorted, one hand slipping around my waist to pull me tighter to his body. "Viva, I love Hendrick, and that man is a bona fide manwhore who's had more orgies than a rockstar in the eighties. Trust me when I say your body count means less than nothing to me. Turn and rinse." I spun again, and he was staring down at me with his deep blue eyes. "But even if we were your hundredth, that doesn't mean that sex can't mean something different each time. It isn't like building up a callus until you feel nothing."

I let out a shuddering breath. "I've felt nothing for years, Otto. Feeling nothing wouldn't be the problem."

Now it was his turn to still. Fuck, I'd said too much. "Do you feel something?"

I shook my head beneath the water, my hair longer when it was wet and flowing straight down my back. "I didn't say that either. I barely know you guys."

It wasn't a no either. I just hoped Otto would let it drop. He continued to look at my face, searching it for the real answer, but I tilted back my head and kept my eyes closed, rinsing out my hair for longer than necessary.

"If you do feel un-okay, tell me?" He tilted my head down so I was forced to look at him.

I met his eyes with a frown. "You're a dangerous man, Otto."

He leaned forward, kissing me gently. "Never to you, Viva."

He was wrong, of course. Especially to me.

It was late afternoon by the time I emerged from the bedrooms, completely starving. The guys were all sitting around the apartment, even Evan, who was sitting on the couch cleaning his gun.

"So, the Librairie Jules Verne?"

Hendrick froze. "You still want to look for Nemo?"

I raised my eyebrows and ignored the slight note of hurt in his voice. "Newsflash, Hendrick, but your dick isn't so magical that I'd forget any other hopes and dreams I've ever had."

He pointed a finger at me. "That's because you've actually never had my dick, Viva. Just you wait. You'll be so dick-possessed, your head will spin 360 degrees like that kid in *The Exorcist*. You'll basically be a cock zombie."

I snorted a laugh, and somehow, I found his insane confidence more humorous and less grating today. Otto was right; he did grow on a person.

I looked at Sampson, who was watching me with that unnerving intensity again. Finally, he nodded, standing. "Let's go. We'll grab something to eat while we're out."

He left the room, and I watched him go. Had I hurt his feelings? Did he want the sex to mean something more? Or maybe it was the opposite. I'd met guys like Sampson before—once the chase was over, the shine wore off.

While the guys went into the bedroom to get their stuff, I walked over to Evan, who was reassembling his gun. "Did you see anything cool while you were sight-seeing?" I asked, plopping down across from him.

He slipped the gun back into the holster under his arm. "No."

"Oh. Okay." I thought we'd bonded after our drinking session in London, but maybe not. Maybe he was just doing his job, returning me safely to Sampson like I assumed he was ordered to do.

Maybe I was entirely wrong—maybe his opinion of me had changed somewhere between England and France, when we were speeding through a tunnel and Sampson was, uh, speeding through my tunnel.

I stood, turning away from Evan so he couldn't see the hurt on my face, and walked over to look at the Eiffel Tower, right there in front of me. It was amazing. A hundred days ago, I could never have imagined that this was where I'd be right now. I'd been drowning, and now I was finally coming up for air.

Otto appeared beside me, dressed in a duffle coat with his hair still slightly messy from his shower. He kissed my temple, and I got the feeling that perhaps Otto was the touchy-feely type. It was... nice. My parents weren't huggers, my ex-boyfriend had been extremely against PDA's—except after sex—and everyone else had been a 'hit it and quit it' kind of setup.

This casual intimacy was new, but not entirely unwelcome. I leaned into his touch, and he wrapped an arm around my shoulders. "What do you want to eat?"

I shrugged. "French food?"

Hendrick laughed. "You're the cutest basic bitch

I've ever met in my life, Viva. Luckily, I have just the place. I found it last time I was here in Paris." He hesitated in front of me and Otto, then leaned forward and kissed me quickly. Then he kissed Otto, very much not quickly, and grinned.

Probably laughing at my stunned expression.

"Let's go, lovebirds."

I looked up at Otto, and noted he was just as shocked. Hmm. He shook his head, ushering me out of the apartment.

Luckily, our apartment had underground parking because the French did not believe in leaving a buffer space. It was nose to bumper if you had to park on the street. Sampson climbed into the front of the car, and I was sandwiched between Otto and Hendrick in the back.

Let me just say, it was an enviable position to be in.

Librairie Jules Verne was in the Latin Quarter, and I was going to beg Evan to drive past the Pantheon and Notre Dame on the way back to our apartment. We finally made it to the right area and drove past the actual bookstore five times looking for a parking spot in the narrow, one way streets.

Evan was beginning to mutter under his breath before he finally found a place to park, and while it was a little walk away, I didn't mind. The streets were beautiful here, the setting sun making the white stone buildings look blush-colored. My breath caught in my chest as I took in the moment.

Paris. I was in Paris.

Sampson rested his hand possessively on my spine, walking closely beside me as we strolled down an honest-to-goodness French lane.

The bookstore was everything you'd want a bookstore to be. It had a brown and tan striped awning over a huge plate window displaying secondhand books. Hand-painted lettering on the glass declared it the Jules Verne Bookstore—but in French.

"I'll wait here," Evan grunted, and Sampson slapped him on the shoulder.

Hendrick pushed open the door, and a little bell tinkled above it. It smelled musty, like that indescribable antique book scent, and I inhaled deeply. Used bookstores had a magic that normal bookstores lacked. It was always like being transported to a sepia-colored paradise.

"Bonjour." A pretty woman with straight blonde hair and red lipstick greeted us. Gosh, she was beautiful. I wished I had the confidence to pull off her understated sensuality.

I winced, because I was about to sound dumb. "I'm sorry, I—"

Otto let out an easy flow of French that had me gaping. The woman happily answered, directing us toward the back. "You speak French?" I whispered, and he chuckled.

"Yep. And Mandarin, Spanish and German."

"Show-off," Sampson muttered, and Otto punched him in the back.

We weaved in a single file through the shelves of books to an entire section for Jules Verne. "Holy shit, there must be a hundred books here," Hendrick whispered, and I looked at it, disheartened.

How were we going to find the right fucking book?

Sampson nodded. "Otto and I will take the top corner; you two start at the bottom corner. We'll meet in the middle."

I shrugged off my jacket and pulled out the first book.

Chapter 26
Hendrick

I slumped back against the shelves, watching Aviva as she checked books, mainly so I could look at her ass. It was a great ass. I wasn't nearly done with it yet.

Sam looked over his shoulder at me. "You could help, Drix."

I raised both brows and waved a hand toward the gloriousness of Viva's peach butt. "And miss the view?"

She gave me a dirty look, and I grinned back at her. I kept having vivid flashbacks to her mouth wrapped around Otto's dick, and Sampson buried deep inside her. I wanted that too, fuck it. I wish we could forget this Vernian bullshit and just stay in Paris, fucking and eating, drinking and laughing. Better than this goddamn wild goose chase for some pompous asshole who thought he was Hemingway.

"Found it," Sampson muttered, a book flipped open in his hands. He studied Aviva as she snatched the book out of his hands. Her eyes scanned the words like she was gobbling them up like candy, and for some reason it irritated the hell out of me.

"Out loud, Viva. Don't leave us in suspense."

"It says, 'There's a fine line between courage and insanity. Penny Lane, Calcutta.' That's it."

"India? You have to be joking. I thought we were hitting up Europe."

Viva snapped the book shut, giving me a sour look. "Then go. I can do India by myself."

I frowned, her words like a punch to the chest, but I quickly smoothed my face into a neutral expression. "Go for it. I'm pretty sure your black AMEX won't work on the Air France website though."

Otto huffed, ushering us both out of the back of the bookstore. "Not going to lie, I thought it might've been Suez."

I followed along behind him, now checking out both his ass and hers. "Why the hell would anyone go to Suez? I mean, Egypt is nice, but Evan would have a fucking coronary." Sampson snorted, but didn't disagree.

Otto gave us both a disappointed look. "Well, if either of you picked up a book, say *Around the World in Eighty Days*, you'd know that we aren't the first people to do a mad dash across the world in order to win a ridiculous prize."

Viva cut him an angry look, and I was going to bet that none of us would be getting laid tonight. She slammed the book down onto the counter, and the bookstore owner looked at us, alarmed.

Viva forced a smile onto her face. "Just this, please."

The owner smiled, picking up the tattered illustrated copy of *From the Earth to the Moon*. "Oh," she said, her face creasing between the eyes. "I didn't think this one would ever sell. Too worn. But he said someone would come to collect it eventually." She gave our group a considering look. "I didn't expect you though."

Aviva's whole body basically vibrated with excitement. "You know him? The man who wrote these notes?" She flicked open the book and pointed to the inscription in the back. The writing was loopy and smudged, like he'd done it quickly. "What was his name? How long ago was he here?"

Sampson reached out, wrapping a hand around her forearm. "Easy, Aviva."

The bookstore owner's gaze bounced around us once again, confusion painting her features. "I didn't get his name. It must have been, oh, nearly a year or two ago now. Maybe a little longer?" She shook her head. "Said I had to add this book to the collection. That someone would ask for it eventually. He was very compelling."

"You must know something else? What did he look like? Did he leave an address or a number to contact him? There must be something!" Aviva's voice rose an octave, and she gripped the counter.

"I'm sorry, *mademoiselle*. He was American, tall. Dark hair and eyes. I cannot tell you much else. He was... intense, *oui*?" She said something in a flurry of French to Otto, who nodded and smiled politely, his words soothing. She pushed the book at him, refusing the money from Sampson. "No. Take it. I was just holding it anyway."

"*Merci,*" Otto replied, before grabbing Aviva's shoulders and pushing her out the door.

"Otto, she had to know something else. He's got to be here, in Paris—we have to ask more questions, check more of the books."

Evan was leaning against the stone shopfront, but snapped to attention when a stressed-looking Aviva appeared in front of him. "What the fuck happened?" he growled.

I tilted my head at him, trying to work out if he was being derogatory to Aviva or was just worried about her wellbeing. Evan had been with Sampson as long as I'd known him. He was a big brother to us at times, a safety net a lot of the time—not just for Sam but for us all. But he was old as fuck.

"Nothing," Sampson snapped. "We found what we were looking for. Let's go."

Hmm, tense... What was that about? I didn't think about it too much more as Evan hustled us all back to the car, like the threat to us was anything other than the five-foot-two ball of crazy striding in the middle of our group.

She slid into the backseat of the car, the paper bag-encased book clutched to her chest. She was like fucking Smeagol with his precious—she was losing it. I looked at Otto. "Never thought I'd say this, man, but is she taking her meds?" I muttered under my breath, and he nodded.

"Yeah, I synced your schedules. She's just..." Yeah, I didn't have a word for how she was acting right now either. Like she was hopped up on coke and sex with six flight attendants and a performer from Cirque du Soleil.

Not speaking from experience or anything.

"Jesus, is this what I'm like?" I mused, walking to the other side of the SUV.

"Worse," Otto called, sliding into the car so he missed me telling him to fuck off. Evan and Sampson were arguing quietly in the front seats, and I strained to hear what they were saying. Guess Sampson was breaking the news we were leaving the first world to galavant through freaking Kolkata like Mother Theresa.

"Let's go! I'm starving, and I get grumpy when I'm hungry," I yelled at them, and slid into the car beside Aviva. Her wild energy was starting to affect my own. Like bears and bees, my own problems fed off the emotions of the people around me. So I did the only thing I could think of. I grabbed Viva, pulled her onto my lap, and kissed the hell out of her.

She squeaked with surprise, which was adorable as fuck, and then she kissed me back. Her soft, pillowy lips danced across mine, tantalising and making promises her body was backing up.

She rolled her hips, and I groaned into her mouth. I kissed the crazy right out of her, sucking it in like it was my favorite poison. Maybe it was, because I felt like I could kiss her for hours. Days.

I stroked up and down her back, soothing her and me, and I made a humming noise under my breath as my heart rate both sped up and evened out.

Nice. This was nice.

"I hate to break this shit up, but Good Girl needs her seatbelt. Get back in your seat, Viva."

Mmm, Sampson wasn't amused. I gripped her delectable ass and squeezed hard, making her let out another little moan, then dropped her in the center seat.

I pointed at Sampson. "Don't be a hypocrite, Sam. Sharing is caring, or didn't your nanny ever teach you that?" He muttered under his breath, while I just laughed. "We're heading toward the Pantheon, Rue Descartes."

I'd feed her and then later, I'd fuck her. I reached out, wrapping my hand around her thigh.

Everyone would be happy, but mostly Viva. And definitely me as well.

Chapter 27
Aviva

We ate dinner in a quintessential French bistro, complete with red-checked table-cloths and food that made you want to spontaneously orgasm. After we left, we walked down to the Seine River, night falling and making the whole place like a dream.

"I can see why they call it the city of romance."

"Mmm, if you don't look at the trash, pigeons or people sleeping under the bridge down there," Sampson replied casually.

"Sampson is the last true romantic," Otto teased, and I leaned into him. My new Verne book was tucked in my bag, I was full of good food from the most romantic place I'd ever been, and I was hopped up on happy hormones from the orgasms.

I stopped, looking at Notre Dame, lit up from the

inside. Boats motored softly up and down the river below us, and I just breathed it all in. The guys kept walking slowly, but I just wanted to take a moment. Otto paused to stand beside me, his shoulder touching mine.

"You okay, Viva?"

I nudged him with my hip. "You've already asked me that once today, Otto."

He wrapped an arm around my shoulder. "Pretty sure I'm going to ask it ten more times this week, so you better get used to it."

"I'm fine. Excited. It's been a while since I've felt that."

He made a noise of agreement, and just stood with me as we gazed into the swirling water. Even this late at night, there were tourists about, though I guess that applied to us as well. A man smiled at me as he leaned on the wall a few feet from us.

We stared at the scene before us a little longer, and then I sighed. "Come on. We better catch up."

Otto wrapped his arm around my shoulder again, and stepped away from the wall. The tourist beside me stepped off the wall, and in a movement too quick for me to comprehend, held a switchblade to my stomach.

"Your purse, *mademoiselle*. And your wallet," he said in a low voice to Otto. Otto looked confused for three seconds, until he looked down at the guy's hand,

and back up to his face. The mugger—because there was no doubt in my mind we were about to be a statistic—was a generic-looking guy, blond but not attractive, with a hat pulled down low over his face. "Now," he hissed, and it shook Otto from his stupor.

He pulled out his wallet, handing it to the guy, and I slipped my purse from my shoulder. "There's a book in there..." I started, but the guy just pressed the knife harder into my stomach and the words dried up in my throat.

He looked back at Otto. "Your phone and watch too, into the bag." He said it all with a smile on his face, like he was having a friendly conversation with us about Notre Dame.

"You need to back the fuck up before I rip your head off, asshole," Otto growled, but he was still removing his watch, dropping it into my handbag. Then he pulled out his phone and placed it in there too. "This isn't going to end well for you."

The man shrugged. "What will happen? You will describe every man under forty in Paris to the police, they will give you a number to claim on travel insurance and we are all happy, *oui*?"

Otto started laughing. "Yeah, *oui,* motherfucker."

The guy's face went pale, and when I looked around his shoulder, Evan was there. The look on his face was calm, like this was a regular occurrence. "I am holding a 9mm Sig Sauer to your spine. You so much as move, I'm going to use a bullet to sever it and eviscerate more than a few of your internal organs. Do you understand?"

"*Oui*. Y-yes," the guy stammered.

"Good. Now give back their stuff." The guy handed over my bag, and I clutched it to my chest. "Aviva, Otto, walk around me and back toward Hendrick, please."

I did as I was told, and once I was behind Evan, I sprinted toward Hendrick and Sampson. Hendrick grabbed me up, spinning me so his body was between me and Evan with the mugger.

"Are you okay? Fuck, I was scared as hell, Viva." He clutched me to his chest too tightly, like he was still scared something would go wrong and we'd be dead. Otto came up behind us then, and Hendrick gently pushed me into Sampson's arms to grab Otto into a tight hug. Then he leaned back, scowling at his full-time friend and part-time lover. "What were you thinking? Did you forget all of Evan's training? Give them what they want. Disengage and walk away with your damn life."

"He had a knife pressed into her stomach, Drix. A fucking knife. One accidental bump from a pedestrian and she would've been dead."

Sampson's hand ran up and down my spine, and I

was pressed tightly to his chest as he spoke to the police on his phone. Quickly, the blue flashing lights and high-pitched siren of the police cars arrived.

I looked around Sampson's shoulders and noticed that Evan had the guy facedown on the ground, which had to be gross. Two French policemen hopped out of the car, and Otto detangled himself to go speak to the police. "I'll make a statement. Take her back to the hotel. Evan and I will grab the car and meet you back there."

Sampson nodded, hailing a cab down, and Hendrick just watched Otto go. "It makes me so fucking hot when he's all authoritative like that. I want to tell him 'fuck you' because he's not my boss, but on the flip side, I kind of want him to fuck me at the same time."

A slightly hysterical laugh bubbled out of my throat, and I could see Sampson roll his eyes in the moonlight. He hustled us both into the car, Hendrick squashing me close to his side. Sampson gave the cab driver the address of the apartment, and the driver grunted. Guess that meant he knew where it was.

The guys squished closer to me than necessary, but I didn't care. I was still clutching my purse and it wasn't until I dropped it in my lap that I realized I was shaking. Actually, my whole body was shaking. I'd almost fucking died; Otto had been right.

My breathing became labored and the walls of the car seemed to creep in. Sampson leaned forward. "I will give you an extra hundred euros if you can get us there in less than ten minutes."

The cab driver grinned, said something in rapid French, and hit the gas.

My breathing was getting choppy again, and it felt like someone had placed a bowling ball on my chest. "I'm having a heart attack," I wheezed, and Sampson went pale.

"Should we take her to a hospital?"

I felt more than saw Hendrick shaking his head. "She isn't having a fucking heart attack. She's having a panic attack. Textbook presentation—I should know. Viva, I'm going to hold your hands, is that okay?" When I nodded, he gripped my hands. "I want you to squeeze them as hard as you can, and we'll breathe in time." I was shaking my head, but Hendrick just laced his fingers in mine and pulled them to his lap. "Squeeze. And tell me something. Tell me about Nemo. Tell me how he's more romantic than I am."

I heard Sampson's thumping punch. "Really? This isn't the right time to stroke your ego."

"It's the right time all the time," Hendrick snarked back. "Come on, Viva. Tell us about what you hope for when you find him."

My thoughts around Nemo were already disorganised, and I shook my head more, still gasping shallowly. "I can't."

"That's okay, Viva. We're here," Sampson whispered in my ear. "We will keep you safe. Listen to my voice, feel how certain I am that I will never, ever let anyone harm you. Not even the men I love the most in this world. I *will* protect you, Good Girl. Always. Do you believe me?"

"Yes," I whispered.

"Do you trust me?"

"Yes."

He stroked his hand up and down my thigh. "Good girl... We're almost back at the apartment, and then I'm going to tuck you into bed and we'll pretend this whole night was just a bad dream. Tomorrow, we'll book a flight for Kolkata, and when we get there, we'll track down that damn book. I've always wanted to go to the flower markets. Do you have a favorite flower?"

"Not magnolia."

Hendrick snorted, and I remembered that he'd read my file. "Definitely not the magnolia."

"What is it?"

"Dahlia?"

Sampson made a noise of approval, and it warmed something in my chest. Or maybe cooled the burning heat that was threatening to suffocate me. "Beautiful choice, Good Girl. We will buy enough dahlias to fill the hotel room. Every color they have. Would you like that?"

I was nodding, the panic receding until I no longer felt like I was being strangled.

Hendrick squeezed my hand again, and I realized I'd been flexing my fingers in his. "Ready to breathe with us, beautiful? In..." He sucked in a lungful of air, and I found myself inhaling with him. "And out..." The air whooshed out of my nostrils, and my heart rate calmed a little. We did it a few more times before the cab skidded to a stop outside our apartment building.

"Nine minutes and forty-five seconds," the cab driver announced, and Hendrick laughed. He slid from the cab as Sampson paid, picking me up in his arms and clutching me to his chest.

The ancient elevator creaked as it reached the top floor, and Sampson unlocked the front door, ushering us in and locking it up tight behind him. Hendrick didn't even slow his step, walking into the bedroom we'd had sex in earlier and laying me down on the bed. I sat there like an invalid as he pulled off my shoes and socks, peeling off my jacket and lifting my shirt over my head.

"Lift your butt. Holy shit, did you pour yourself into these jeans? They are tiny," he huffed, tugging them down my thighs. Reaching into the suitcase we were yet to unpack, he pulled out one of his Henleys.

"Wear this if you want, beautiful. Or nothing. I'm totally good with nothing too," he teased, and I couldn't help but give him a weak smile back.

I scooted up the bed and Hendrick pulled back the blankets for me. Looking over at the doorway, I saw Sampson leaning there, taking in the whole scene with eyes that saw way too much.

Hendrick tugged the soft blanket up to my chin and kissed me on the forehead. "Rest, Viva. It'll be better in the morning."

He stepped toward the door and panic seized my heart again. "Wait!" They both froze. "Will Otto and Evan be okay?"

Sampson nodded. "You still have Otto's phone, but Evan messaged to say he was done with the police already and they're on their way back to the car."

I bit my lip, my gut still burning and my heart still thumping, despite the fact that my brain knew I was fine now. That nothing had happened. These guys had my back, all of them.

"Will you guys stay with me until I fall asleep?" I asked quietly, and Hendrick was back across the room with no shirt on before I'd even finished the sentence. "No sex. I, uh, just don't want to be alone."

Hendrick looked affronted, but nodded. "Viva, despite the rumors, I'm not about to jump a girl who just had a panic attack. My dick can cure many things, but not that." He paused. "I mean, at least I don't think so. I've never actually tried."

Sampson slapped him on the back of the head, before standing over the bed and taking in my face. "Are you sure you're okay?"

I nodded, sitting up to pull Hendrick's shirt over my head.

"Wait!" Sampson yelled, making me jump. He moved to the bed, his fingers running gently down my stomach. "He cut you."

I looked at my stomach, and sure enough, there was the slightest scratch on my stomach. It had obviously bled at some point, but I hadn't noticed, probably because of the amount of adrenaline flowing through my veins.

Sampson's eyes were molten with rage. "He. Cut. You." Oh shit. The fury in his voice was palpable. Reaching into his pocket, he pulled out his cell. "I'm calling Evan. I want the fucker locked up. I want him shanked and thrown in the motherfucking Seine. Fuck."

Oh shit. He was having a full-blown meltdown. "Sam, I'm fine."

"You aren't fine, Good Girl. You had a fucking panic attack in the cab. You got cut with his fucking knife. Have you had a tetanus shot? What if there was something disgusting on that fucking blade?"

He was beginning to pace, and I looked over at Hendrick, who was staring at Sampson with eyes as wide as mine. I mouthed, *What do I do?* He just shrugged. Hopeless.

"Sampson." Ignoring me, he just kept walking back and forward. "Sampson!" He spun on his heel and looked at me, his eyes immediately going to the minor scratch on my stomach. "I'm fine. Please, hop into bed and hold me for a while?"

He sucked in a deep breath and let it out slowly, but took his clothes off until he was just down to his boxers. As he climbed in beside me, Hendrick sauntered to the other side of the bed before sliding in. They both pressed close, and I was sandwiched between their warmth—Sampson curled around my back, and my legs tangled in Hendrick's.

I let the adrenaline crash pull me under before my crazy body could take advantage of the sandwich I was currently in.

Chapter 28
Otto

It was painful to look at her. Sampson and Hendrick were both wrapped around a sleeping Aviva. Neither of them were asleep though, both just staring silently at the ceiling. As I watched them, they slipped out of bed, though how they could bear to do it was beyond me.

She reached for Hendrick, but he tucked the pillows and blankets around her and she settled back down to sleep. They tiptoed into the main room, and I stood aside to let them pass. I just wanted to watch her for a few more moments, to appease my mind that she was okay.

When her breathing evened back out, I met the guys in the living room. "How is she?"

Hendrick shook his head. "Freaked out. Had a panic attack in the cab home."

"He cut her," Sampson growled, and my heart clenched. I wanted to go back in there, search her entire body for injuries. "She says it's fine, that she's up to date on her shots, but what if there was something on that blade?"

Evan shook his head. "I looked at it. The guy might have been a piece of shit, but he kept his weapons clean."

Sampson huffed, only slightly appeased. "What did the cops say?"

Evan shook his head again. "Not much. It's an unfortunate occurrence—we've lived in New York for long enough to know that. They took Otto's statement, dragged the guy away, will probably charge him tonight, and then he'll be out on bail before lunchtime tomorrow. It is what it is."

Sampson punched the back of the couch, and I watched him cautiously. Normally, it was Hendrick with the anger, but Hendrick seemed bizarrely calm right now. Had they swapped bodies?

"I want you on her at all times," Sampson snapped, and his long-time bodyguard tensed.

"That's not how it works, Sam. You're my priority."

Sampson got up in his face, and I stepped forward just in case I had to pull him back. "I pay your salary. I am reprioritizing you."

"Sampson." Evan looked around at us all. "I'm not

leaving you vulnerable because you want me to take care of some random girl you guys just picked up," he said in a quiet voice. "I've seen you guys do this time and time again. You find a girl to obsess over. You fuck her and two weeks later, you forget her. I am not watching her ass and leaving you vulnerable because you're getting your dicks wet."

I let out a surprised yell as Sampson threw a punch at Evan, but the guy was a former Marine. He was fast, and Sampson's swing barely grazed his cheekbone, which just infuriated him more. "It's not fucking like that."

Evan stepped back, looking at us all with something akin to disappointment on his face. "What's it like then? You're passing her around like she's a cheap bottle of beer and not a human being."

Now it was my turn to be mad. "You've got it fucking wrong."

Evan bared his teeth at me. "Explain it to me then, because you kidnap a fucking girl from a psych ward, drag her across the fucking ocean and then all fuck her. Unless I'm going blind and she wasn't spread out on Sampson's lap in fucking public this morning?"

"I like her," I hissed. I'd never heard Evan speak to us like this. Normally he was completely professional, or more like a big brother—cool but firm.

"Obviously."

Sampson cocked his head to the side, watching Evan's face closely. "Why do you care?" he said softly, and I knew that tone. He was about to go in for the kill.

Evan swallowed hard and shrugged like he didn't give a fuck. "She's a nice girl."

Sampson made a rude noise. "So were the others, but you didn't get self-righteous over them. And don't give me some bullshit about my safety. We both know that you've been giving me fucking disappointed looks since London."

Evan pressed his lips together, but didn't answer. We stood there in silence, the object of contention sleeping blissfully unaware in the other room. Finally, he sighed, all the posturing leaking right out of him. "She's broken already, Sam. Anyone with two eyes can see it. She's a good person under all that damage, and I don't think she could survive the usual bored rich boy treatment you give women." He paused. "When she ran away, she looked so fucking sad. Like she'd been kicked around every day of her life and didn't know how to stand back up. It doesn't sit right with me to just let that happen again."

Sampson frowned. "You like-like her."

Hendrick snorted. "What are we? Ten?"

Sampson waved him off. "You *want* her. You're nearly a fucking decade older than her."

A light flush touched Evan's cheeks, but the rest of

his face stayed impassive. "Just looking out for her. I'll hire extra security for the whole group." He turned and left, pulling out his phone as he went.

We watched him leave, and Hendrick was laughing softly beneath his breath. "He has it bad."

Sampson shook his head. "He needs to remember his place. He can't bitch at me about watching her back and then whine that he likes her. What could he give her anyway?"

Oh shit, now Sampson was jealous. "A normal life? One without bulletproof glass and paparazzi?" I couldn't help but poke the bear a little bit. I'd never seen Sampson like this before; he usually was the very essence of a fucking insouciant overlord. Rarely did he get this worked up, unless someone crossed him, or it related to me and Hendrick.

"He made a good point, though." Both Hendrick and Sampson whirled on me. "She is different, and you guys are different too when she's around. You better figure your shit out, because if you don't, Evan will be right. We'll ruin her for no other reason than that we're selfish."

With that, I strode into Aviva's room, stripping off to my boxers and climbing in beside her. I needed to hold her, because Sampson, Hendrick and Evan might not know how they felt, but I did. Aviva had captured something in me, and I was fairly sure it was my heart.

.   .   .

We were stuck in Paris for another day while Evan cobbled together another bodyguard or two. Not giving Aviva time to overthink, we hustled out of the apartment early and down to a Parisian bakery to pick up pastries that were insanely good. We sat on the grass beneath the Eiffel Tower and ate, and I watched the tension flow from Aviva's body as I played with her hair in the sun.

Even Hendrick looked more relaxed, his hand wrapped around her ankle as he dozed. Sometimes getting out from beneath his dad's thumb really helped. He opened one eye and looked up at me. "Maybe we should just stay here. I like Paris. I'm sure we could buy the apartment."

Aviva snorted. "Sure, we should buy a Parisian apartment that probably costs more than the GDP of a small country, just because you like lying in the sun."

"What makes you think you were included in that 'we,' Viva?"

She stiffened beneath me, and I was about to chew Drix out but Viva just gave him the stink eye. "The way you haven't stopped touching me since we got to Paris. And you look at me with those big 'fuck me' eyes all the time."

Hendrick rolled onto his hands and knees,

crawling up over her body. "If anyone is giving out 'fuck me' eyes, Viva, it's you."

"You're right," she purred, and then bucked her hips, throwing Hendrick off balance so he rolled down the small embankment we were sitting on.

Sampson chuckled and I laughed, pulling Viva back up into my arms as Hendrick stormed back up the hill. She was laughing, crawling around my body to hide behind me. "Protect me, Otto."

"Ha, no way. Between you two, I'm Switzerland."

She sprung up, hurtling over Sampson's body like a gazelle as Hendrick chased after her. When she ran behind Evan, who was sitting a little bit away, Hendrick stilled.

Aviva was oblivious to the tension though. "Save me, Evan."

Hendrick narrowed his eyes, trying to judge the bodyguard's mood. Evan shook his head. "You poked the bear, Chaos. You're on your own."

Hendrick laughed, ducking around Evan and scooping Aviva into his arms. She wrapped her legs around his hips, and laughed. People turned to look at them, and god, together they were beautiful. Their moods fed off one another, so when one was joyous, so was the other, and it infected everything and everyone around them.

Knowing Hendrick, and getting to know Aviva, I

knew that it would work the other way too. That when one spiralled, it would suck the other down with them. But right at this moment, they looked picture perfect, and everyone around us envied them—like they were some sort of golden couple—totally oblivious to their struggles.

"They look good together," Sampson said in a low voice, as he watched Hendrick spin her around. "Like a magazine cover rolled up in the mouth of a Molotov cocktail."

I huffed a laugh at the accuracy of that. I recognized that a normal man would feel jealous, but I didn't. It was like, if it was hard for me to be everything that Hendrick needed, then maybe another set of hands would help. Especially if they were soft and sweet and attached to a smart mouth and beautiful brain.

Sampson groaned. "Stop looking at them like they're a candy-coated wonderland, asshole. I'm going to puke over the sweetness."

I kicked him in the thigh, but dragged my eyes away, looking up at the sky with a smile on my face.

Chapter 29
Aviva

The guys had been overwhelmingly protective since the first night in Paris, and being in India wasn't going to make them relent on that. Evan had gotten two more bodyguards, including a woman who was around his age. She was pretty, with straight brown hair and a body like a fitness model. I kind of hated her on sight, but she was professional and sweet, and that made me hate her a little more.

The other bodyguard was built like an elephant, and I was pretty sure he could strangle me one-handed. Normally that would turn me on, but this guy just made me want to run in the other direction.

We still had to fly first class, and had to stay in the best hotel in Kolkata. When I screwed my face up, Hendrick told me it cost less than the apartment in

Paris due to the exchange rate, and I found it hard to argue with that.

Driving into Kolkata from the airport to the hotel was an entirely unique experience. It wasn't like anything I'd ever seen; it was both drab and vibrant. Poverty and glittering excess just right there on the street. Traffic was chaos, but the private driver hummed softly along to the radio like this was just another day.

Even pulling up to the hotel was unlike anything else, with hundreds of people milling about stalls that had been roughly constructed under the awning of the huge, imposing hotel. People were yelling, the smells were heady, and I could see why this country would be overwhelming. The entrance was clear however, with a guard standing at the wrought iron gates and ushering us through.

It was hot. So fucking hot. But inside those gates was a little oasis: palm trees, perfectly manicured gardens, and lawns that were clipped within an inch of their life.

The bodyguards stepped out first, their eyes roaming in every direction before we climbed out. It was overkill, but I didn't blame the guys. If they'd been scared, I'd been terrified.

My phone chirped, and I realized I hadn't checked in with my parents yesterday.

. . .

Aviva: Sorry guys. Forgot to check in with you yesterday. I'm in India, but don't worry, I have security and it's beautiful here. Love you both.

I snapped a quick picture of myself in the courtyard, sent it off, and then shut off my phone. I couldn't answer their questions any more today than I could two weeks ago.

A beautiful receptionist greeted us and led us to what I learned was the Presidential Suite. I gave Hendrick the stink eye, and he just grinned. Four-poster beds, overhead fans and an insane amount of flowers and fruits greeted us. It was gorgeous.

I flopped onto a bed, tired from the long flight, despite the fact it was another first class trip where I'd slept most of the time.

Evan and the new bodyguards had the suite beside ours, so it really just was the four of us, alone. Excitement built in my stomach about what we could do, and when Hendrick dropped down on the bed beside me, I resisted the urge to grin. I rolled over until I was straddling him, and he looked up at me with a comical look of surprise.

"Hendrick Kenley, I just realized something."

"Flying makes you horny?"

"No. Well, maybe." I leaned closer until my lips were just an inch from his. "I don't think you're such an asshole after all."

He laughed, leaning up to capture my lips. His hands ran down my sides as he gripped my ass, pulling me firmly against his hardening dick. He fucked my mouth, grinding me down on his cock until I was panting.

"Fuck me," I moaned in his ear, and he groaned. He rolled me onto my back until he was poised above me.

"Aw, Viva. I'm not going to deny us both the best part." He scooted down the bed until his head was between my thighs. "I'm going to eat your delicious pussy like it's dessert. God, I've missed you," he told my vagina.

I laughed, but it cut off quickly as he tore off my underwear, which probably cost more than a month's waitressing pay. Still, I didn't complain as he bit my thigh with a growl.

"Promise me that one day you'll smother me to death with these."

I gripped his hair that was just enough to be a fistful, and pulled his face up. "Not funny, Drix."

His eyes hooded at my use of his nickname. "Not

joking, beautiful. Now let go, I have a mission before the main course."

Couldn't argue with that, I guess. I relaxed my grip on his hair as he ran his tongue over my folds, sucking and nipping and literally making nom-nom noises over my clit. The man was ridiculous, but he soon had me coming all over his face.

He lifted himself up on his elbows, staring smugly down at me like he'd just done a good job, his grin ridiculously wide. He unbuttoned my linen shirt dress like he was unwrapping a present, kissing each inch of skin as it was revealed. I felt worshipped by the time he got to my breasts, sucking my nipples into his mouth through the delicate lace.

"Fuck," I breathed, clawing at his shirt to get it off. He happily obliged, and he was goddamn beautiful. All that smooth golden skin—like he never spent any time with a shirt on—and hard muscle. I wanted to taste every inch of him. "Pants off," I said quietly, and he rolled up from his position, making his abdominals flex. Ooh, pretty.

He stood back, peeling off the last of his clothing, and my mouth went dry. No one had any right to be that pretty.

"Gimme, gimme." He laughed and dived onto the bed, making me bounce. I rolled, so I was straddling his hips, and ran my hands down his chest. "These are nice."

He lifted his arms and grabbed my boobs. "So are yours." I ground down on his cock, and he threw his head back, closing his eyes. "Fuck, that feels good, Viva."

It felt so good, so right, and my good sense left me. I wanted to bury him inside me, feel every inch of him stretching me wide.

A condom flew out of nowhere and hit Hendrick in the forehead. I looked over my shoulder at a grinning Otto.

"Uh, sorry to interrupt, but remember the manwhore conversation?"

Hendrick huffed. "Seriously, man?"

Otto nodded, and left. I was laughing beneath my breath as I grabbed the condom and slid it on. Hendrick was still grumbling. "Mood killer."

I leaned forward, kissing him softly. "He's just looking out for you. Out for us. An STD or a baby would make this experience really, really permanent."

Hendrick frowned, opening his mouth to say something stupid, so I grabbed his dick and held it at my entrance. He couldn't help himself but thrust up until he was deep inside me. We both groaned, and I sat up, riding him in a slow, leisurely manner.

The look he was giving me though, it was making

me feel... something. He was looking at me like I was the best thing since porn, his hands on my hips guiding my movements so he could bury himself balls deep.

He looked worshipful. Is this why he got so many girls? Did he look at every girl with this kind of reverence?

"Mmm, get out of your head, Viva. I have about four more minutes until I blow my load inside your fucking gorgeous body, and I've never come first." He slipped a hand around, his thumb tapping my clit, and my thighs turned to jello.

Sweat slicked across my body as I moved to my feet, pistoning my body over his at the perfect angle so he was hitting all the good places inside me.

"Fuck, Viva," he grunted, thrusting up, meeting me movement for movement. "Come for me, beautiful." Another stroke of my clit. "Now. *Come.*"

I did as I was told, impaling myself tightly on his cock and falling forward to kiss him hard as he held my hips, thrusting up into me until he too was coming with a groan.

"Best dick ever," I murmured, and he chuckled.

"Hear that, guys?!" he yelled toward the door. "Best dick ever!"

I slapped his shoulder with a laugh. This was nice.

Chapter 30
Sampson

Whose fucking idea was this?

Aviva was buffered on all sides by us, but still, people were too close. I wanted to take her back to the hotel, seclude her in her room, maybe give her a few dozen orgasms until she forgot about all this. Forgot about this stupid trek around the world, forgot about Nemo, forgot about everything but us.

On the flip side, her absolute wonder was addictive. She stopped at every stall, touched a flower of every shade, talked to every vendor even though she didn't understand what they were saying.

The food stalls at the end of the market smelled amazing, and we watched as one street vendor cooked dumplings, folding them in front of us before putting in a large steamer. "Oh man, I love dumplings," Aviva said, her eyes wide with delight.

I held up ten fingers to the vendor and he nodded, fishing out the dumplings and piling them high on a rough foil plate, a little dollop of chutney beside them. "Momos," he said with a grin, smiling widely and missing more than a few teeth.

Aviva thanked him and took a bite of one of the dumplings. "Holy shit, this is so good. Try some?"

I shook my head. Street food had never been my thing. Hendrick had no qualms whatsoever, plucking two from the plate and eating them in one bite. "They are good," he said around a mouth full of food. He looked at Otto. "You should try one."

Otto shook his head. "You're gross, Drix. I'm good."

We headed to Penny Lane bookstore, which was a short ride away from the market. Most of the people who worked this market lived here too, in makeshift tarpaulin tents, and they bathed in the Hooghly River. It made me appreciate what I had, even with the risks of being tortured to death for my money. Again.

The bookstore was a weird little hole in the wall, filled to the brim with engineering and science textbooks. "Are you sure we're in the right place?"

She shrugged. "It's what it said in the book."

We walked in, and the owner didn't even look up from his lunch. Okay, that was fine; I didn't want him hovering anyway. Curmudgeonly bookstore owners were a cliché that crossed the cultural divide, apparently.

Books were stacked floor to ceiling, and while they were loosely grouped into subjects, I couldn't find anywhere with fiction novels. "Find a translator. We'll start from the back and work our way forward," I told Evan, and he nodded, stepping back out onto the street.

Aviva reached behind me and squeezed my hand. "Thank you."

We set to work, and I silently began to curse out this Nemo guy. Fuck, I should just get a private investigator to find the guy, go straight to the source so Aviva could see he was just some self-obsessed asshole like the rest of us, and then we could all move on with our lives.

The other side of my brain knew that if this ended now, she'd go back to school, become beige again. She wouldn't stay with us. I couldn't blame her, really.

Three hours later, we were no closer to finding the book, and it was so hot I thought I was going to pass out. Aviva was looking pale and sweating profusely, and I decided that was enough.

"Good Girl, we'll come back tomorrow. Let's head back to the hotel."

She shook her head, looking at a stack of books but barely staying upright. "We have to be close."

Otto stepped toward her, holding her shoulder as she weaved on her feet. "Then we'll be just as close tomorrow. Come on, you're looking a little pasty."

She stood up, and I got a good look at her. She was worse than pasty. She looked gray. "I'm fine," she argued, which would have been a hell of a lot more convincing if she hadn't buckled over and puked on my shoes.

Fuck.

"Viva, are you okay?" Otto asked, as the owner of the store finally emerged, yelling angrily.

I spun around to him, pushing my finger in his face. "Fuck off." I looked past him at the bodyguards. "Get a car, now."

Aviva was swaying softly, and I scooped her into my arms. "Sam, I don't feel good."

"I know, Good Girl. We'll get it figured out."

Evan appeared from nowhere, directing us to an idling town car. I climbed in, and Otto and Hendrick climbed in beside me. She was sweating so badly now that she was shaking in my arms.

"Let's go!" I demanded.

Evan climbed in the front, and slipped the driver a stack of bills to hurry. "I'll call the hotel, tell them to get a doctor."

I nodded, but my eyes were back on Aviva. "How are you feeling now?" I asked softly, pushing back the curls that suddenly sat limply around her face.

"Feel like shit," she said, panting. "Like I'm going to puke, and my stomach, argh..." She moaned, curling into a ball on my lap. I rubbed her back, feeling fucking useless as she groaned. Eventually, her groans turned to sobs. "I'm gonna throw up." Hedrick yanked off his hat and passed it to her, and she vomited in great heaves.

"No sick in the taxi!" the driver yelled, and Evan growled something in a low voice that I missed, but had the driver weaving in and out of traffic. Hendrick threw his vomit-filled hat out the window before we rolled through the gates of the hotel. Otto hopped out first, and I passed him Viva.

"Get her to our room. I'll see where the doctor is." He took off into the hotel, his eyes wild with worry. I strode up to the reception desk. "I need that doctor now."

The employee nodded. "One is en route now, sir. He should be here any moment."

I wanted to yell at her that 'en route' wasn't good enough, that I wanted him here now. Instead, I calmly said, "I need bottled water and some kind of electrolyte replacement liquid sent up to my room. Soup. Anything you can think of that might make her better."

"Yes, sir," she replied, but I was already striding

toward the elevator. I mashed the button, and Evan slid between the doors before they closed fully. We stood there in silence, my heart pounding at how sick she was, and how fast it had happened.

"I shouldn't have taken her to that market. We shouldn't have come to this country. I should have sent her home after Paris."

Evan shook his head. "I don't think you have as much control over her as you'd like to think. But I agree, you should have sent her home. You never should have brought her in the first place."

I pushed open the door to the suite, and was greeted to the sound of dry retching and moaning.

Otto appeared in front of me. "She's still throwing up in there. She's pale and sweaty, but freezing cold. She has a fever."

"Virus?"

He shrugged helplessly. "I don't know, I'm not pre-med. How far away is the doctor?"

I shook my head. "They said he's en route."

Hendrick stumbled out of the bathroom. "She kicked me out. It's, uh, coming out from the other direction now." He screwed his nose up. "I, uh... I think I might love her."

I gaped, and Otto took a significant step back. "What? Why?"

Hendrick stumbled forward and puked into the

fruit bowl. Otto reached for him, rubbing his back, and he lifted his head out of the bowl. "Same reason you're trying to make me feel better right now. I just saw a person I've had sex with vomit and shit at the same time, and yet I'd still fuck her once she feels better."

I let out a strangled laugh, but he continued vomiting.

"Come on, Drix. Thank god this suite has two bathrooms." Otto managed to get a shoulder under Hendrick, and led him toward the bathroom. "You go and check on Viva. I got Drix."

I nodded, making my way to the other bathroom. "Good Girl, are you okay?"

"Go away. I'm embarrassed enough." There was more moaning, and I opened the door. Aviva was curled in a ball on the ground, her eyes wet with tears.

"It hurts, Sam. I swear, I'm not usually this, ah..." She panted a little. "Not this wimpy, but it hurts."

I squatted down beside her. "I know, sweetheart. The doctor is coming and he'll have meds to make you feel better. Hendrick is sick too, so I'm going to say it was probably the food. Now I'm kind of glad I didn't eat the dumplings."

"Oh god, don't mention the dumplings..." She lurched toward the toilet bowl, and if there was anything left inside her, I couldn't imagine how.

I held back her hair, worried but oddly not as disgusted as I would normally be.

Maybe there was some justification to Hendrick's hypothesis after all.

Chapter 31
Aviva

I was dying. If I wasn't dying, I wanted to. My whole body ached. I'd only just stopped shaking and I'd expelled every ounce of liquid inside me. However, if whatever the fuck this was didn't kill me, the embarrassment just might.

I buried my face further in the pillow, groaning. Sampson had scooped me off the bathroom floor and held me in the shower as I washed off all the filth coating my body. Otto had held my hair as I prayed to the porcelain gods.

I'd vomited in Hendrick's hat, and he'd actually watched me shit myself. I wanted to cry in self-pity. I'd have to go home, because there was no way I could look any of them in the eye ever again.

Yeah, I knew it wasn't my fault. The doctor who'd come to visit had told me that it was either a gastrointestinal bacteria or food poisoning, but the outcome was basically the same.

I was miserable.

At least he'd given me a couple of shots, so I no longer had to throw up or shit every three minutes. Turns out that Hendrick had gotten it too, lending credence to the possibility it was food poisoning. Though if it was some kind of bug, he'd had his tongue in my mouth—and other places—only hours earlier, so who knew which one it was.

Didn't matter really, because the advice was the same: fluids, rest, and ride it out. If it wasn't better in three days, go to the hospital. If I hadn't peed in two days, go to the hospital. If I started to see Jesus, avoid the light, and you guessed it, go to the hospital.

There was a knock at the door, and I closed my eyes, pretending to sleep so I didn't have to look any of them in the eye. I almost hoped I was contagious so I could justifiably keep them at arm's length.

"Viva?" Otto's soft voice whispered into the darkened room, and I lay so still, I probably looked like a corpse. "Viva, I know you're awake. Your breathing is too light."

Fuck. "Knowing how I sound when I'm asleep is just creepy, you know."

"Come on. I ran you a bath. It'll make you feel better."

Actually, that did sound nice.

"But first, you need to drink this," he crooned, closer now, and I pulled back to see him holding out a bottle of what looked like watered-down Gatorade.

My stomach flipped, and I covered my head with the blanket. "I don't want to puke again."

"You won't. Come on now, sit up." He pulled back the blanket and manhandled me into a sitting position. I was dressed in one of Sampson's shirts that he'd sacrificed to the gods of food poisoning.

Taking the offered bottle with arms that still shook, I drank it down slowly. Thankfully, it stayed where it was supposed to be. For now, at least.

"How's Hendrick?"

"Whiny," Otto grumbled. "You're a much better patient."

I kept sipping slowly, exhausted. "I'm sorry."

He hugged me close, and I was fairly sure that despite my shower with Sampson yesterday, I still stank like sweat and other things I didn't want to think about. "You have nothing to be sorry for. Absolutely nothing." He scooped me out of the bed and set me on my feet. It was like walking on jello, but I managed. When I made it to the main bathroom, the tub was filled with an opaque liquid and rose petals.

I burst into tears.

"Shit, what's wrong? Do you need to go back to the bedroom?"

I didn't know how to tell him that being sick had just cracked my normally apathetic exterior. My emotions were running closer to the surface, and right now, I was overflowing with emotion for Otto.

"No, it's beautiful. Perfect. Sorry I'm being a crybaby," I said, wiping my face on the sleeve of my shirt. "It's just so nice."

Otto reached out and pulled me into his arms, wrapping me in a hug that encompassed me completely. "You deserve nice things. I'm sorry if we haven't shown you that over the last couple of weeks."

Well, thanks for the extra miles I'm about to get out of my tear ducts, Otto. I just nuzzled into his body and let him hold me up for a while. He slipped his hands under the hem of the shirt, and pulled it up over my head.

It left me standing in a pair of Otto's underwear. Yes. I'd even borrowed their underwear. Because have you accidentally pooped yourself in a lace thong? I had, and 100/10 did not recommend. He hooked his fingers in the waistband, tugging them down smoothly. Then he scooped me up and laid me in the bath.

I couldn't help the sigh that left my lips. It was perfect. It smelled divine, but it felt even better. I let my eyes close as my body floated in the water and all the gross feelings washed from my skin.

There was a small step that ran around the edge of the bath, and Otto sat down on it. "Want me to wash your hair?"

I opened one eyelid and gave him a small smile. "I'm beginning to wonder if you have a fetish for bathing with your lovers."

His crooked grin and dimples did something to my insides. They felt like they were in a tumble dryer, all warm and fuzzy. "Is that going to be a problem?"

I shook my head. Otto made me feel cared for, and I wasn't sure a man had ever made me feel that way before. It was wonderful and terrifying in equal measures. I floated in the water as he washed my hair, which was lank and gross, and I had to resist the urge to purr.

"Sampson and Evan have the other bodyguards at the bookstore looking for Nemo's book. They weren't impressed, but honestly, it wasn't like we were going anywhere with both you and Hendrick so sick." He paused, his fingers still threading through my hair. "I was worried."

I didn't apologize again, because it wasn't like I could have known those dumplings were bad and we both knew it. They'd tasted fine.

"Tell them I said thank you. I know this isn't what you guys signed up for. Any of you."

Otto shrugged. "We didn't really know what we were signing up for. Maybe Hendrick? But Sampson and I were just along for the ride." He tipped my head back slightly, pouring water from a small cup over my hairline. "Mostly, it's been amazing. I don't have any regrets."

I chewed my lip, but didn't say anything else. I just soaked up the peaceful silence, Otto not needing to fill the space the way that Hendrick did, or control the moment like Sampson. With Otto, I could just be me. Aviva. Fucked up, a little neurotic, but me. I don't think he knew how much I really appreciated him.

After I'd thought about nothing but the warm water for thirty minutes, Otto helped me out of the bath, wrapping me in one of those fluffy, expensive hotel towels.

Someone—I was going to guess Sampson—had laid me out fresh clothes, including another pair of Otto's boxers. I flushed, but Otto didn't seem to care.

He kissed the top of my head and left me to dry off. "I'll let you get dressed, and go and get you something to eat."

I groaned but didn't protest. I spent a moment brushing out and braiding my hair, and by the time I was done, I was exhausted. The door to my bedroom opened, and Hendrick shuffled in. He looked gray, but freshly showered. He was only in boxer shorts, and his whole body seemed smaller somehow.

"You look how I feel," I teased, and he gave me half a smile. He climbed into my bed, snuggling under the covers, and grunted.

Well, guess we were snuggling then. I climbed in beside him, and he dragged me closer to his body, so he was hugging my back to his chest like I was a teddy bear.

He inhaled deeply. "You smell pretty. And how the hell are you so soft?" he grumbled, stroking softly up and down my stomach.

"Vagina magic."

He huffed a laugh. "I fucking believe it. Gotta have some magic, Viva. Nothing else explains it," he mumbled.

I frowned. "Explains what?"

But he was already asleep. His body was warm, his arm over my waist a comforting heaviness. I fell asleep, wrapped in the encompassing presence that was Hendrick, before Otto even returned.

Chapter 32

Hendrick

F uck, I could murder a hamburger right now. Probably not the time or the place to ask though. I was an asshole, but I could respect people who believed in something, even if I didn't. Hell, I was almost envious. For my entire life, I hadn't put my faith in anyone who wasn't in this cab with me right now, and definitely not in some higher power.

Sampson might believe he was a god, but I was fairly sure he was still a man.

We were heading to the airport once again, on our way to Japan. Yokohama, to be exact. This asshole, Nemo, definitely thought he was some globe-hopping Verne wannabe. When the new security douches got back from that nightmare bookstore with a copy of *Five Weeks in a Balloon,* I'd wanted to throw it in the sparkling fucking hotel pool. I thought we'd be done.

It should've been impossible to find a single book in that store, because it was a mess. Viva had been too sick to look herself, and we could have just said 'oh well, better luck next obsession.' But no, Evan was a fucking perfectionist, and he wouldn't let this crap rest. Like he'd made it his own personal mission.

Maybe he just wanted to go home to his wife or girlfriend or goldfish. Whatever the hell he had. He was a good-looking guy, I could admit that much. Not the kind of gem you'd pick from a jewelry store, but the kind of shiny stone you found on a nature trail, took home, and kept as a paperweight forever.

Maybe I should buy Viva some jewelry. Girls liked jewelry. Though not a ring—wouldn't want her to get the wrong idea. Maybe a necklace. Maybe an opal.

"For fuck's sake, Hendrick, stop thinking so loud," Sampson grumbled from where he was napping beside me.

"You can't hear me think, dickhead. Right, Otto?"

Otto laughed sheepishly. "Well, you kind of can. You grind your teeth and tap your fingers on your thigh. Sigh a lot."

"You can hear your two brain cells crashing together like symbols," Sampson added, and I reached over Aviva and punched him in the thigh. She gave a husky chuckle that made my dick hard, and I resisted the urge to pull her onto my lap.

I pouted and stared out my window, frowning until Viva laced her fingers with mine. She looked a lot better, and I never wanted to see her that sick ever again. Fuck, I never wanted to *be* that sick again, either. Though I hadn't minded spooning with Aviva while we spent the last five days recuperating in bed. We'd all binge-watched a Henry Cavill series together, which had enough violence to keep Sampson entertained, and enough Cavill in leather to keep the rest of us riveted to the screen. Honestly, it had been the best five days I'd had in ages, and we didn't even leave the room. It was all because of her.

Fuck, I didn't deserve Aviva. She'd been right when we first met. I was an entitled asshole who ruined everything and everyone around him. I'd ruin her too. Hell, I'd wanted to ruin her.

I shook her hand free to scratch my chin, and then just let my hand fall back to my lap. I could feel her eyes on my face but pretended I couldn't, continuing to stare out the window.

"We should go out in Yokohama. I haven't hit a club since New York. I need booze and beats." I felt Aviva stiffen against me, and the car was unnaturally silent. "Isn't Firth still in Tokyo? Get him to come down and give us the grand tour of the place. Or at least of the nightlife."

Sampson scoffed. "Dude, you just shit out things

you ate when you were ten. You sure you want to go out drinking?"

"Fuck off, Sam. You know I do."

I couldn't see Otto's face, but I knew the tenseness in his shoulders. He didn't approve. He'd get over it. Aviva wouldn't be hurt. She knew she was too good for us; that's why she was still chasing goddamn ghosts.

We pulled into the airport, and security hustled us straight to the terminal lounge. I needed more sleep, more food, more alcohol. More everything. No sooner had we sat down than an announcement came over that our flight was delayed by two hours. Dammit.

I headed straight to the bar, ordering a cognac, neat. It was an old man drink, but fuck it. It was smooth going down, so I could knock back four before I even felt it.

I should have known Otto would appear beside me like the Ghost of Boyfriends Past, Present and hopefully Future, if he didn't get sick of my bullshit.

He grabbed my drink, taking it straight out of my hand and replacing it with my meds. "Water, please," he told the bartender, who reappeared with a sealed bottle of water. Otto pushed it toward me. "Take them."

I rolled my eyes but downed the pills. "Such a fucking nag, Otto." I opened my mouth, proving they were gone, like we were back in the institution and not at an airport a whole world away.

He shook his head at me, handing me back my cognac. "You've been violently sick. Your meds haven't been as effective as they'd normally be. Don't fuck this up just because your brain is all out of sync. Don't fuck it up for all of us."

With that, he just walked away, not giving me the chance to argue. I would have argued that it wasn't my bipolar that was fucking with me right now. No, it was reality, that dark fucking dominatrix. She was beating me with her studded paddle of truth.

Okay, even mentally I'd taken that metaphor too far.

I walked back to the small group of people who would be sad if I died. I liked to think Aviva would be sad, and even Evan might shed a tear. My father would rejoice, my mother would be too fucking stoned to notice, and life would go on.

Aviva rested her head on Sampson's shoulder as he spoke to Otto about stock figures and MMA fighters, her eyelids heavy with sleep. Her full pink lips were slightly parted, like it took too much energy to keep them pursed.

Without even pausing his conversation, Sampson pulled her onto his lap, letting her lie against his chest like it was the most natural thing in the world. She didn't protest, just laid her head on his shoulder and closed her eyes. She was still recovering. She should have had another couple of days building her strength back up, but she'd wanted to go, wanted to find the next clue in the next city.

We were all so pussy-whipped that we'd caved. I don't know why though. We'd fucked her less than a handful of times, but somehow, that was enough. I was quickly learning that was the real magic of Aviva.

They kept talking and I kept drinking until our flight was called. Viva kept casting me worried looks, which I ignored. I didn't want to talk about my cursed brain right now, and I was kind of hoping that Otto was right and the meds would magically even me out. Otto deserved better too; they'd all be better off not being dragged under by my bullshit.

It was a long flight to Yokohama, and I breathed a sigh of relief when I was next to Sampson and not beside Otto or Aviva. Sampson gave me a worried glance. "You alright, man?"

I nodded. "Still a little green from the food poisoning, but nothing that killing my liver with sake won't cure."

He looked at me for a little longer, then shrugged and stuck his earbuds in his ears. That's what I loved about Sampson. He didn't worry. He did what he could, supported when he had to, and the rest he just let go. He didn't try and change me, didn't expect anything from me except for me to be my usual, insane self.

The flight attendant poured me a champagne, and I followed Sampson's lead, putting in my earbuds and closing my eyes. Maybe I'd fall asleep and dream of a world where I was a normal man, who went to work, loved his girlfriend, and was not constantly stalked by the shadows of his very own demons.

Chapter 33
Otto

I watched Hendrick out of the corner of my eye, that heavy feeling in my chest one I knew all too well. If I was honest with myself, I'd known the crash was coming, but I'd kind of hoped I was wrong. Falsely hoped that this last stint at rehab had done some good. Which was naive of me because Hendrick didn't need rehab—he needed regular therapy and chemical intervention. His giddy happiness was usually a precursor to his lows, though those usually came when he had too much downtime to think, or was adjusting to new meds.

On the other hand, I watched Aviva, who was far more perceptive than anyone gave her credit for. She knew something had shifted on the cab ride to Kolkata airport, but she didn't know what, because she didn't really know Hendrick. She only knew the confident, arrogant, playful Hendrick. She didn't know the Jekyll to his Hyde. Didn't know he was bipolar at all.

No one did, except those closest to him. Though I was fairly sure his father knew—it would have been in any number of psychiatrist reports. Didn't stop the fucker from beating his son though, and causing his bipolar to double down with a side of PTSD. God, I hated that son of a bitch. I hoped that one day he'd get hit by a bus and rot in the pits of Hell where he belonged.

Yokohama was exactly as I remembered it, and as we pulled up in front of the hotel, Aviva was pressed tightly against the glass window of the cab. "Holy shit, it's huge."

We all looked at Hendrick, waiting for the inevitable dick joke, but he was staring at his phone with a glazed expression. My heart constricted in my chest, but I pasted on a smile for Aviva. "It's not the fanciest hotel in Yokohama, but it's okay and has an amazing view of the Cosmo Clock wheel."

She gave me a knowing look, but she didn't protest. Maybe she was becoming more comfortable with us as well, learning that when we stayed in fancy hotels, it wasn't because we were trying to impress her. It was legitimately because Hendrick and Sampson were whiny rich boys who didn't sleep on anything less than thousand thread count sheets.

We all climbed out of the cab, and bellhops hurried over to collect our baggage. I wouldn't say it to Aviva, but I was getting tired. I wanted to go home, and I wanted to see my parents. Hopping from hotel room to hotel room, bookstore to bookstore, was starting to wear me down. I wasn't like Sampson, who was literally at home in a hotel, or Hendrick, who'd never really had a home where he felt comfortable and safe. I'd grown up loved, and secure in the knowledge that I'd always have a safety net to fall back on.

Hendrick hung back, and Aviva sidled up to me while Sampson checked us in. "What's wrong with him?"

I swallowed hard, and looked at the man who had my heart in a vice. "He's bipolar."

Aviva didn't gasp with shock, or look horrified. She just nodded, like I was confirming all her suspicions.

"You knew?"

She shrugged. "I suspected. You don't spend ninety days in an institution and not learn the difference between a personality quirk and an actual illness." She looked at him, not with pity, but with empathy. I guess that was one possible perk of dating a girl who also suffered from mental illness—she understood. "What can I do?"

I sighed, because that was what was so hard about mental illness, from a bystander's point of view—the helplessness. "His self-talk gets really dark. Just let him know you're there. That you aren't going anywhere just because he's a little fucked up." I paused. "Forgive him for the stupid shit he'll inevitably do once he decides you're too good to him. He'll try and drive you away, because obviously it'll be easier than owning up to his bullshit."

She nodded as Sampson came over, the room key clutched in his hand. "Let's go up. This jet lag thing is killing me." We walked to the elevator, and Evan slipped in beside us. The guys would be horrified, but I could tell Evan wanted Aviva. Wanted her badly, but he was a professional. He would never act on it, especially because he'd sound like a fucking hypocrite after that stupid speech he gave us back in Paris.

"Firth texted me while we were on the flight. He's coming down on Saturday to hit up the clubs with us," Sampson stated, looking back down at his phone as the doors closed.

Hendrick nodded, and in the reflection of the elevator mirror, I could see him scrolling through some Insta posts. Following the pattern like a champion, just like he always did. He'd lose himself to meaningless hookups that made him feel like shit, because then he wouldn't have to face the fact that I—that *we*—meant something. Like he could just push us away. It hadn't mattered to me before, when it was just me and him, and we were only a casual hookup between friends. But I wasn't sure I could stand back and let him purposefully hurt Aviva like that.

Our suite was actually two connected rooms, and Hendrick grabbed my arm, pulling me into the first one. "I'll sleep with Otto. Sampson won't rub my dick in the middle of the night."

Sampson gave him a sharp grin that was all teeth. "You've never asked," he teased back. "Come on, Good Girl. I want a nap and a spooning buddy." He dragged her into the other room, not bothering to shut the door.

I looked at Hendrick but he raised a hand. "No lectures, Otto."

I tilted my head at him. "Maybe you should have bunked with Sampson if you didn't want lectures. Or maybe you could have had Aviva all to yourself."

He scratched the back of his neck in a gesture I knew meant he was about to give me an excuse that I wasn't going to like. I'd known this man too long.

"About Aviva..."

I held up a hand to stop him and went over to shut the adjoining doors. Finally, I waved for him to proceed. Honestly, I couldn't wait to hear what his fucking excuse was for this.

"I like her. I like being around her. But we aren't good for her. Our—I mean, *my* life wouldn't be good for her. It isn't even good for me. Getting attached, or letting her get attached, will only lead to bad shit."

Fuck, he wasn't even spouting selfish lines that I could shoot down as his illness talking, because I'd actually thought those very things myself. Hendrick's life was complicated, not just with the bipolar, but with the constant attention he'd received ever since he was young. Him and Sampson, they were the darlings of the tabloids. That was without the added pressure of Hendrick's family, especially his fucking dad.

I was silent, and Hendrick took that as confirmation. "We both know I'm right."

I shook my head. "No, you're not. You definitely don't have the right to make those decisions for her, or for me either. Or for Sampson, who—in case you've been blinded by yourself these last couple of days—might actually be in love with her. It's hard to tell with Sam." I stepped closer to him, pulling him against my body so he'd be forced to look at me. "If I've learned anything about Aviva, it's that she does what she wants. You can try pushing her away, but in the end, I think she'll love you whether you like it or not." I lifted his chin a little so I could kiss him. It was a soft kiss, a rope that I could wrap around his body and use to keep him tethered tightly to me. "You deserve to be happy, Drix."

He just grunted, and I knew that was about as

much as I was going to get out of him. I hung up our clothes, watching as he lay down on the bed and closed his eyes, pretending to go to sleep despite the fact he'd slept the entire fourteen hour flight here, and it was now the middle of the day.

This was the beginning, but I was determined to drag him out of his spiral before he hit the bottom. I stripped down to my boxers and climbed into bed beside him, holding him to my chest so he knew that he had me, no matter what.

Turns out, the bookstore we needed to visit for this little expedition was about forty minutes away, so we hired a car. Evan left the other two bodyguards at home for a well-deserved rest day, and chaperoned us himself down south.

Hendrick seemed a little better today, handing out his usual dirty one-liners and smiling brightly, even if it didn't quite make it to his eyes every time.

I'd done some research while everyone recovered from the flight yesterday, and while I couldn't find the exact address for the bookshop, I knew its general location. We'd unanimously decided that shopping was also in order, because so far we hadn't done much on these trips other than sleep, eat, and chase down a ghost.

Evan parked, and we all piled out. Instantly, you could tell that this area was off the tourist trail. The locals eyed us with surprise, but just kept going about their day. It was your average, working class neighborhood, complete with a shopping strip. Except unlike the US, everything was insanely clean.

We ducked in and out of back alleyways as a group, exploring and laughing. Sampson bought several silk scarves in jewel colors and when he handed them to Aviva, he gave her a look so hot it even made me hard. Somehow, I didn't think they were for his great-aunts back home.

If Aviva noticed though, she didn't let on. She skipped ahead, giving Evan a heart attack as he kept one eye on her, and one eye on us. Bet he was regretting not bringing the rest of the security now.

"Relax, Evan. It's fine. Enjoy yourself," Sampson grumbled, and Evan just gave him a droll look before going back to scanning the street for potential threats. Aviva ducked down one of the alleys, and we all strode after her.

"Guys! I think this is it!" she called, following the narrow walkway. There was a hand-painted black and white sign, the word *Tabi* painted like a title on the front of a book. I caught up to her in a few long strides, and grabbed her hand, keeping her with me. I was being overprotective—it was just a store after all—

but I'd feel better if one of us was with her all the same.

As we stepped in, a little old man behind the counter greeted us with a smile and a bowed head. He looked about a hundred, but blaring over the speakers was a Red Hot Chilli Peppers song. I laughed before I could stop myself.

Aviva stepped forward, bowing respectfully. "Do you have any Jules Verne?"

The old man smiled, but didn't answer. She pulled a book from her bag, pointing to the name. The old man smiled wide and yelled loudly in Japanese. Aviva squeaked in surprise, jumping slightly, but the man kept smiling.

From the back, another guy appeared. He was about our age, maybe as young as Aviva. He said something in rapid Japanese to the old man, then looked over at us. He was handsome, with a jawline so sharp it was basically a work of art. Aviva's mouth dropped open and she stared—at least, she did until I nudged her with my elbow.

"Hi, I'm Kato. My grandfather says you are looking for a particular book?"

Aviva continued to blink, and I cleared my throat. "Yeah, a Jules Verne novel."

He gave us both a bright smile with perfect teeth, and honestly, I totally got his dazzling appeal. He didn't compare to Hendrick, but he had that easygoing, sweet book nerd thing going for him with those thick-rimmed glasses and a t-shirt that was just this side of too tight.

"Sure, come on back."

Aviva finally found her voice. "Thank you."

"You are welcome." His English was great, only slightly accented. "This is our English classic section here. I apologize that there is no specific order."

Aviva flushed. "No, that's okay."

Kato smiled. "Are you all together?"

Aviva went beet red. "No. I mean, yes, but not seriously. I mean, I don't really know what we are, it's not like—"

Sampson put his hand over her mouth. "She means yes, we are all shopping together. Thank you."

Kato bowed and left, and I lost it. I laughed so hard I could barely hiss, Hendrick and Sampson laughing right along with me. Aviva's face went impossibly redder, and she punched me in the stomach.

"Shut up. Help me find this book so we can leave, and I can throw myself off that pretty bridge by our hotel and never face the world again."

Sampson curled his arm around her shoulder and pulled her close to his chest. "Come on, Good Girl. Find your book so I can take you back to the hotel and show you how together we really are."

Chapter 34
Aviva

I spread the gloss over my lips with precision. Tonight, we were going out for dinner, then on the Cosmo wheel, finishing off the night by meeting one of the guys' college buddies at a club. I was nervous about that.

Somehow, I knew that meeting their friends meant things would change. I couldn't be sure how, I just knew it would. So I put my makeup on with extra care to ensure I looked worthy of their attention, as stupid as that sounded. I'd spent a ridiculous amount of time on my curls after my shower, and they fell in soft ringlets around my face. My lipstick was red, my lashes long, and my dress sparkled softly under the bathroom lights. It would have to do.

I even put on heels instead of my Converse or boots, which I felt was probably good aesthetics but terrible practicality. Still, I couldn't argue with the fact my legs looked long and shapely, and I felt confident. Not just confident, but beautiful, which wasn't something I'd ever felt before this trip.

Pushing my boobs up in my dress to give me better cleavage, I took a deep breath. These guys had all seen me naked. Hell, they'd all seen me worse than naked. They still liked me.

So what if Hendrick had been different over the last couple of days? Otto had explained. It didn't have anything to do with me. At least, that's what my head told me. That stupid voice that might be my heart told me that he'd fucked me, seen me at my very worst, and now he was done. Disgusted with me. Men like Hendrick expected perfection—the girl at the club in New York had proven that. She'd seemed like the epitome of perfection to me, but even she hadn't been good enough for Hendrick.

I shook my head, my curls bouncing around my ears. No. It didn't matter now; I wasn't going to let the doubts creep in. I was going to go, have a nice night with the guys, and thoughts of the future could just fucking wait.

I opened the bathroom door, and walked through to the living area. I saw Otto first, his shoulders encased in a stiff white shirt that stretched across his back like a caress. His slacks were very obviously tailored, and they made his ass look divine.

I cleared my throat, and he turned, his mouth dropping open. "Aviva. You look beautiful."

He stepped toward me, and I could see around his shoulder to where Sampson sat sprawled on the couch. He was in tight black jeans and a black button down shirt. A classic leather jacket hung over the arm of the couch beside him.

A choked noise to the left had me turning, and Hendrick was gaping at me. "Jesus, Viva. I can nearly see your ass cheeks in that dress."

I flipped him the bird, falling back into our old antagonistic roles easily. "Then don't look, you pervert."

He looked achingly handsome tonight, a sports jacket giving him an air of propriety paired with his ripped, dark wash jeans and a khaki t-shirt. It made him look both dressed down and effortlessly fashionable. Asshole. It shouldn't be that easy.

"You all look nice too," I said with a smile.

Sampson uncurled himself from the lounge, and he made it look so graceful that it was definitely a turn on. Considering I was only twenty-one, I felt like I was ninety-nine some days, especially after the accident.

He strode over to me, getting into my personal space until he was staring down at me with those dark, quicksand eyes. "You look sexy as fuck, Good Girl." He ran the back of his fingers down my exposed shoulder. "Now go and take it off, because there's no way I'm letting you out in public looking so fucking beautiful."

I snorted, pushing his chest. "You chose this fucking dress, Sampson Rubio. Now you can wallow in your shitty, high-handed attitude." I grinned, because revenge was a sweet dessert. "Let's go. I don't want to miss our dinner appointment. Why are we going to a French restaurant in Japan anyway?"

"It's a three star restaurant, Good Girl. Who cares where it is?"

As we left the suite, Evan was waiting with his team outside the doors. They were all dressed to go clubbing as well, probably so they didn't stand out in the crowd. Evan looked up, dropping his cellphone, and it landed at my feet.

"Whoops!" I bent forward to pick it up, but Hendrick was there, swiping it out of my hands.

"For the sweet love of god, Viva, do not bend over in that dress." He sounded physically pained, and I laughed. Yeah, I didn't wear many skin-tight minidresses.

"Fuck this, I'm calling Firth and telling him we're cancelling," Sampson added.

Someone else muttered an agreement as I straightened my dress, and I frowned. "Listen, I just spent three hours getting ready, so don't be assholes. I promise I won't bend over again, though I'm not sure squatting down in this dress will be any better." Hendrick groaned, and I just smiled. "Loosen up, guys—no one's going to care. Besides, if it really is the End Of Days and I'm swarmed by eligible bachelors, I have Evan to beat them off."

"He'll be beating something off," someone murmured, making Evan clench his jaw.

I decided to save him from further embarrassment. "Let's go. We'll miss our reservation."

Dinner was amazing. Dammit, when this was all over, I could live without the first class travel and the fancy hotels, and the expensive as hell clothes. But the food— that I would miss.

We walked across the bridge that ran around the bay and over to the Cosmo Clock wheel. "Are we going up?"

Sampson chuckled. "If I just wanted to look at it, we could be doing that naked against the windows of our suite. You could watch it go around as I fucked you from behind."

Hendrick went over and bought tickets, while security took up separate positions around the entrances. Directing me up a set of stairs, Sampson moved to my side and Otto came up behind me.

When I was a few steps up, I felt fingers running lightly up the inside of my thigh. I gasped and stumbled, Sampson's arm around my waist the only thing keeping me steady.

"Otto," I hissed, and he just smiled cheekily up at me. Fuck, he was cute. "Stop it or I'm going to trip and topple us both back down the stairs." I looked past him to Hendrick still on the bottom step. "Hurry up, Drix. What are you doing?"

He grinned, and it was that same smile that had completely undone my defenses in the first place. "The view is better from down here."

"You are all perverts, and I hope you know it."

We made it to the gate, where the signs announced that the Ferris wheel didn't stop. We had to jump on when the doors opened. I mean, it was moving slow as hell, but still, I was in six-inch heels. I wasn't the most coordinated person at the best of times and moving vehicles wouldn't help. Arms suddenly wrapped around my waist as Otto picked me up, pressing me tight to his body and walking us both on.

"I could have done that."

Otto shrugged. "I just wanted a good reason to have that tight little ass pressed against my crotch and still seem chivalrous."

I laughed and wiggled my ass against his dick as he slid me back down to my feet. Hendrick stood at the door, eyeballing the attendant, daring him to let anyone else into our capsule. Eventually, the doors slid closed and we moved up.

"So, I read that it takes fifteen minutes for this to go around," Sampson said lightly, though there was no mistaking the undertone of lust in his voice. "You know what that means, Good Girl?"

I smirked at him. "That I better appreciate the view?"

He wrapped an arm around my waist, pulling me tightly to him. "No, Aviva. It means I can only make you come twice."

He slid his other hand down my side and over my ass, lifting my thigh so my leg hooked around his own, opening me to him. His fingers traced over the crease of my thigh and then brushed across my underwear.

"I've imagined all the ways I want to fuck you in this tiny dress all night long. Bent over. On your knees. Up against the bathroom wall at the restaurant. Then I imagined peeling it off you slowly, so I could taste every inch of your flesh and claim it as mine."

Oh god. His words were their own kind of foreplay, raising goosebumps on my skin and dampening my core until I ached with every brush of his fingertips. Slipping beneath the lace lines of my underwear, he stroked his fingers through my folds, making a satisfied noise at how wet I was. He teased around my clit, just enough pressure for the promise of pleasure, but not enough at all. The fucker was tormenting me.

"Please," I begged, and he laughed. I clawed his back. "I thought you said we were in a hurry?"

One of the other guys grunted out a curse as Sampson kissed my neck, placing soft bites there. "But I love that noise you make when I tease." He let out a put-upon sigh. "Fine. Hard and fast it is, like the dirty girl you are." He rubbed his thumb across my clit, making me buck into his hand.

"Yes," I breathed, as he slid two fingers inside me, his thumb still gently working me. God, this man was good with his hands. Almost as good as Hendrick was with his mouth.

Maybe this was why women didn't have more than one lover—if they nailed the basics, a woman would be an amply pleasured puddle instead of a constructive member of society.

He rolled his fingers inside me, and I gripped him tightly as he hit all the right spots. "Sampson," I gasped, clawing him closer. "Oh god..."

I tilted my head to the side as he kissed and nipped my neck, my body thrumming with pleasure that was building at the same wild tempo as my heartbeat. He continued to stroke and tease, thrusting hard enough that it was just this side of too much, and it was so, so good. I looked over to see Otto and Hendrick watching me with hungry eyes, like they were taking a mental porno reel of the moment to use later. Hendrick adjusted his cock in his pants, his tongue darting out to wet his lower lip.

Sampson bit harder, making me gasp and moan at the same time, which was a fucking weird noise. "Concentrate. I want you to come for me, Good Girl. Come for me here, where anyone down on the ground could see your delicious ass pressed against the glass and my fingers buried inside you."

Hendrick muttered something about a telescope, but I didn't care as my orgasm washed over me and I muffled my scream behind my lips.

I slumped back against the glass. Well, as much as Sampson's tight grip around my back would allow. My head fell to the side and I realized we'd reached the pinnacle of the ride. The lights of Yokohama glowed below, looking like a glittering fairy kingdom. "The world's perfect from up here."

Sampson leaned forward, kissing my lips softly so he didn't ruin my makeup. "Yeah, it really is."

Chapter 35
Sampson

The club where Firth was meeting us was already insane. We'd waited in line for thirty minutes, because we meant less than nothing in Japan. Honestly, it was as annoying as it was refreshing.

The club played a mix of Japanese and American house music, and everyone was dancing like this was a fucking pop music video. I checked my phone and saw a text from Firth, telling me he'd gotten us a seat in the VIP area. No idea how he'd managed it, but I was glad. I guess I'd become accustomed to not being in the crush of humanity.

Firth saw us standing on the other side, and came over, saying something to the bouncer in rapid Japanese. The guy stepped aside, letting us past the barrier, and Firth grabbed my arm and pulled me into a hug. He was always overfamiliar.

"Sampson, it's good to see you, man!" He moved past me to Hendrick, grabbing his arm and dragging him into the VIP area. "Drix! Otto! God, it's good to see you guys. It's been forever."

"You've been here six months, Firth."

Firth waved his hand, like that was a lifetime. "Come on, I'll introduce you to my friends." He completely ignored Aviva, and I tried not to be annoyed. Tried and failed. But she rested a gentle hand on my arm and shook her head.

We followed Firth through the tables to a small set of couches where two guys and a girl were laughing over drinks. The girl was a Brit; I could tell from her high, screeching laugh as she joked with the men. The guys looked like Firth: plain, loud, and filled with enough desperate confidence that it came off them in waves.

"Guys, this is Sampson Rubio, Hendrick Kenley and Otto." Yeah, no last name for Otto, because he wasn't trying to name-drop him to sound more important. I was quickly remembering why Firth annoyed the fuck out of me, though I knew Hendrick liked him.

The girl ate me up with her eyes, and I gave her a blank stare back. Putting my hand on Aviva's spine, I directed her into the seat between me and Otto.

Hendrick sat on the occasional table between the couches and poured himself a heavy dose of sake.

"Guys, this is Torielle. She's in the same young entrepreneurs exchange program as I am. This is Goro and Asa; they work in the office with me. I told them I was coming down to party in Yokohama, and they asked to come. The more the merrier, right Drix?"

"Call me Elle," the girl said pleasantly.

Drix grunted something that might have been agreement, or might have just been from the burn of the sake. He pointed the bottle at Good Girl. "That's Aviva. She's poor and we're chaperoning her around the world."

Aviva stiffened beside me, the barb obviously hitting the mark. "Fuck off, Hendrick. It was your idea, you asshole."

Firth threw back his head and laughed. "She certainly has a mouth on her." There was an undertone of desire in his voice as he took in her long legs in that dress, her perky breasts, and that perfect pink mouth.

I waited until he looked at me and I gave him a silent warning. It was all he'd get. If he even thought about hitting on Aviva, I would beat the ever-loving shit out of him. Then I'd systematically ruin his fucking life.

I didn't examine the reason why. I didn't need to. She was mine.

Firth proved he wasn't a complete idiot by averting his gaze back to the British girl. "Let's get more sake. I haven't partied with you guys in nearly a year."

More bottles were bought, and I didn't miss them waiting for me to put my card on the tab. Whatever. I could afford it, and Hendrick looked happy. Even Aviva was laughing at something Goro was saying. I let myself relax.

Evan was at the bar, drinking water and watching the crowd. The girl behind the bar was trying hard to chat him up, but he was barely giving her anything. That happened at almost every bar we went to though. It wasn't that Evan was attractive—well, not that I could tell anyway. No, the reason women always flocked to him was two-fold.

One, he wasn't interested. He was polite, and would answer direct questions, but gave off no signals whatsoever. He was a professional. He had a job. Women were just like men, in that they wanted the things that didn't come easily. Wanted the challenge of wooing someone into letting us in. Not in a fucking sleazy way—no means no, always. The challenge lay in getting past the little voice that society implanted in your brain. The one that said you shouldn't, that a person was out of your league, that it would end in heartache. Anyway, Evan presented that challenge in a way no other man in this club would.

The second reason that he was catnip on nights like this was that Evan had an air of danger. It was just in the way he held himself. Despite the pleasant mediocrity of his face, his eyes held a coldness that was like a beacon to girls with daddy issues or who liked it a little rough.

"Isn't that right, Sampson?" Firth said, and I dragged my thoughts back to my current company. I raised an eyebrow until he repeated himself. "I said our nights out were legendary. You remember that time Drix was banging... fuck, was it Shauna? Sheena? Fuck, I can't even remember her name. Whoever she was, Drix had her in the back of her daddy's Rolls, and then the paps opened the car door. You couldn't look at a newsstand for weeks without seeing her tits on the front page of the tabloids."

"She got disinherited," Otto murmured, always the conscience for those of us who didn't possess one— Firth included.

Hendrick shrugged. "She knew what she was doing."

Aviva frowned but didn't say anything, sipping her drink. Elle stood up, dragging up Firth and Hendrick as well. "We should dance," she screeched, and looked down at Aviva. "Come on, girl! Why come to a club if we don't shake it?!"

Aviva gave a tight laugh, but stood too. Otto was in

an intense conversation about robotics and the future of communications with Asa and Goro, and waved us off. I sighed, standing. I hated dancing. But I wasn't going to let my Good Girl go out there with just Hendrick and some strangers. He'd either fuck her, or piss her off, and neither of those options boded well for the rest of the night.

Hendrick grabbed the bottle of sake off the table, glaring at security as if daring them to stop him from taking it out into the main area of the club.

We moved down to the sunken dancefloor, with its strobing lights and smoke machine haze creating an epileptic's nightmare. But it did seem almost surreal, like a frenzied orgy of sweaty limbs. Our group managed to find a spot and began to dance. I gripped Aviva's hips as she swayed and bounced to the music, completely focused on how beautiful she looked as she let go of her inhibitions and just danced.

She got that same euphoric look on her face when she came.

One song turned into another, and then another, and finally I pulled her closer to my body, kissing her as I ground my body into hers in a way that couldn't be construed as anything but foreplay.

Someone whistled but I ignored them, but then Aviva's entire body stiffened. I looked over to see Hendrick had his entire body pressed against Elle's, and the way they were dancing was similar to fucking with your clothes on. From what I could tell, they weren't actually fucking, but it was awfully goddamn close.

"Cut it the fuck out, Drix," I yelled over the sound of the music, and Hendrick cast me a petulant look, his eyes glazed with too much alcohol. I knew what was about to come out of his mouth would be bad.

"What? You were basically fucking Aviva on the dancefloor—what am I supposed to do? Wait with my hand on my dick until she's ready to screw her way back in my direction?"

I felt more than heard Aviva's gasp. "Fuck you, Hendrick Kenley. I screwed you once and that was uninspiring enough."

"Ah, Viva. You lost your appeal as soon as I got my dick inside you. Been there, done that, don't need a repeat performance."

I sucked in a ragged breath of shock. I looked down at Aviva, and her look of pain, and shame, made my whole chest ache. Then a red haze came down over my vision.

"You fucking son of a bitch," I growled, launching myself at Hendrick, my fist connecting with his jaw. His head snapped back, but while the alcohol in Drix's system stole his coordination, it made up for it in pain tolerance. He barely stumbled back before he was springing forward again, tackling me around the waist and taking me down onto the dirty club floor. I dodged his swinging fist, because it was sloppy, and leaned up, headbutting him in the face.

Out of the corner of my eye, I saw Aviva running off and Evan wading through the crowd toward me. "No! Go after her," I shouted, as Drix roared, spattering blood on me. I didn't have time to see if Evan listened or ignored me.

I rolled Drix onto his back, and slapped him hard. Honestly, nothing shocked a man like being bitch-slapped. "You fucking idiot," I yelled in his face. "What the fuck do you think you're doing?"

He slumped back to the floor, and that was when I realized he was fucking manic. Bloody and manic on the dirty dancefloor, with hundreds of people watching the spectacle.

"It's for the best," he said, his eyes glazed and far away. "She deserves so much better than us, Sampson. Can't you see that? Don't you understand?"

I climbed off him, sick to my stomach. "No, Drix. You don't understand. You're so fucking wrong, and now you've fucked it up for all of us, asshole."

Otto had appeared in the circle, his worried eyes bouncing between us. I climbed to my feet, nursing my aching face, but I didn't look nearly as shit as Hendrick. Elle, the girl, stared between us all, horrified, while Firth looked on like this was the most entertaining thing he'd seen in forever. I was surprised he wasn't filming it.

I walked toward Otto, angry, sad and nearly sick to my stomach. "Clean him up. I'm going to find Aviva."

Otto nodded, as the crowd went back to dancing, like they hadn't just witnessed the disintegration of something that had nearly been perfect.

Chapter 36
Aviva

I ran out of that club with the burn of Hendrick's words still coating my skin. Pushing past the bouncers and people hanging around the front of the club, I turned back toward the bay. I knew if I followed the water toward the Ferris wheel, I'd eventually make it to the hotel. I didn't have the key, but I'd figure that out when I got there. Maybe they'd have another room so I could have some space and just breathe.

I wished I was wearing my Converse instead of these stupid heels, but I'd wanted to impress them. Impress Hendrick. I suddenly realized I was crying when the tears cooled rapidly on my cheeks, the wind from the water chilly this late at night. I nearly tripped again, growling at my stupid shoes that probably cost more than my car back home. Leaning down, I slipped them from my feet. Yokohama was fastidiously clean; I'd take my chances that I wouldn't step on anything terrible. Finally able to run, I took off again, my hair loosening from the tight curls to fly out behind me. I ran until the tears flowed into my ears and down my neck.

"Aviva, wait!" I stumbled at the shout, straightening only to see Evan coming up behind me.

"Leave me alone, Evan. I want to be alone."

He caught up to me easily, basically because he wasn't running in a bodycon dress barefoot, and his stride was twice as long as mine. He grabbed my arm, pulling me to a stop. "I'm not leaving you out here alone."

I huffed, because I did feel better with him here, despite my words. And he hadn't done anything to me, not really. "Fine. But I don't want to talk about it."

He grunted. "What part of my personality makes you think I'm a talker? Bottle that shit up, Chaos."

"Why do you call me Chaos?"

He was staring at my bare feet with distaste. "That's what I call you in my reports. All of the guys have code names, and that's the one that fits you best."

A surprised giggle broke past my lips, but then I remembered Hendrick's sneer as he basically called me a whore. Every sliver of mirth left me in an instant. I

316

didn't want to go back there. Didn't want to sleep in a suite with the guys. I was so hurt, because Hendrick had been right. I did expect him to wait for me, yet I was fucking both of his friends. We weren't in a relationship, so what right did I have? From what he said, that had never been his endgame anyway. Just a warm hole, like all those other girls. I was so fucking stupid, thinking I was different. Just like the rest of them.

But that didn't change the fact that watching him dance with that girl had made jealousy course through my veins like acid.

"Probably apt," was all I said as I walked along the promenade. I still wanted to run, but my blood had cooled. "Do you have a room in the hotel?" He nodded. "Are you sharing?"

He shook his head. "Yolanda and Steven are married. They share a room."

My eyebrows shot up. "They're married? But I thought they hated each other." They sniped constantly, always trying to one up each other.

Evan shrugged. "Love is weird."

"A-fucking-men," I grumbled.

We were silent again, watching the people wandering through the street merrily, and the odd fight breaking out on grassed areas. Made sense. No one wanted gravel rash, even if you were drunk off your ass.

"Do you love them, then?"

I stiffened. "I thought you weren't a talker?"

He looked at me with his soft brown eyes that shone with the bright neon lights of the Cosmo wheel. "Just a yes or no question."

"No," I said automatically. While the look on his face said I was full of shit, he didn't contradict me. "Can I stay in your room tonight?"

He hesitated, but nodded. "I'll have to tell Sampson where you are."

I wanted to say no, but stressing out Sampson would be punishing the wrong person. "Okay. But tell him I want space."

He nodded again, but didn't move to grab his phone. Instead, he was looking at the footpath in front of us. "Someone smashed a bottle. Put your shoes back on."

I winced, finally feeling the blister bubbling up on the ball of my left foot. "Can we go around? I don't wear heels enough, especially not brand new ones and, well..." I lifted my foot and showed him the big blister brewing. He heaved an inconvenienced sigh and came to stand beside me, squatting down awkwardly, while I stared. "What the hell are you doing?"

"Get on my back, Chaos. Fuck me, how have you survived this many years?"

Part of me wanted to be indignant, but the other

part of me hadn't had a piggyback ride since I was six. I took a bit of a run up and leapt onto his back. He caught me easily, his hands under my thighs. I wrapped my legs tightly around his waist, trying to ignore the fact that the world could probably see the bottom of my asscheeks.

"If you don't want me to moon the entire city, we might want to make this quick."

"Hang on," he said, and started to jog. I wrapped myself around him like a backpack, clinging tightly. I pressed my cheek between his shoulders, the burn of the alcohol in my system starting to wear off, and sadness rushing up to fill the void.

I should've known better than to think that Hendrick was actually beginning to *like* me. I felt so fucking stupid for forgetting who he was for a moment. For forgetting that he was a selfish, spoiled, rich boy who was used to getting what he wanted, and I was just the last in a long line of girls who thought they were changing him.

But I'd been so convinced. Otto had convinced me. Were they in on it together? Let's break the fucking crazy girl? Sounded sporting.

The pity party bus had arrived, and I was all aboard apparently. The tears came back, and I tried to swallow them down, but I learned another very valuable thing tonight. Sake made me a sad drunk. Once the waterworks started, there was no stopping them.

The message in Nemo's book had been even more desperate today, but I'd ignored it so I could enjoy my time with the guys. Served me right. He was calling to me, telling me to come, and I was busy being pretty for men who saw me as a temporary challenge and nothing else. His message inside *In Search of the Castaways* was rambling, about no man being an island, and that perhaps no one was searching for him at all.

Sampson had said it sounded crazy, and maybe it was. But right now, I could relate to being lonely. The inscription in the book had listed a store in Hong Kong, and for the first time in weeks, I wondered if I should just go home. Give this whole crazy thing up before it consumed me completely.

But I couldn't, not yet. Nemo was waiting for me, and I knew he was the answer. He would see my madness as a reflection of his own, and we could heal together. My mirror.

Evan slowed as we got to the lobby of the hotel, and he walked straight in, ignoring the looks from the reception staff, while I just buried my face in his neck. He smelled really good. A soft, manly smell that was both reassuring and arousing.

"How old are you?" I asked, and felt him stiffen underneath me. He lowered me to the ground, and I tugged at the hem of my dress, pulling it back down my thighs.

"Too old for what you're thinking."

I frowned, sniffing and scrubbing my eyes on the back of my arm. "What am I thinking?"

The doors to his floor slid open, and he frowned at me. "Revenge sex."

I stepped past him into the hall, ignoring his words. He pointed down the hall at a door, and I tried not to wince with every step. Now that the sake had worn off, I was really feeling that blister. "Do you know what it feels like to be empty? To feel like a vampire, missing something integral that I have to leech from the people around me. Sometimes I feel like I was born empty, and nothing I ever do fills me up. Maybe that's why I relate so well to the guys. We're the same, yet different. Except Otto. He's a blood bank, pouring himself into us all. Soon, he'll be nothing but a husk too."

I chewed my lip as I looked up at Evan, his brown eyes a soft caramel in this light.

"The guys, they filled that emptiness for a while, but eventually they realized what everyone does. I'm a black hole, and I suck everyone down into that emptiness with me."

He grabbed my elbow, turning me to face him. "That's not true, Chaos. They like you."

I laughed, and it was a sad sound even to my own

ears. "They don't know me." I paused, my eyes watering no matter how hard I blinked. "I'm not asking for a ring, Evan. I just want you to fuck the feelings back. I want to be full for just a moment. Please." I winced at how my voice cracked, and I dropped my eyes to the floor.

"Aviva..."

I was already shaking my head. "I'm sorry. Forget it. I'm going back to my room—"

But his hand wrapped around the back of my head and then he was kissing me. It was a kiss filled with self-flagellation, which was hard to describe. He was devouring my lips, but holding his body stiff, and I could almost hear his internal thoughts about how bad of an idea this was. My body curled toward him naturally, and I sighed as his warmth soaked into me.

"You wanna know how old I am, Chaos? Old enough to know this is a terrible idea. To know that this won't make you feel better tomorrow."

He kissed me again, his tongue slipping past my teeth to stroke mine as he walked me backwards to the door, resting me against it as he held out the door key to the scanner. I pushed the handle down when it clicked, and then we were slipping into the dark room. The door shut behind us, but neither of us reached for the lights.

He pulled his mouth away. "Are you sure about this, Aviva? Really, really sure?"

"Yes," I breathed, gripping his hair to pull him in for another kiss. "Fuck me, Evan. Make me feel nothing but you for a little while."

Chapter 37
Aviva

Evan knew his way around a woman's body. He was apparently also going to talk me through the entire process, which should be annoying but was somehow arousing.

"I'm going to take your dress off now, Chaos. I'm going to see all that creamy skin that has taunted my dreams for so many fucking nights." That last bit was more muttered at himself than at me, but as he unzipped my dress, I didn't ask questions about how many nights he'd been thinking about me.

He peeled my dress down, and his eyes were hooded with lust. He sucked in a gasp as he realized I wasn't wearing a bra, and my breasts spilled out into the moonlit room. "So goddamn beautiful."

He kissed down my collarbone and over the swell of my left breast. I tugged at his shirt, letting him know what I wanted too. He threw off his jacket, unbuttoning his shirt, and my clumsy fingers helped him along. I wanted to touch his chest, feel the thudding of his heart beneath my palm.

As I reached for the button of his dress pants, he stilled my hand. "Thirty-four. I'm thirty-four. I'm more than a decade older than you. Fuck, this is wrong."

He went to move away, but I gripped his pants. "How do you see me?"

"You're too damn young. I'm a fucking predator."

I laughed, because I couldn't help it. "I'm old enough to drive, drink, vote, and go to war, Evan. I'm pretty sure I'm old enough to pick my own sexual partners."

"You're depressed. What kind of monster does that make me? Using you like this?"

It was hard to stand there and argue that I was an adult when I was in just a thong. "Do you care if I live or die?"

"Of course I do!" he growled, stepping toward me.

I wasn't done. "Do you care if I'm happy?"

"Yes."

"Would you stop if I said stop?"

"Fucking hell. Yes."

"Then you're already three times better for me than the majority of my ex-lovers, Evan. I promise, it's not just the depression that wants you. *I* want you. Me. Chaos."

He groaned and kissed me again. "God, you're killing me." He lifted me back into his arms, pressing me against the wall so he could dip his head and capture my nipple. I moaned, wrapping my legs around his waist. He moved to my other nipple, biting it softly, and my gasp echoed around the silence of the room.

I buried my hands in his short hair, holding on as he played my body like an artist. He was a lot broader than I'd thought, the slight roughness of his chest hair scraping my belly. Obviously, those slightly too large suits weren't just hiding his weapons, they were hiding a ripped body too.

He held me easily as he dropped one hand between my thighs, his fingers dipping inside me as the weight of our bodies ground his palm hard into my clit.

"Oh god," I breathed, as his fingers curled inside me, stroking me to perfection as he licked and sucked at my breasts. I held on for dear life, shuddering through my orgasm, crying out as I soaked his fingers.

He pulled back until he could see my face. "We can stop now. There's no pressure for anything more. Take this moment, climb under the sheets of the bed, and sleep off the night, Chaos."

I couldn't tell if he was begging me to tell him to stop, or begging me not to. But I didn't want to stop.

"More, Evan. I want more," I whispered into his ear, and his whole body shivered. I launched myself at his lips, our kisses no longer tentative. No, this was the chaos he accused me of as he lowered my feet to the ground and I kicked off my lace thong, while he shrugged off his shirt. I reached for the button of his pants, tearing it open and reaching into his boxers for his cock. It was hard and thick, and I wanted it.

I fell to my knees, and he moaned. "Fuck me, you look so pretty down there."

I grinned and took his cock, stroking it just to hear him grunt and flex his hips toward me. I licked the head, running my tongue along the underside. Then I slid him deep into my mouth, and tried not to laugh at the sound of his cursing. Taking him as deep as I could, I twisted slightly on the way back up, and he buried his hands in my curls.

"Jesus fucking Saint Joseph, Chaos."

I wanted to tell him that he was probably going to Hell for that, but you know, my mouth was full. He thrust slightly in time with my head bobbing on his cock, making me gag a little before he drew out of my mouth. "I'm going to come if you keep doing that."

"That's kind of the idea."

He growled, pulling me back up into his arms. He

pressed me to the wall again, his cock notching against my core, and I held my breath. He paused, and I knew he was about to ask again if I wanted this, but I could barely breathe, let alone talk him into this. I wanted him so goddamn bad.

So I wrapped my legs around his waist and pulled him tight into my body, and he slid in with a moan. Or maybe it was my moan, or a combination of both, because holy shit.

"You feel so fucking good. Better than I could have imagined," he groaned. He slid all the way out and then slammed home, and this time there was no doubt whose moan it was as the sound that left my throat bordered on a scream.

"Yes. Fuck, Evan. More."

Holding my thighs, his body pressed tight to mine, he fucked me into the wall. I moaned his name, my nails raking over his shoulders as he pounded into me. Fuck, I felt sorry for the people in the room next door.

I let out a high-pitched whine as I got closer and closer. He buried his face in my neck, biting it gently, and pleasure pulsed through me.

"Oh, god. Fuck," I chanted.

"Come for me. I want to feel you milking my cock," he growled in my ear, and that was it. I was helpless as I clutched him tightly to me and rode out the waves of pleasure as my orgasm rocked me.

Evan continued to fuck me, his movements wild and fast, until he was coming too. His hand slammed onto the wall above my head, and his body pressed tightly into mine like it was the only thing still keeping us standing.

We were both panting, and I had a cramp in my thigh that would probably ache more if the endorphins from that orgasm weren't coursing through me like a drug.

"Hold on, I'll walk us to the shower."

Fuck.

"What?" he said, pulling back to look at my face.

I flushed pink, or at least, I felt like I did. My face was probably already an unattractive shade of red. "No condom."

His whole body froze. "You aren't on the pill?" I shook my head. "You aren't on the pill and you're fucking all three of them?"

Now it was my turn to stiffen. He swore, rubbing a hand up and down my back. "I didn't mean it like that. It's just an accident waiting to happen, is all."

I swallowed hard, fighting back the post-orgasm mood swing. "I'm usually careful. Don't worry, I'll take care of it in the morning."

He gripped my chin, still holding me tightly to his chest, his dick softening inside me. "I'll do it, Chaos.

I'm sorry. I should have taken better care of you. You deserve better from me."

This time I did cry.

Which was how the guys found us. The hotel room door slammed open, with Sampson silhouetted in the light from the hallway. Me crying, still on Evan's dick.

The relief on Sampson's face quickly turned to shock, which rapidly devolved to anger. "You son of a fucking bitch," he roared, and Evan quickly put me down, setting me to the side and accepting the fist to the face. I grabbed Evan's shirt and wrapped it around myself, running from the room. Otto was just outside the door, looking pale as he watched Sampson fighting on my account for the second time in one night.

I froze when I saw Hendrick leaning beside the elevators. "Is three not enough dick for you, Viva? Or are you finding my replacement already?"

The world went red, and I strode toward him, lifting my knee and driving it into his balls as hard as I could.

"Argh!" he yelled, falling to his knees, grabbing his testicles.

"You have no fucking right, Hendrick Kenley. No fucking right."

A hand touched my shoulder, and I spun, ready to throw punches. Otto was there, his face soft. He threw a sad look at Hendrick, and leaned down to whisper something in his ear. Whatever he said made Hendrick flinch away like it had been a punch.

"Come on, Aviva. Let's get you cleaned up and put to bed," Otto murmured softly as he led me into the elevator and held me as I cried, Evan's cum leaking down my thighs.

How had I fucked this up so royally?

Chapter 38
Otto

Sometime, around three in the morning, Aviva had fallen into an exhausted sleep. We'd fucked this all up so badly, just like I knew we would. We'd ruined her, just like I'd warned them would happen.

I was just as much to blame as Hendrick and his self-destructive behaviour, and Sampson with his petty fucking jealousy.

Evan was a surprise though.

A knock on the main door had me standing, hurrying so it didn't wake her. I'd locked the connecting door between the suites as soon as I'd gotten Aviva back to the room, and I had no intention of answering that one. Hendrick and Sampson could fend for themselves for once.

I opened the door, not particularly surprised to see

Evan there. He was sporting a black eye and a split lip, and generally looked like shit.

He held up a small white bag. "For Aviva. I had to pull a lot of strings. Apparently, they don't hand these out over the counter like they do in the States."

"What is it?" I knew what it was, but I wanted him to say it out loud.

"None of your fucking business, Otto," he hissed, and I shushed him.

"You didn't even protect her. You fucked her when she was feeling low, like she meant nothing."

His face went red, and for a split second, I thought he'd take a swing. Instead, he sucked in a breath. "She begged me, Otto. How could I fucking resist when she begged me to make her feel better, after you three played with her emotions like she was a sex doll and not a person?"

I gritted my teeth. We'd all screwed up, and it was Aviva who would shoulder the brunt of it. "I'll make sure she takes it so she isn't paying for your mistake forever. You should know better," I shot at him, and closed the door in his face.

I was going to have to wake her up to take this. The earlier the better, or so I remembered from our very basic sex-ed class. I grabbed a glass of water, tiptoeing back into the bedroom.

She looked like a bedraggled angel on the white

sheets. Her hair stuck up at odd angles from not drying it before going to sleep, combined with all the tossing and turning she'd done once she'd fallen into a restless slumber. She hadn't even gotten all her eye makeup off properly, so it had smudged a little under her eyes like a raccoon. Her lips looked puffy and her eyes were swollen from crying. There was a goddamn hickey on her neck taunting me as well, and I went back to cursing Evan under my breath.

However, it just confirmed I definitely loved her, because none of that really mattered to me. Well, the puffy eyes did, because I hated that we'd hurt her that bad. But the shit with Evan, the fact she looked like she'd been dragged through Hell backwards—none of it lessened the shine of her soul.

I sat down beside her, shaking her shoulder softly. "Viva. Wake up."

She blinked groggily, her eyes running around the room as she got her bearings. "Otto," she whispered, and it sounded pained. Yeah, downing sake like water would do that to you.

I popped the morning-after pill from its foil packet, and shook out a couple of aspirin into my hand. "Here we go, sweetheart. Painkillers from me, and Plan B from Evan." She took them and threw them all back at once with the efficiency of someone who took regular medication. I handed her the water, and she downed the whole glass in a single gulp.

She groaned, slumping back onto the pillows. "Tell me that whole thing was a nightmare."

I stroked her wild hair. "Afraid not."

"I fucked up so bad. Sampson will never forgive me. Evan will never let it happen again. And I probably stole Hendrick's ability to have children."

I huffed at that last one. "No great loss. He deserved it."

"You warned me, Otto. You can't be mad at him."

I lay down beside her. "Don't forgive him too easily, Aviva. Just because he's fucked up, doesn't give him the right to treat people like shit. Not you, and not me."

She closed her eyes with a sigh. "But you think I should forgive him."

I nodded. "If you want to. I definitely won't pressure you. He could use some consequences for his actions."

"How do I face them now?" She paused. "Should I go home? I could probably scrape up enough to get a flight back to the US."

I automatically wanted to say no. Because if she went home now, I knew that would be the end. There would be no future for us. That was selfish though, and honestly, she probably should go home. Start her life again, away from this craziness.

"Whatever you want to do, I'll support you. Pay for your flight home, or wherever you want to go." Fuck, I was so pussy-whipped.

She snuggled into my chest with a sigh. "I'm sorry. Sorry that I had sex with Evan without even consulting you. That wasn't right of me, and it's disrespectful of what we had."

I kissed the top of her head, trying to ignore the fact she was talking in the past tense. "We aren't in group therapy now, Viva. We are human and we all make mistakes. Not that I think you and Evan were a mistake."

She snorted and buried her face in my neck. "Yes, you do."

Well, maybe the timing was shit, but I wasn't about to confirm that out loud. "No, it was inevitable. Sampson has been keeping you two apart as much as possible because Evan wanted you—it was obvious as hell to everyone but you." I let out a humorless laugh. "The problem is that Evan is a nice guy. The antithesis of us. I think Sampson was worried that if you got too close, you'd realize that someone like Evan is a thousand times better than any of us."

She shook her head against my neck but didn't

move away as she mumbled, "It wasn't like that. You're good guys too."

"I didn't say good. I said nice. No one's ever accused Sampson or Hendrick of being nice. Even I can be a prick when I want to be. Evan is safe. Respectful." I stroked a hand down her back. "You crave safety, even if you don't know it."

"I thought you said this wasn't group therapy," she grumbled, and I laughed. God, she was cute. "You're nice, Otto. You're the kind of man I always imagined I'd end up marrying."

I tried not to stiffen at the pain in my chest. Even though she hadn't said it out loud, I knew she'd made her decision. She was going to leave us behind. I didn't blame her and I wouldn't try to convince her to stay, but I knew I'd carry the hurt of it around for a long time.

"Sleep, Viva. We'll work it out when you're rested."

I stroked her back until she fell asleep again, and lay there with her until her whole body was floppy and lax, and she was snoring lightly. I moved out from underneath her, tucking her in tightly. She looked so peaceful in her sleep, the sadness in her eyes hidden behind those pale eyelids and thick, brown lashes.

I moved to the interconnecting door and unlocked it quietly. Slipping into the adjoining room, I closed the door softly. Hopefully it was soundproof, because shit was about to get loud.

Both Sampson and Hendrick were awake, sprawled at opposite ends of the room, and the tension between them was palpable. I guess they hadn't kissed and made up either. Good.

I was pretty sure Hendrick was nursing a mimosa, even now. Hair of the dog to cure a hangover, that's what he always said. Ridiculous. It just confounded your damn liver; you still got a hangover eventually. That was Hendrick in a nutshell though—double down on the things that'll kill you, so you don't have to face your problems.

I felt coldness wash over me as I looked at my best friends. Drix had the good sense to look guilty. Damn right. He should feel fucking guilty.

"I love you guys, and before twelve hours ago, I don't think there's ever been a moment in our friendship when I felt ashamed to be your friend." I let my coldness spread through my body until ice was dripping from my tongue. I looked at Hendrick. "I can't say that anymore. If she leaves, it will be because of you. You got your wish. You made that decision for us all, just because you were too scared to let yourself feel anything." My voice got louder and louder. "I love her, and you stole that from me. I'm not sure I can ever fucking forgive you. I will always love you, but this will always be a festering wound between us, just because you couldn't fucking let us be *happy!*" I yelled. I slammed my hand down on the table, making him jump.

Drix dropped his head into his hands but didn't defend himself. He knew what he'd done, the self-destructive bastard.

I turned my eyes to Sampson. "I know what his excuse is—he's just a giant fuck-up—but what's your goddamn excuse?"

Sampson scowled at me. "I didn't do anything wrong. I found her fucking my security guard, Otto. I think I have a right to be pissed when I find my girl-friend screwing another man."

I raised my eyebrows incredulously. "Your fucking girlfriend? She isn't your girlfriend, Sam. She was a convenient plaything for you. Oh, the mighty fucking Sampson Rubio, who can't do commitment, who plays with women like they're mice in a trap, just expects a woman to know when she's finally worthy of girlfriend status? Do the goddamn angels sing and a heavenly light shines down on her head? She's not a fucking mind reader, you pompous goddamn prick." I took a deep breath before I said something else just to be cruel. "She was—I mean, *is* single and can screw whoever she wants, and if I was her, it wouldn't be you ever again."

I was breathing hard as rage coursed through me. Silence filled the room, an unbearable rift spreading between us.

Sampson broke first. "I fired Evan."

Even Hendrick whipped his head toward Sampson. "You idiot," he breathed.

I wasn't surprised though. It was just the kind of jackass thing he'd do when his pride was hurt.

Sampson didn't look even a little remorseful. His jaw was set in that stubborn line and his eyes were blank.

I slow-clapped in his direction. "Well, congratulations, Sampson. You lost a girlfriend and a lifelong friend all in one testosterone-fuelled overreaction. She's going to leave. I'm going to pay for the rest of her trip. Now that you've fired him, maybe I can convince Evan to stay with her so she doesn't end up dead on some city street because of you douchebags and your self-obsession. Pack your shit. We can go home now."

I left the room, not even looking back at them. I locked the door between the two suites, Aviva still sound asleep. I climbed back into bed with her, curling around her body and trying to stop my heart from breaking.

Chapter 39
Hendrick

I stood outside the door, willing myself to knock. I needed to do this, to repent for my sins in some way. Sucking in a fortifying breath, I lifted my hand and rapped my knuckles too hard on the wooden door. I needed the pain, but I kept my face impassive as the door swung open.

Evan looked like shit. There were deep bags under his eyes, and he looked worn out. The huge shiner on his eyes showed that Sampson's self-defense training had paid off.

"What do you want, Hendrick? If you want to take a swing, Sampson already got the free shot, so I will hit you back."

I kept my thoughts about the whole Sampson thing, and how shit Evan looked, to myself. "Can I come in?"

"No." He tried to shut the door, but I stuck my hand in the doorjamb. Evan might be pissed at us, but I knew he'd never hurt me. I knew it in my soul, because Evan was the best humanity had to offer. He'd seen a scared boy and left his job to become his personal bodyguard. He'd beaten the shit out of paparazzi who took photos of two best friends kissing, when it could have made him millions. He'd come to our defense over and over, and Sampson had just thrown him away. I didn't agree with Sam even one bit, but that was neither here nor there right now.

"Come on, Evan. I swear, it will only take a moment."

He sighed, pulling open the door and standing to the side. His suitcase was on his bed, and he looked like he was packing. Fuck, I'd been kind of hoping he'd just ignore Sampson's hissy-fit and stay. But this worked better right now, anyway.

He went back to the bench where his weapons were spread out, ready to be cleaned and packed.

"You fucked her," I said impassively.

Heat flushed his cheeks. "If you are here to talk shit about Aviva, you can get the hell out, Hendrick." He sucked in a breath. "I warned you. But you cocky little shits thought you knew so much, when really, you haven't been around long enough to know how to tug

342

your own dicks right, let alone how to form a healthy relationship. I should have stopped it."

Now it was my turn to snort. "Like you could stop Sampson from doing anything he wants to do. Don't get ahead of yourself, Evan."

I watched the older man's jaw work. "If that's all you need, you can go."

Ugh, I was fucking this up too. "I need to hire you."

The look he gave me could have flayed the skin from my bones. "Sampson fired me. I have no interest in going to work for you."

I shook my head. "Not me. Aviva. I need you to stay with her."

He froze, his eyes raking over my face for something—answers, probably. "What do you mean?"

I chewed my lip, slumping down on his bed. "She wants to go on without us. Otto says we've fucked it up beyond repair. I want you to stay with her, make sure she's safe. Crazy knows crazy, and there's something off about this Nemo guy. If he is at the end of this wild goose chase, I don't want her to meet him alone. And if he's not, I don't want her to be alone then either."

Evan continued to stare at me silently, and then his face shut down. He turned on his heel and went over to his guns, pulling one apart and cleaning it silently. He didn't say anything else, and I wondered if I should leave.

When he moved onto the second gun, he finally spoke. "I thought she'd go home."

I snorted. "She's stubborn. She's come this far, and Otto said he'd fund the last of her trip if that's what she wanted. He's firmly Team Aviva, but he'll stay with us regardless. With me. I don't think he'll forgive me, but he'll stay out of duty."

Sadness washed over me at the thought. I was so fucking selfish. Ruining what I had with Aviva on purpose was the extent of my selflessness, and look how that had turned out.

Evan waved a hand. "Otto is angry, but he loves you. He'll forgive you eventually."

"He might love her more. At least, he could have, if I hadn't, you know..."

He sighed heavily but continued the reflexive task of cleaning his weapon. I'd seen him do it so many times over the years that I knew it was almost like yoga for mercenaries. Centered the mind, but you know, without the spandex-covered camel toes.

He looked up, catching my eyes and drilling a hole in my skull with his glare. "I'll talk to Aviva. You guys have coerced her into enough shit. She is capable of making her own decisions—she's not a damn child."

"I'd fucking hope not, considering you had your dick in her twelve hours ago."

He ignored me, though his lip curled in distaste. "If

she wants me to stay, I'll do it for her. I don't need your money, Hendrick Kenley. You don't need to buy me to assuage your guilty conscience. Now get the fuck out of my room."

I stood, stepping toward the door, but I couldn't help but give him one last piece of parting advice. "You'd be good for her, Evan. Don't make my mistake and ruin it because you're afraid." I shut the door gently behind me.

I wanted to find a bar and drown myself in numbing liquor. But that would mean facing people, so instead I'd go upstairs and drink my way through the minibar. Sampson still wasn't talking to me, and I hadn't seen Otto since he chewed me a new one.

When I got to the room, it was empty. I had no idea where Sampson was, but it didn't matter. This room was still too claustrophobic, even without the heat of his anger stealing the oxygen.

I grabbed the bottle of sake from the minibar, and walked back out of the room. I needed to get out of here and breathe. Skipping the elevator, I took the fire escape. It didn't appear to be alarmed, so I headed up. I was pretty sure I could get onto the rooftop of this place.

At the top floor, there was a locked door preventing access to the roof. Yeah, fuck that. I lifted my foot and aimed my designer biker boot at the bottom half of the door, kicking it hard. They might be made of Italian leather, but they were still shit kickers.The door slammed open, and I grinned. I was probably going to have to pay for that later but I'd consider it money well spent.

The roof was a mish-mash of cooling units and clear blue sky. I sucked in a breath, and felt it fill my lungs. Walking to the edge of the building, I looked down. My stomach revolted at the height, but I made my feet hold me there, reveling in the instinctual fear. If I fell from here, I would just be an unrecognizable stain on the sidewalk. It would be painless.

Sitting down, I hung my legs over the side. My heart thundered as my brain tried to drag me away from the edge. Well, most of my brain—that niggling little part that was the monkey on my back taunted me, telling me to just throw myself over. I wouldn't, though. I'd been to enough therapy to know that voice was bullshit. Besides, I'd never do that to Otto. He'd never recover if he had to scrape my body off the sidewalk.

I opened the sake bottle and put it to my lips, dragging down the alcohol and letting it burn through my system. I watched the boats come in and out, watched the Ferris wheel spin around and around constantly without ever stopping.

"What are you doing out here, Drix?"

I jumped at the sound of Viva's voice. I looked over my shoulder at her, and my heart clenched so tightly I thought I was having a heart attack. I should say something mean, send her away, but I just couldn't do it again.

"Drinking. Not throwing myself off the edge, you don't have to worry." I paused. "How'd you find me?"

She shrugged. "Otto has a tracker on your phone. It said you were here somewhere. He went to the bar, but I had a suspicion you'd be up here."

"Crazy knows crazy, I guess."

She huffed a humorless laugh, sitting down beside me. "You're not wrong, Hendrick Kenley."

She didn't look mad, just really, really sad. I scooched closer to her, so I could grab her in case she tried to throw herself off the building. Not so I could save her, but so she'd take me with her.

I passed her the bottle, and she drank without hesitation. "Sorry I'm an asshole."

She shrugged. "It's not like it's a surprise that you're a dickhead." She looked up at me. "I forgive you."

I swallowed hard. "But?"

"No buts. I forgive you." She paused. "Okay, one but. You aren't ready for what your heart wants to give me. Maybe I'm not ready either. We were always just tinder in a box, just waiting for a spark to burn our shit to the ground. I know it, you know it. Otto knows it."

"I don't deserve your forgiveness."

"Well, you don't get a damn choice in the matter, so suck it up and take it." She grabbed the bottle and knocked it back.

I laughed, remembering why she fucking stole my heart in the first place, like a thief in the night. "Little klepto." Let her think I meant the booze and not my heart. She rested her head on my shoulder, and I was fairly sure I'd never be the same after this. "You could still patch things up with Otto and Sampson. You don't have to cut them all out," I said softly, and hoped she couldn't hear the sound of my pain.

"Nah. You guys are a package deal." She looked up at me, her pretty blue eyes filled with too much wisdom and drowning in pain. "You need them too, Hendrick. Even more than me. Otto would never be happy with just me, because you're his first love. Sampson..." She trailed off, and I knew what she was thinking.

I turned my head and kissed her temple. "He'll forgive you. Though, as Otto pointed out when he was verbally eviscerating us, there's nothing to forgive. No one made any commitment outside us all being on this cursed trip. You can fuck whoever you want against a wall."

She jammed her elbow into my ribs. "Thanks for your permission."

We let silence consume us again, and it was beautiful. Heartbreaking perfection. I would remember this moment forever, suspended on a knife's edge between life and death. Happiness and pain.

I felt the cool trickle of Aviva's tears on my arm, but I pretended that I didn't. I could tell her that this wasn't the end, that it wasn't goodbye, but that would be one more lie. There wasn't any need for lies between us anymore.

"Drix! Viva!" Otto's panicked voice made me turn, and I saw him frantically walking toward us, probably to drag us from the edge. I smiled at him, and his feet stilled.

"It's okay, Otto. We'll come in now." I slid back, swinging my legs back from the edge. Aviva grabbed my arm, anchoring me to the roof. Or maybe I was anchoring her.

I laughed at the irony. Pulling her to my chest, I kissed her softly. "I'm sorry again."

She smiled up at me, her eyes red and puffy. "I'm not."

When we got close to Otto, I leaned forward and kissed him too. "Safe and sound, Otto. I'll just be in my room, packing."

I felt Otto's eyes watching me until I was inside the

stairwell, like he was worried I wasn't really going inside, and instead just getting a good run up. I slowly descended the stairs and let myself into my room. Sampson was back, his eyes taking me in, ensuring I was in one piece.

"Otto was worried."

"Not you?"

Sampson shook his head. "Sometimes, I think maybe you've got your shit together more than the rest of us combined."

I scoffed, because that was the craziest thing I'd heard ever. "We're all just fuckups, making shit up as we go along, Sam. I just embrace it better." He let out a grunt of agreement. When the silence settled over us again, I turned away. "I'm going to shower."

I undressed, set the water to scalding and climbed in. Once I was sure that the water was hot enough to wash away my sins, I let the tears fall down my cheeks. God, I should have brought the sake into the shower to numb the pain. Then I remembered Aviva still had the bottle.

A little laugh escaped me as I realized she'd managed to keep my booze and my heart forever. Bitch.

Chapter 40
Aviva

My chest felt like it had been through a meat grinder. Seeing Hendrick up on the roof, teetering on the edge, had sent panic unlike anything I'd ever felt before shooting through my veins. But in the end, our goodbye had been much like our first meeting—all kinds of fucked up.

That was the nature of Hendrick, I think, and maybe me too.

I packed my stuff, and each item of clothing that I folded and placed into my bag was like a dagger to my heart. I'd have to get rid of it all when I returned to the US; I'd never be able to wear any of it again without thinking of Sampson and the betrayed look on his face.

A knock at the door had my heart pounding, and I sucked a deep breath as I opened it. On the other side stood Evan, and I gasped as I took in the mass of bruises on his face. "Holy shit, Evan. Are you okay?"

He gave me a soft smile. "It's nothing. Can I come in?"

"I think you already did that last night," I said, then immediately slapped a hand over my mouth. "I'm sorry. That was terrible. God, why is this so awkward?" I stood to the side so he could enter the suite.

A laugh burst from his chest, and he shook his head. "It's been a long twenty-four hours."

When he was chest to chest with me, he paused, leaning down to brush the softest kiss across my lips. When he pulled back, I just stared up at him. Hell. What did I do? What did I say? Why wasn't I better at this?

He frowned, reading my silence as something else. "I'm sorry, I shouldn't have assumed—" I lifted up on my toes and kissed him hard, without any finesse whatsoever.

"No, it's fine. I mean, it's good. Ugh." I walked to the bed and just threw myself facedown onto the mattress, silently screaming. When I was calmer, I sat up, looking at Evan where he still stood near the door. "I'm sorry."

He shook his head, crossing the floor to me in two huge strides. "No, Aviva. You have nothing to be sorry for. I should have had better restraint. Protected you better. Not taken advantage of how vulnerable you were. Fuck, so many things I should have done better." He waved his hand at his face. "I deserved this."

I frowned. "We've been over this. I'm not stupid—I knew what I was doing. I'm a consenting adult. I'm depressed, not crazy." I grinned. "Maybe I should have protected *you* better. I'm the one who's been fucking a whole friend group. I could have given you the clap. Besides, you got me Plan B. I mean, it might be protection after the fact, but it still counts."

He gave me an unamused look. "Don't talk about yourself like that, Chaos. We both know what you feel for those three isn't casual lust. I've been watching it from the outside." He paused. "And Plan B isn't a hundred percent effective."

I screwed up my nose. "Are you about to give me the afterschool special about contraception? Because I can promise you, I was a straight A student. Pretty sure I aced that Health class in high school, and can put condoms on a banana like a champion. Apparently, it's just dicks I struggle with."

"Aviva," he rumbled. He had a great voice. Deep and growly. I kind of loved how he said my name. Not as much as I loved how he moaned 'Chaos,' but it was close.

"Tell me what you need to say, Evan. Rip it off like a bandaid." I was waiting for the inevitable 'this was a mistake, you're too young, I'm too old, it can never happen again' spiel. I'd hardened myself to the words already. I'd had this entire conversation in my head twelve times since last night.

"Sampson fired me. I'd like to stay with you, if you want that too."

Well, plot twist. I hadn't planned for that in any of my imaginary scenarios. I blinked at him, trying to wade past my shock. "He fired you for having sex with me?" He nodded. "I can't pay you to be my security."

He growled, and dragged me into his arms. "I don't want you to pay me. I don't want to be your bodyguard, Chaos." He let go of me and stepped away, running his fingers through his hair. "I like you, despite the fact that trouble follows you like a magnet. You're something special, and if you want to as well, I'd like to see where we go. Even if it is only until the end of this trip and then you go back to your old life." He grunted and turned away. "I'm fucking this up, putting you on the spot. I'm shit at words. Pressuring you again."

I raised my hand. "If you could take a break from the brooding self-flagellation for a moment, I seem to remember that it was me putting the pressure on you." I reached out, grabbing his shoulder that still bore the gouges from my nails peeking out above the collar. "Are you just sticking around to make sure I'm not knocked up? Because I promise to call you if I am. I don't know fucking jack shit about babies."

A smile curled his lips. "No. Not just for that."

I bit my lip. "The guys didn't put you up to this? Otto?"

He shook his head. "No. Well, both Otto and Hendrick approached me about it, but I'd already decided I want to court you."

I snorted. Who the hell 'courted' anymore?

He gave me an exasperated expression. "I know it sounds old school, but you know what I mean. This is what *I* want, if you want it too."

I sucked in a few deep breaths, looking up into his brown eyes that seemed to swirl with emotion. Earnestness was so refreshing, yet terrifying. The thing about the other guys was that we'd always expected it to end badly. It didn't feel like Evan was going into this with quite the same pessimistic outlook.

So despite the age difference, the tumultuousness of our beginnings, and the fact my heart still belonged partially to three men I'd never have, I found myself saying, "I'd like that."

A sigh of relief flowed from between his pretty lips, and he gave me a genuine smile. Leaning forward, he kissed me hard. "Thank fuck."

. . .

It didn't seem real until we were all standing in the lobby of the hotel, two different cabs waiting for us. I stepped into Otto's arms, and he pulled me tightly to his chest. I could hear the pound of his heart, even though mine was breaking. But I held it together, barely.

"Be good, Viva. Call me if you need anything, anything at all. Hell, message me every day anyway." He kissed the top of my head. "I'm going to miss you, sweetheart."

My eyes welled, and I blinked them rapidly. "I'll miss you too."

I pulled away, swallowing the lump in my throat, as Hedrick grabbed me up in his arms. "Bye, Viva. Live long, okay?" He kissed my temple, his arms encompassing me against his solid warmth. Despite the fact he'd been the detonator for this relationship, I found it hard to stay mad at him.

"It's not goodbye forever, Hendrick."

He just made a low humming noise, holding me tighter before letting me go. I stepped back, looking over at Sampson. I swallowed back the emotion, clenching my back teeth to keep my face from crumpling.

"Bye, Sampson."

He gave me a half-smile. "Be good."

The pain in his eyes tore at my heart, but he was

the first to move away, his eyes snagging on Evan who stood a few feet behind me. I was stealing the one constant in his life, and I felt miserable. They all climbed into the cab, and I watched the car pull out into traffic. The other bodyguards were on point until Sampson made it back to the States, where the rest of Evan's team could pick up the slack.

Evan bundled me into the other cab, directing the driver to the airport. My hands shook as I tried to buckle myself in, and when Evan's warm, strong fingers took over, buckling me in easily, I burst into tears.

He slid closer and held me to his chest as I cried. He didn't give me empty consolations, just stroked my back while I soaked his shirt with tears. This was stupid. This wasn't what I was here for. I wasn't meant to fall in love with those assholes. I was meant to find Nemo, but it was like chasing a dream, when what I needed had been standing in front of me the whole time. Then I'd lost them, simply because I was dumb and didn't figure it out until too late.

When we arrived at the airport, we waited in line to check our bags. Evan bought us both coffee and some bread-like pastries, and we walked to the gate that would take us to Hong Kong. Despite Otto's insistence that he could afford to fly us first class, I told him I was happier in coach. It was where I belonged, with the average people, not in the glittering world with rich princes. These people were just as special, but they weren't wrapped in the falsity of the upper class. They were average people who were just worried about surviving. A woman juggled her baby, and several businessmen typed on their laptops, but most people just stared at their phones, looking for a connection.

Evan stroked his hand down my spine. "Are you okay?"

I nodded. "I will be."

"We can chase them down. I've watched romance movies. We win over the kind-hearted gate attendant, burst onto the plane and then you sing them a song about how much you love them."

I smiled sadly. "This isn't that kind of story, Evan. I'll be okay, I promise." I reached out and grabbed his hand, lacing our fingers together. "I'm glad you're here though."

"Me too, Chaos. Me too."

Chapter 41
Sampson

Everything in me rebelled at the fact that Aviva wasn't here with us. How had everything gone so wrong in such a short amount of time? I wanted to run through this airport to her gate, grab her, haul her over my shoulder and take her home with me. But I couldn't. I hadn't respected any of her other rules, but I could respect this last one. She'd made her decision. She'd chosen Evan.

Every time I closed my eyes, I saw them naked and wrapped around each other, and rage flooded my system all over again. If she stayed, we would destroy each other, and I couldn't do that to her.

I looked between my brothers, my best friends, and they looked how I felt. Miserable as fuck.

As if he could sense my thoughts, could sense me

wavering, Hendrick lifted his head and met my eyes. "This is right."

That was all he was giving me after destroying everything. If she hadn't run, she wouldn't have ended up in Evan's arms. This was all Drix's fault. Though the logical side of my brain argued he'd just sped up the inevitable ending to this story. Good Girl had never been meant for us.

Otto hadn't said a word to either of us, and guilt ate at me. I didn't doubt he would look her up when she came home, because even I knew that they had a connection. He'd resist for a little while, but he wouldn't be able to stay away forever. She was an addiction that was well and truly under all of our skins, but Otto wasn't enough of a masochist to ignore the crawling need to have her.

First class wasn't the same without Aviva wide-eyed in front of us, whispering about the size of the seats and the fluffy pajamas. The world was duller without her barely-contained wonder.

We took our seats, and the flight attendant was a no-nonsense, sixty-something woman, making me breathe a sigh of relief. I couldn't have politely shaken off a flirty attendant today. I would have lost my shit and probably got us bumped from the plane.

Hendrick downed two glasses of champagne straight away, and Otto didn't even lecture him about it. Those two had a distance between them that I'd never seen before, and I was worried about them. They'd been a couple for as long as I'd known them, but this had damaged that. More than Hendrick's cheating, or the shit they copped from the other trust fund babies back home, this had caused a rift that I didn't know if Drix would be able to mend.

"Go easy on the champagne, Drix. I don't want to be thrown off the plane before we get home."

He gave me a droll look that broadcast his thoughts well enough. He didn't give a fuck about what I wanted or my opinion right now. Aviva had done a number on us—or we'd done a number on ourselves—and I wasn't sure our friendship would survive.

I plugged in my headphones and pulled out my phone, ignoring everyone and everything. I looked through my emails, messaging my assistant a list of reports I wanted tomorrow. I didn't care that it was three a.m. there right now—he could get his ass out of bed.

I'd need some recommendations for a new security firm too, and the pain in my chest at the loss of Evan was another thing I was ignoring. So too was the panic that crawled along my skin at not having him close by, watching my back. I hadn't been without him, really, since I was fifteen. Since he'd pulled me out of that basement, bleeding and broken.

I wouldn't admit it to anyone, but Evan had become more than an employee, and that was why his betrayal had hurt so badly. This whole thing was a nightmare, and the sooner we got back to reality, the better it would be for us all.

Fourteen hours later, I dragged myself from the plane. Despite the fact I'd spent the majority of the flight pretending to sleep, I was exhausted. The last leg of the trip had been nearly unbearable, and I'd snapped at the flight attendants until I made one of them cry. I'd felt guilty, leaving her a huge tip, but still, I was at the end of my rope. I was about to lose it.

"Thank you for flying with us, Mr. Rubio. Welcome home." Her mouth smiled, but her eyes told me to go fuck myself. Fair call.

I grunted my response. Otto thanked her softly, and Hendrick just ignored her completely. Hendrick was more than a little drunk now. He'd imbibed steadily since we'd boarded, taken a Valium, and yet still remained awake for most of the flight, so he was now staggering like an alcoholic. Otto strode in front of him, leaving him behind.

I worried that Otto would take off as soon as we were out of customs, and I wasn't sure when we'd see him again. He needed time, and I'd give it to him. I would prop up Hendrick for as long as he needed it. Somewhere in hour twelve of the flight, I'd realized I was just as much to blame for the implosion of everything. I couldn't blame it all on Hendrick being a dick. If I hadn't reacted the way I had about Evan, we could have swept it all under the rug and continued on in blissful ignorance. But I hadn't, so here we were...

There was a bit of a commotion at the top of the ramp, and I sighed heavily. Great. If it was a fucking flash mob, or worse, if someone had tipped off the photographers that we were here, I was going to be pissed.

When I reached the top, I frowned at the group of police hovering around the check-in desk. One of them spotted us and stepped forward, and my heart began to pound. Something was very, very wrong. I instinctively looked for Otto, and found him on the other side of the crowd, staring in confusion. Hendrick was somehow instantly stone cold sober. When I looked behind the cops and saw his old security detail, I knew something bad was about to go down—and that his father was behind it.

Dread crawled up my spine as a cop came over, his face serious. "Sampson Rubio? You are under arrest, charged with kidnapping and human trafficking. You have the right to remain silent. Anything you say can and will be used against you in a court of law..." He continued speaking, but I tuned him out, looking over at Otto, who was staring back at me in horror.

"Call my lawyer," I yelled over the sound of the shocked crowd.

He nodded, just as one of Hendrick's security guards stepped forward. "Hendrick. Your father, Senator Kenley, has been very worried. We are to escort you directly to Mount Sinai Hospital to undertake a mental health and wellness check."

My security was still arguing with the cops, as they spun me and cuffed my hands behind my back. Hendrick backed up, stepping around me and the cop, out of reach of his father's henchmen. "Are you fucking kidding me? You aren't taking me anywhere, especially not to a mental institution."

One of the bodyguards thrust a trash magazine into his hands, his lip curled in disgust. Hendrick looked at it and went pale. His wide eyes flew to Otto. I strained to look at the magazine cover, but when I did, I immediately wished I hadn't.

On the front of the magazine was a slightly blurred photo of Hendrick being fucked against the window of the London hotel. You couldn't see Otto's face in the picture, and I was fairly sure that was the only reason he wasn't on trumped-up charges of kidnapping too. We were in so much trouble.

Hendrick's security leaned forward and snarled,

"Move it, you fucking fag, or we'll take your boyfriend too and beat the shit out of him on the way." He spat on the floor at Hendrick's feet.

I didn't know what the fuck to do. I could tell my security was losing the argument with the police, and I desperately wished Evan was here.

Hendrick, that fucking crazy asshole, reared back and headbutted the bodyguard who'd just spat at him. Then he lurched toward the cop holding my cuffs and cold-clocked him until the other cops broke away, tackling him to the ground and putting him in handcuffs too.

"Son of a bitch. You are under arrest for assaulting an officer," one of them growled. We were definitely going to get the rough treatment on the way to the station, but it was easier to get out of prison than an institution.

I looked at Otto. He was going to have to save us all now. "You know what to do," I yelled, and he nodded.

We'd been planning for Hendrick's dad to make a move for a while now, but the bullshit kidnapping charges to get me out of the way were a surprise. He wouldn't have planned for Otto though; he'd always underestimated him since he wasn't filthy rich—like he was just some weak hanger-on, rather than the glue that held us together and kept us grounded.

The cops frogmarched us out of the airport, and

the paparazzi were right there, snapping pictures. Fuck. Senator Kenley may have made the first move, but he wouldn't win the game. I was going to eviscerate him. When I was done, he wouldn't have a reputation to fall back on. I was going to destroy the man piece by piece.

Thank fuck Aviva wasn't here.

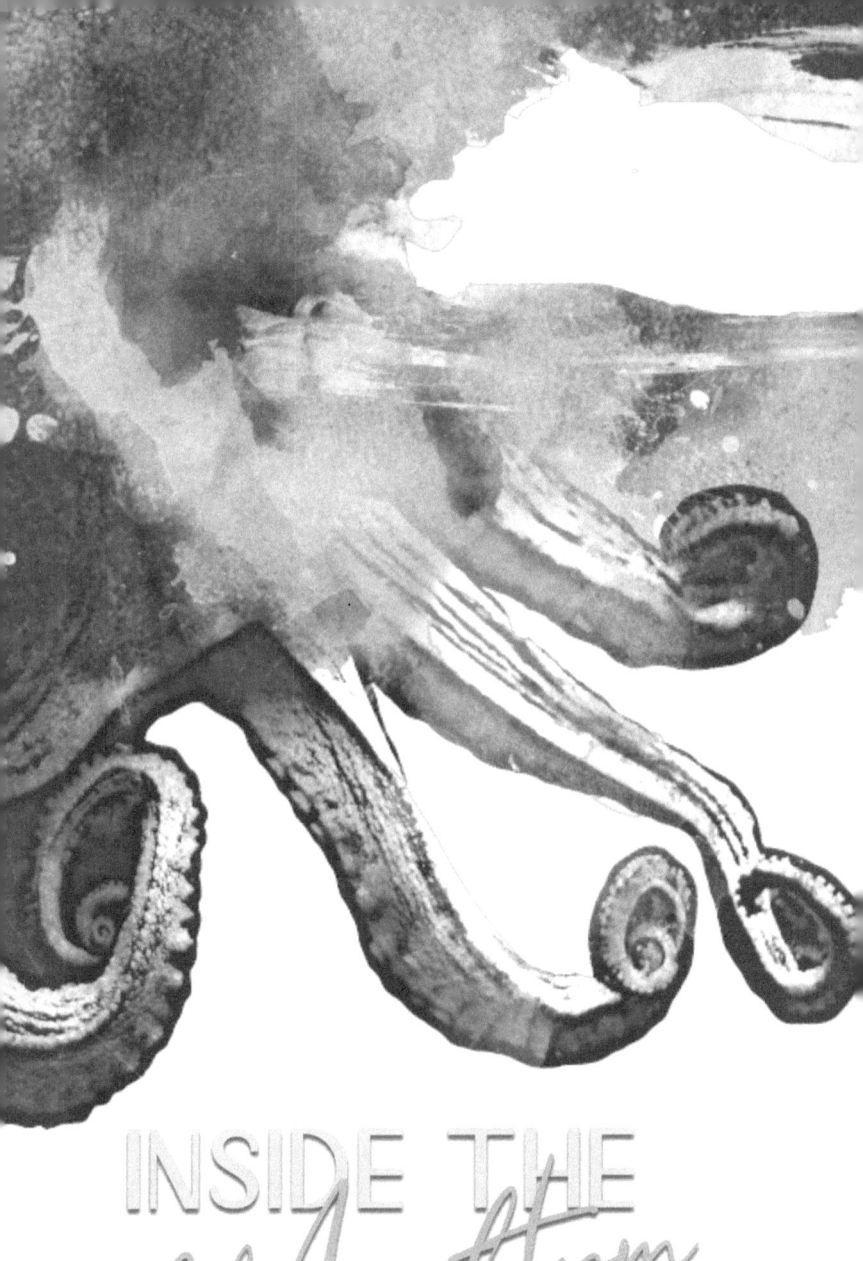

INSIDE THE
Maelstrom

Notes From The Author

Times have been a little wild over the past few years, and it's taken its toll on us all. So, listen to Mama Grace. Take care of yourself. You're important, not just to me, but to countless other lives you touch every single day, and you may not even know it.

You are never selfish or a disappointment for seeking help or needing to talk.

Suicide prevention Hotline America: +1-800-273-8255

Lifeline Australia: 13 11 14

Samaritans UK: 116-123

INSIDE THE MAELSTROM: Part Two (Preorder here)

About the Author

Grace McGinty is eclectic. She has worked as a chocolatier, a librarian, a forensic accountant and finally a writer. Like her professional career, the genres she writes are also eclectic. She writes romance, reverse harem romance, fantasy, contemporary young adult and new adult books.

She lives in rural Australia with her crazy family, an entire menagerie of pets, and will one day be crushed by her giant piles of books that litter every room.

Head over to www.gracemcginty.com and join my mailing list for sneak previews into what I am working on and to stay up-to-date with new releases and giveaways!